A NATION DIVIDED

A NATION DIVIDED

A 12-HOUR MINISERIES

of

THE AMERICAN CIVIL WAR

VOLUME ONE
Episodes 101–104

MICHAEL FROST BECKNER

This is a work of historical fiction. Apart from the well-known actual people, dialogue, events, and locales that figure in the narrative, all names, characters, places, and incidents are the product of the author's imagination or are used fictitiously, and any resemblance to actual persons, living or dead, events, or locales is entirely coincidental.

Copyright © 2022 by Michael Frost Beckner

All rights reserved.
Published in the United States by
Montrose Station Press LLC, Los Angeles.

Cover design by Andrew Frost Beckner
Book interior design by Brooke Koven

LIBRARY OF CONGRESS CONTROL NUMBER: 2022901704
ISBN 9798985597493

Printed in the United States of America
FIRST PAPERBACK EDITION

For Jeannie Blaine,
beloved Grammy

CONTENTS

"A NATION DIVIDED"

PILOT—EPISODE 101

"THE POINT"

BY

Michael Frost Beckner

FADE IN:

CLOSE ON: A GRAND ARMY OF THE REPUBLIC MEDAL

A five-pointed star similar to the Medal of Honor, made from cannon captured in battle during the American Civil War.

The Goddess of Liberty is its center. In the star points are the services emblems: bugle/infantry, cannon/artillery, muskets/marines, swords/cavalry, anchor/sailors. The legend reads: **Grand Army of the Republic, 1861—Veterans—1866.**

EXT. THE EXECUTIVE MANSION—DAY

WASHINGTON, D.C.—May 1, 1869

The medal is worn by Head Coachman, PAUL POREE (40), an Afro-Creole. A carriage arrives. Poree signals his groom, STEVEN MYERS (21), to secure the horses. Poree opens the carriage door for ROBERT E. LEE (62), four years a civilian. Lee notices the medal. Gives a respectful nod. Unexpected.

LEE
Fine bronze. Wear it proudly.

Lee faces the house with the sadness of shattered dreams.

INT. GRANT'S EXECUTIVE MANSION OFFICE—DAY

President ULYSSES S. GRANT (47), cigar clamped in his jaws, watches Lee through the window. Beside him, First Lady JULIA GRANT (43), adored and adoring wife of twenty-one years.

GRANT
I thought this was in a few weeks.

JULIA
His son wrote. The general's ill. He asked if he could
come before the summer swelter.

GRANT
Never wanted this. Never wanted the Army. The war.
Wanted to be a teacher.

Julia strokes his arm. Grant gestures at Lee with his cigar.

GRANT
Heir to George Washington, this place was his for asking. Instead…
(smokes)
He's the one runs a college. Funny…in an awful way.

JULIA
Endeavor to—*be kind*—?

That she emphasizes the last two words draw a wistful, pained smile
from Grant. They both know why she's said this and where he heard
it before. He nods, leans in, kisses her brow.

INT. FRONT ENTRY HALL, EXECUTIVE MANSION—DAY

Grant waits a short distance back as an Executive Mansion POR-
TER opens the door. Lee is framed in sunlight. Grant nervously
puffs his cigar. Lee hands the doorman his card.

PRESIDENTIAL DOORMAN
General Robert E. Lee.

Lee's eyes tighten, a kind of wince, at his former rank. Grant steps to meet his most formidable enemy with characteristic humility OVER THIS:

> MARK TWAIN (V.O.)
> Grant and Lee met face to face on only four occasions.
> Two hours all told—? God knows, less than three.

They bow, shake hands. Grant smiles. Lee cannot. They head for the President's Office.

> MARK TWAIN (V.O.)
> Precious little time upon this hurtling ball of mud for the two men ordered to the most unpleasant, and unwanted tasks two Americans ever undertook.

Entering alone, they shut the door behind them.

OVER THIS: A POUNDING. LOUD, URGENT, VIOLENT AND MECHANICAL.

INT. WEBSTER & CO. PUBLISHERS, NEW YORK—MORNING

THREE MASSIVE STEAM-DRIVEN ROTARY PRESSES.

> MARK TWAIN (V.O.)
> Their last meeting: four years after hostilities.

Each operated by SIX PRINTERS, they convey the "signatures" of a book—those separate portions that ordered and combined compose the entire "text block" body of the work—from PRINTING, to AUTO-CUTTING, to FOLDING.

> MARK TWAIN (V.O.)
> A meeting one might say was the most important in history—

BOOKBINDING SORTERS parade between the presses order-
ing the signatures into text blocks they deliver to TWO DOZEN
BOOKBINDERS, at long wooden tables, who in assembly-line
fashion, prepare the endsheets, flyleafs, headbands and gutters; sew
the volumes together; add the embossed red leather covers; and, finished, crate them for shipping.

> MARK TWAIN (V.O.)
> —it went, inexplicably, unremarked in the Presidential
> Record. Just a calendar entry, a time, the room, and
> two simple names of uncommon complication.

The title of this book is not revealed as a hand reaches in and selects
one for quality assurance. MARK TWAIN (50), smokes his pipe.
He thoughtfully examines the book. The men and women at the
tables and presses gaze at him with expectant faces. He smiles gently at them all, but doesn't utter a word. He walks to a large arched
window that overlooks Broadway.

TWAIN'S FACE: SMILE REPLACED BY AN
UNBEARABLE SADNESS

—reflecting his innermost thoughts:

> MARK TWAIN (V.O.)
> Man is the only animal that deals in that atrocity of
> atrocities, War.

THROUGH THE WINDOW: Every building the length of the
street is draped in black. Large swathes of burlap gathered from
corner to corner, swooped like bunting; course muslin sheeting,
curtained across entire facades; dyed linen tablecloths and woolen
blankets, featureless flags of black. It is unlike anything ever seen in
the City.

A SERIES OF SHOTS: CEMETERY RIDGE,
UNION POSITION, GETTYSBURG—**FLASHBACK**

MARK TWAIN (V.O.)
He is the only one that gathers his brethren about him—

Roughly 6,500 UNION TROOPS behind a low stone wall above a gently sloping valley of high grass, wait with loaded rifles in their hands with up to three, four, five more piled beside each man. Cannon smoke obscures the far side of the valley.

MARK TWAIN (V.O.)
—and goes forth in cold blood and calm pulse—

SEMINARY RIDGE, CONFEDERATE POSITIONS
—**FLASHBACK**

CONFEDERATE SOLDIERS step out from the treeline. They come to attention prior to stepping off into the smoke like ghosts in stately ranks threading between 200 smoking cannon.

MARK TWAIN (V.O.)
—to exterminate his kind.

They enter the field. A mile-long approach to Cemetery Ridge.

MARK TWAIN (V.O.)
Five years Grant and Lee led young Americans to the slaughter of young Americans. The killing of strangers against whom you feel no personal animosity—

CEMETERY RIDGE, UNION INFANTRY POSITION
—**FLASHBACK**

Union artillery is brought forward and loaded.

MARK TWAIN (V.O.)

—strangers whom in other circumstances you would help if you found them in trouble, and who would help you if you needed it... But in Civil War you show no mercy.

The Confederate Divisions emerge through smoke. It is beauty the likes of which the world sees only once: as one man, 12,500 Rebels come forward to the sound of FIFE AND DRUM.

RESUME: WEBSTER & CO. PUBLISHERS

Smoke curls from Twain's pipe.

MARK TWAIN

Sirs, ladies. Put down your work. Come. It's time.

As his workers gather around him and the two windows on either side, REVEAL: EACH OF THEM WEARS A BLACK ARM-BAND, A BREAST RIBBON, OR ROSETTE OF MOURNING. These devices are not new, each having been worn before for loved ones lost in recent past.

Mark Twain and his workers look down upon an awesome sight: THOUSANDS OF DIGNITARIES... 60,000 MEMBERS OF THE U.S. MILITARY... 18,000 VETERANS OF THE GRAND ARMY OF THE REPUBLIC who fought to victory in the Civil War form a procession.

INSERT: CEMETERY RIDGE, UNION POSITION
—FLASHBACK

At this battle the Confederates do not give the Rebel yell. Instead, they concentrate on keeping their advance perfect.

MARK TWAIN (V.O.)
Cut down by lead, obliterated by explosives, burned
up and frozen, drowned. Cut down by sword, knifed,
clubbed, beaten to death and strangled and gored,
trampled.

THEIR FLAGS unfurl in the breeze. They SNAP and the color in
the blinding sun of this July afternoon is gorgeous.

MARK TWAIN (V.O.)
Firing squads, hangings, lynchings, suicide, starvation.
Infectious disease, pestilence, diarrhea, dysentery.

At the sight of this, from behind the wall, rises the SINGLE,
AWE-INSPIRED GASP OF EVERY UNION SOLDIER who is
there. (Survivors will refer to it as "the loud quiet moan").

MARK TWAIN (V.O.)
It seemed when we used up all the death God created
for us we invented more kinds of our own.

THE EMMITSBURG PIKE—**FLASHBACK**

The Confederate Army now running forward. They reach a sunken
road, rail fences on both sides of the roadbed. They crowd in, pile up.

CEMETERY RIDGE, UNION INFANTRY POSITION
—**FLASHBACK**

THE FIRES OF HELL BREAK LOOSE as lanyards are pulled
to cannon BLAST, every Union soldier FIRES THEIR RIFLE.
FREEZE FRAME ON THIS FIERY HURRICANE OF DEATH.

MARK TWAIN (V.O.)
Figuring in the women and children, the aged and
infirm: over 750,000 Americans white, black, red,
(MORE)

> MARK TWAIN (V.O.) (CONT'D)
> brown, yellow who five years earlier we're all eager
> for Civil War were uselessly killed.

RESUME: WEBSTER & CO. PUBLISHERS—VIEW OF
BROADWAY BELOW

Lining the sidewalk: HUNDREDS OF THOUSANDS of American men, women and children of every race and creed, Northern and Southern hold little American flags. *It is the largest funeral in American history before or ever since.*

> MARK TWAIN (V.O.)
> Add to that the number permanently maimed, physically and mentally destroyed from battle and from grief: the casualties were our entire nation.

REVEAL WITHIN THIS CROWD: THOSE WAR WOUNDED—
AMPUTEES, CRIPPLES, BURN VICTIMS, THE HIDEOUSLY
DISFIGURED.

> MARK TWAIN (V.O.)
> Grant could not have saved the North without Lee. Lee
> could not have saved the South without Grant.

EXT. BROADWAY, NEW YORK CITY—MORNING

Cobblestones shimmer in an August sunshine. The CLIP-CLOP
RING OF HORSESHOES; THE CREAK OF CARTWHEELS.
The tail end of the procession, the final components of the cortège.
The highest ranking SENIOR WEST POINT CADET (20), in full
uniform, leads a PAIR OF HORSES pulling a caisson.

> MARK TWAIN (V.O.)
> To understand one we must understand the other.

Upon the caisson lies a coffin. Behind the coffin walks a riderless horse, a pair of boots backwards in the stirrups.

MARK TWAIN (V.O.)
The only way to understand America, is to understand what we allowed to do to ourselves.

The coffin rolling into view, the riderless horse behind...

MARK TWAIN (V.O.)
What must never happen again.

The pallbearers step in on both sides of the coffin. Union generals: WILLIAM T. SHERMAN, PHIL SHERIDAN and dark-skinned last chief of the Iroquois: General ELY PARKER; Confederate generals: SIMON B. BUCKNER, JAMES LONGSTREET and JOE JOHNSTON. This Band of Generals, the deceased's closest friends in life.

INT. WEBSTER & CO. PUBLISHERS, NEW YORK—DAY

Twain grips the book to his heart. On its spine: *"Personal Memoirs of U.S. Grant."*

As the coffin passes below, its crystal window comes into view. PUSH SLOWLY UNTIL...

EXT. BROADWAY, NEW YORK CITY—MORNING

VISIBLE INSIDE THE COFFIN: a wreath of oak leaves and red flowers preserved in lacquer over his chest, is the man known to the world as ULYSSES S. GRANT (63).

HOLD ON: GRANT'S PEACEFUL FACE

MARK TWAIN
(reads from the Memoir)
"My family is American, and has been for generations…"

FADE OUT:

OVER BLACK:

GRANT (V.O.)
(blending with Twain)
For generations—

MARK TWAIN (V.O.)
—in all it branches…

GRANT (V.O.)
—in all its branches, direct and collateral.

A BLACK HORSE

lit by a shaft of moonlight in an otherwise dark space. In SLOW
MOTION it collapses to a sawdust covered wooden floor.

GRANT (V.O.)

In June, 1821, my father, Jesse R. Grant, a successful
tanner by trade and a lifelong abolitionist, married
Hannah Simpson of Ohio.

Another horse: SLOW MOTION, falling dead like the previous
horse, lands hard on the killing floor, bloody head bouncing in a
swirl of silver-lit sawdust in shafts of light.

GRANT (V.O.)

I was born on the 27th of April, 1822, at Point Pleasant,
Ohio. Six weeks later, by slips of paper drawn from a
hat, I received a name: Hiram Ulysses Grant.

Another horse...flanks quivering... BANG! A PISTOL BLAST. The slow motion ended, this dead horse crumples quickly and gracelessly. TANNERY WORKERS (20s, all of them white), load it onto a wooden skid and drag it away.

INT. JESSE GRANT'S TANNERY—NIGHT

JESSE GRANT (30s) reloads his pistol as another horse is led onto the killing floor. BOOM! THUD!

> GRANT (V.O.)
> My earliest memories are filled with sights and smells of blood and lumps of flesh, raw animal fat and the boiling skins of horses, cattle and other animals.

As Grant narrates, SLOWLY PULL BACK TO REVEAL: a room hellishly lit, flickering with fires boiling vats of bloody animal skins. Everywhere are the carcasses of horses either being skinned or, already-skinned, seeping blood and fluid.

TODDLER ULYSSES GRANT: horrified in the door.

> GRANT (V.O.)
> In rebellion against my father and the death surrounding him that frightened me...

EXT. JESSE GRANT'S HOME, GEORGETOWN, OHIO—DAY

A modest house beside the tannery works. There is a field for farming and a corral of work horses and other animals.

> GRANT (V.O.)
> I have always had a strong regard for animals, especially horses...

In the corral, toddler Grant scrambles between horses' legs and happily swings from their tails. TWO WOMEN on the lane see his deadly game and, alarmed, rush to the kitchen door. HANNAH GRANT (20s) listens to the women, looks to her boy.

> GRANT (V.O.)
> ...and, as my mother would point out...horses understood me back.

Hannah Grant shrugs and goes inside. The women are stunned.

INT. JESSE GRANT'S TANNERY—DUSK

Ulysses Grant [YOUNG GRANT (17)] stands, scowling, at the entrance to the grim room. Jesse wearily approaches.

> JESSE GRANT
> I didn't know you were there.

> YOUNG GRANT
> You know I won't come inside.

There is little fondness between father and son.

> JESSE GRANT
> It may interest you to know you're going to receive an appointment.

> YOUNG GRANT
> What appointment?

> JESSE GRANT
> To West Point. I made it for you.

> YOUNG GRANT
> I won't go.

JESSE GRANT
I think you will.

GRANT (V.O.)
And I thought so too...if he did.

EXT. WEST POINT PARADE GROUND—DAY

WEST POINT—May 31, 1839

Gray-uniformed UPPERCLASSMEN range from sneering to amusement as they watch the confused arrival of PLEBES gathering on the 40 acre parade ground surrounded by the looming, Gothic facades of the Academy buildings. Among the upperclassmen: an exuberant, easy-going South Carolinian, James "Pete" Longstreet [YOUNG LONGSTREET (18)], and William Tecumseh Sherman [YOUNG SHERMAN (19)], red-haired and whip smart. OVER THIS the VOICE OF WEST POINT'S COMMANDANT:

SMITH (V.O.)
West Point's role in our nation's history dates back to the Revolutionary War when General Washington considered West Point the most important strategic position in America.

Longstreet and Sherman can't help but laugh at the smallest, most unqualified of the new arrivals: farm boy Grant.

SMITH (V.O.)
The oldest continuously occupied military post in America, in 1802 Thomas Jefferson established this United States Military Academy.

INT. WEST POINT BARRACKS, CORRIDOR—DAY

The plebes formed into a line before upperclassmen Sherman, Longstreet and RICHARD EWELL (22)—a Virginian with an eagle eye and a lisp—who assign rooms...and nicknames. The youth in line before Grant, YOUNG BUCKNER (17) steps forward.

YOUNG SHERMAN

Simon Bolivar Buckner, Kentucky..?

A glance to Longstreet and Ewell.

YOUNG EWELL

"Buck the Kentuck'."

YOUNG SHERMAN

"Buck." You'll room with... U. S. Grant, Ohio.

YOUNG LONGSTREET

"United States" Grant?

YOUNG EWELL

Mite small for nation status.

YOUNG SHERMAN

How 'bout "Uncle Sam" Grant?

YOUNG LONGSTREET

Welcome aboard, Sam, without tripping over those clodhoppers, follow Buck to your assigned room.

LAUGHTER. Embarrassed, Grant hurries off with Buckner.

SMITH (V.O.)

Of the two hundred fifty cadets you have entered with, a third will not make it through your first year...

INT. A LECTURE HALL—DAY

Before the plebes (who now wear cadet gray), is Commandant of Cadets, 1st Lieutenant CHARLES F. SMITH (35).

> SMITH
> Half that number will not reach graduation. For those who do: you shall be counted the forty-first class to benefit from the best education this nation can offer...

His stern eyes bore into the plebes—it seems each one—to make sure they have no illusions. Satisfied...

> SMITH
> How many of you have heard of Captain Robert E. Lee of the Great State of Virginia?

Hands of TWO HUNDRED FIFTY CADETS shoot high in response.

> SMITH
> Family heir to George Washington, in his four years at this academy Captain Lee was at the top of his class in every class.

Grant, in the back row, pencil moving across note paper.

> SMITH
> In four years, this Man of Marble did not accumulate a single demerit. No sloppy salutes, never tardy for formation; never a button that didn't gleam.

He comes around behind Grant to spy over his shoulder—

GRANT'S DRAWING—INDIANS ON HORSEBACK

> SMITH
> Your name, Cadet?

> YOUNG GRANT
> Grant, sir—Hiram Grant—

> SMITH
> *Cadet* Hiram...

> YOUNG GRANT
> *Cadet* Hiram Ulysses Grant, sir. But I prefer Ulysses.
> To Hiram.

Cadets SNICKER at Grant's confusion. The oldest of new cadets, William Rosecrans [YOUNG ROSECRANS (20)] of Ohio—Grandson of a signer of the Declaration of Independence, privileged, disdainful, imperious—cracks—

> YOUNG ROSECRANS
> "Useless" Grant, I'd say...

> SMITH
> Mister Grant, when I speak you will listen.

> YOUNG GRANT
> Yes, sir. It's... I understand that Captain Lee is perfect.
> But Lee is Lee. Shouldn't we be aspiring to our own
> potentials?

Flip yet insightful, the laughter cools as the cadets look to see how Commandant Smith will take this...

INT. ADMINISTRATIVE OFFICE, WEST POINT—MORNING

Grant stands humbly before Lieutenant HENRY HALLECK (25): bug-eyed and already portly. A brilliant academic brought onto the West Point staff after his graduation, Halleck is ambitious and conniving, with a repellent habit of crossing his arms to scratch his elbows when worried or lying.

> HALLECK
>
> It's been brought to my attention, Mister Grant, that you are causing confusion. Is it your intention to be ejected from this Academy?

> YOUNG GRANT
>
> No, Lieutenant Halleck.

> HALLECK
>
> Tell me: what does your middle initial "S" stand for?

> YOUNG GRANT
>
> My middle initial is "U", sir.

He consults Grant's application for admission.

> HALLECK
>
> Not according to the U.S. Government.

> YOUNG GRANT
>
> Governments can make mistakes, sir. My name's Hiram Ulysses Grant.

Halleck scratches his elbows.

> HALLECK
>
> No mistake. Your application, approved by Congress, provides for one cadet from Ohio: one Ulysses Grant, to
>
> (MORE)

> HALLECK (CONT'D)
>
> whom your Congressman made perfectly clear the middle initial is "S." This leaves you a decision. You may leave this Academy by whatever silly name you choose, or remain as whom your country says: Ulysses S. Grant.

> YOUNG GRANT
>
> What does the "S" stand for?

> HALLECK
>
> Nothing written here... It cannot be allowed to stand for a'thing.

INT. THE ACADEMY STABLES—EVENING

CLOSE ON: YORK, A MASSIVE, SORREL STALLION

A red rope across the stall door offers a warning: "KILLER."

> GRANT (V.O.)
>
> As H-U Grant I did not take hold of U-S Grant's studies with avidity.

Grant pulls a bridle from his tunic and unlatches the gate.

> GRANT (V.O.)
>
> At the end of my first year, the only manner by which I might have found comparison with Lee would be if my class had been turned bottom to top... One challenge, however, did engage my interest.

INT. ACADEMY INDOOR RIDING ARENA—MINUTES LATER

York stands, eyes blinkered, a red cord (indicating his dangerous status) braided into his tail. Grant leaps into the saddle. Noticing are Longstreet, Sherman and Ewell.

YOUNG LONGSTREET

See that, Sherman? That's the North-South difference a'temperment we're talking about. A Southerner wants to get thrown outta here, he puts some other fella on a stretcher.

YOUNG SHERMAN

Pete, Sam's not trying to get thrown out of anything.

YOUNG EWELL

Gotten to know this muddle-head?

YOUNG SHERMAN

Only that "Uncle Sam's" an Ohioan same as me, and when a man from Ohio gets on a horse there's only one thing anyone needs know.

Sherman slaps a silver dollar on the rail.

YOUNG SHERMAN

He aims to ride it.

Longstreet, a lover of whiskey and cards and never one to turn down a bet, matches the coin as also stepping up—

YOUNG ROSECRANS

I, too, am from Ohio. The mistake you've made here, Mister Sherman, is ascribing the prowess of Ohio manhood to..."Useless" Grant.

Rosecrans throws down a gold Half-Eagle. Although Longstreet hardly likes Rosecrans, he enjoys Sherman's discomfort. Sherman digs in his pocket, matches the five dollar bet. The PRUSSIAN RIDING MASTER (50s) charges into the ring.

PRUSSIAN RIDING MASTER

Mister Grant! Off that horse!

YOUNG GRANT
After I break him, sir.

PRUSSIAN RIDING MASTER
He'll kill you.

YOUNG GRANT
Guess I can't die but once.

Grant pulls the blinkers from the horse's eyes. Seeing his predicament, York takes off for the rail. Inches from it York stops, attempting to throw Grant over his head, but Grant's knees grip tight. York bucks and jumps; he drops to roll over Grant; rears and BELLOWS. The only constant in this struggle is Grant holding on... And Grant puts York through his paces.

EXT. WEST POINT PARADE GROUND—DAY/NIGHT (SUNSHINE AND RAIN)

Grant and his fellow plebes exercising, marching, the manual of arms [**handling your musket**], formations, bayonet drills—all under the harsh orders of upperclassmen "officers."

A SERIES OF SHOTS FROM WIDE TO CLOSE UP ON GRANT'S STOIC FACE

UPPERCLASSMEN
(*a growing cacophony*)
Salute! Throw out your chest! MIS-ter Grant! Say "Sir!"
Eyes front! Can't you hear that drum?! You're a helluva
Uncle Sam! Demerit! You're an animal! Pull your chin
down, you beast! DE-merit: MIS-ter Grant!

Grant never flinches as they try to break him.

INT. WEST POINT, SHERMAN'S QUARTERS—NIGHT

Three hens hang in a small fireplace, slowly spin and cook.

> YOUNG SHERMAN (O.S.)
> Sam, if you mean to stay in this Academy, make it into
> the Army—

Grant, Sherman and Longstreet sit by the hearth. Blankets tacked
over the door and window hide the light of the fire.

> YOUNG SHERMAN
> —you'll have to find yourself something you're as good
> at as horseflesh.

Longstreet shuffles cards...

> YOUNG GRANT
> I don't plan to stay in the Army.

Sherman pulls a flask from its hiding place behind a brick.

> YOUNG SHERMAN
> None of us do.

Longstreet drinks deeply.

> YOUNG LONGSTREET
> Speak for yourself, Cump.

He passes the flask to Grant who has a "first whiskey" reaction, as—

> YOUNG SHERMAN
> Pete sees himself better'n Lee.

Longstreet grins—why not?

> YOUNG SHERMAN

But Sam, you and I are here to benefit from this education. For that you have to complete it...as I've done. What else you like?

Longstreet deals cards.

> YOUNG GRANT

Algebra—comes easy.

> YOUNG SHERMAN

Then make mathematics your own. My parting words of wisdom.

Grant nods, takes another drink. *Drinks more deeply.*

> YOUNG LONGSTREET

The game is Brag, gentlemen. Penny ante. Sam let's you and I see if we can make Cump part with a little coin as well as he imparts advice.

INT. A CLASSROOM/ACADEMY INDOOR RIDING ARENA— A SERIES OF SHOTS OVER TIME

- *A math formula; Grant volunteers and is handed the chalk.*
- *Grant training Academy horses.*
- *Grant drilling poorly but hardly abused on the parade ground. He's begun to get a reputation for himself...*

EXT. WEST POINT PARADE GROUND—MORNING

A NEW CLASS OF PLEBES arriving. Grant and Longstreet are among the amused upperclassmen; Rosecrans among the sneering. The first two they notice are: George Pickett [YOUNG PICKETT (16)], and George McClellan [YOUNG MCCLELLAN (15)]...

YOUNG GRANT
Letting 'em in younger and younger.

YOUNG LONGSTREET
George Pickett, there—a Virginian—rumor is came here on the advice of one of you Westerners. Congress-man from Illinois named Lincoln.

YOUNG GRANT
The other boy have political connections as well?

YOUNG LONGSTREET
George McClellan was a "boy" when he attended the University of Pennsylvania at thirteen. Word 'round the faculty is he'll be running this Army one day.

YOUNG GRANT
Thought Halleck had that job.

YOUNG LONGSTREET
So does Halleck… There's someone reminds me of you.

Thomas Jackson [YOUNG JACKSON (18)]. Wearing saddlebags over his shoulders, he is twice the country bumpkin Grant was when Grant arrived. He carries a well-used Bible.

YOUNG GRANT
Got a story for him?

YOUNG LONGSTREET
Tom Jackson, another Virginia boy…although at the other end of the spectrum from Pickett.

YOUNG GRANT
I can see that.

> YOUNG LONGSTREET

Not the manner of living—the *how*. The Picketts own property.

> YOUNG GRANT

Slaves.

> YOUNG LONGSTREET

Which is why you'll appreciate Jackson. Word is he's running from a warrant. Been teaching his uncle's slaves to read.

> YOUNG GRANT

What do you think of that?

> YOUNG LONGSTREET

Where I grew up, slaves taught us how to shoot. What's *reading* to be scared of?

**INT. CLASSROOM/INDOOR RIDING RING/
GRANT'S QUARTERS—SERIES OF SHOTS OVER TIME**

- *Grant teaches trigonometry to new plebes.*
- *Grant teaches McClellan and Pickett how to take the heads from dummies in a mounted saber charge. McClellan, more interested in how he looks than how to kill argues, but Pickett takes to it gallantly.*
- *Buckner sleeps as, Grant tutors Thomas Jackson in math...*

EXT. WEST POINT PARADE GROUND—DAY

Grant with Longstreet, carrying their trunks, moves through cadets departing for summer. Graduated, Longstreet wears the uniform of a 2nd Lieutenant of Infantry.

YOUNG LONGSTREET
Wish I could get you to my uncle's place at White Haven
for summer.

YOUNG GRANT
Missouri so much better than Ohio?

YOUNG LONGSTREET
White Haven could be for you.

As Grant puzzles that, Longstreet's uncle, "COLONEL" DENT
(56)—a heavyset, irascible man who never held military rank in his
life—waves from beside a carriage. Col. Dent's slave, DEAR OL'
BOB (20s), comes for Longstreet's trunk.

COL. DENT
Grant. Another year 'mong Southern men has begun to
fill you out.

His smile, like his words, isn't particularly kind.

YOUNG GRANT
Yes, sir.

COL. DENT
Pete tweren't able to convince you to summer with us?

YOUNG GRANT
Thank you, sir, I...

The carriage door opens revealing Julia Dent [YOUNG JULIA
(16)]. While not beautiful she has a magnetic loveliness all her own.
She embraces Longstreet, laughing and TALKING—

YOUNG JULIA

Why, Sam Grant, you're as pretty as a toy. Pete, I see why you've kept him away: you're afraid your cousins will steal him.

Julia is a Southern belle. Grant is speechless—Longstreet's intention; he gives an encouraging wink. Grant quickly gives Dear Ol' Bob his trunk. Col. Dent frowns.

INT. WHITE HAVEN, THE FAMILY DINING ROOM—SUNSET

Col. Dent at the head of the table pours Madeira for his guest, General ALBERT SIDNEY JOHNSTON (39) of Texas. Johnston stands, raises his glass to Longstreet and Grant.

JOHNSTON

Whether you choose a military career like Lieutenant Longstreet or not, Mister Grant, there is no better path to success than West Point. This nation is expanding. Take my Texas: we're building cities now—we're a Republic—maybe soon, part of the United States. And it's men from the Point who are making it happen.

Pete Longstreet clearly buys into this; Grant is skeptical.

JOHNSTON

To the Point.

Meanwhile, Julia and her THREE YOUNGER SISTERS assist their mother, ELLEN (40), clearing dishes alongside slaves AUNTIE MARY ROBINSON (18) and Dear Ol' Bob. Lighting his pipe—

COL. DENT

Sam Houston's a great leader, a fine president for Texas, General Johnston...

(smokes; reflects)

(MORE)

COL. DENT (CONT'D)
Makes me think about *my* country; the trouble with
the Yankee North... John C. Calhoun had it right. Two
presidents: one for the North. One for the South.

Grant clears his throat. Col. Dent scowls, but—

JOHNSTON
Mister Grant?

YOUNG GRANT
As the west continues to open, sirs, would you then
allow three American presidents?

COL. DENT
If that's what it takes.

YOUNG GRANT
Then wouldn't America as a unified nation—the nation
General Washington fought to create—cease to exist?

COL. DENT
A broad statement, young man.

YOUNG GRANT
As is the idea of two presidents.

Johnston smiles politely, but Col. Dent won't have it... Longstreet,
however, enjoys debate as much as cards.

YOUNG LONGSTREET
Maybe, Sam, you'd share with us a Yankee solution to
our predicament?

INT. WHITE HAVEN, THE KITCHEN—SUNSET

[Note: kitchens at this time are single room buildings, usually stone, detached from the house/dining room.]

> YOUNG JULIA
> Papa doesn't like him.

> ELLEN DENT
> I've seen him eject men for challenging him with less.

> YOUNG JULIA
> I'm going to marry him.

> ELLEN DENT
> If that's what you want...

> YOUNG JULIA
> *You* like him, mother?

Ellen realizes this isn't idle chatter.

> ELLEN DENT
> He does have a rare common sense... Julia, you know, I believe that young man will be heard from.

Julia beams, while across the short stretch of yard from the kitchen and visible through the open dining room windows—

> COL. DENT
> Under the present system, the South is taxed unfairly for success in agriculture to pay for Northern failure to compete with the European textile industry.

> YOUNG GRANT
> The tariffs are unfair, but many have been repealed. To dismantle our Constitution over bad taxes—

JOHNSTON
And our right to our property?

YOUNG GRANT
Your slaves, sir.

JOHNSTON
An American right much older than your Constitution,
Mister Grant.

COL. DENT
Here-here!

Grant drinks—a bit sullenly—too young to notice that the Texas
general actually admires his pluck. Amused—

YOUNG LONGSTREET
Uncle, perhaps Sam and I can take the girls for a ride?

EXT. WHITE HAVEN—EVENING

Blue light, fireflies, chestnut trees, three horses. Longstreet hustles
out with Julia's two younger sisters.

YOUNG GRANT
Where's saddles for Julia and me?

YOUNG LONGSTREET
There's a rig waiting. You take Miss Julia for a ride, tell
her how you feel. Get a kiss, get a slap—the rest of us
are gettin' bored.

Before Grant can answer, Longstreet and the girls—GIGGLING
because they're in on it—ride off. Julia comes outside.

YOUNG JULIA
Why, Mister Grant, they've left without us...

INT. TWO-HORSE BUGGY—EVENING

Grant and Julia ride down a lane between cotton fields.

> JULIA
> *(re: the horses)*
> Two in hand comes easily to you.

They continue on, Grant too tongue-tied to speak.

> JULIA
> Neighbors had a wedding today. Would you like to go
> to the dance?

> GRANT
> I don't dance.

> JULIA
> *(laughs)*
> I do. Would you take me?... It's just over the stream.

They ride on. Presently, they reach the swollen stream. Grant heads into the water. Edging closer to him.

> JULIA
> Maybe the water's too high. The horses will shy.

> GRANT
> Not with me.

And he urges them gently; the water is up to the wheel hubs.

> JULIA
> Isn't this a tad dangerous? I know the horses won't go
> any farther.

GRANT
They will.

JULIA
If anything happens, remember I shall cling to you, no
matter what you say to the contrary.

Grant urges the horses further into the stream. Julia clutches Grant
desperately.

GRANT
We'll make the other side, Miss Julia, but when we do I
don't want you to let go.

Their eyes meet.

GRANT
I never want you to let go.

JULIA
Sam Grant? Is this a proposal?

GRANT
I'd like your promise that one day you will be Missus
Grant.

JULIA
Father would never let me marry a soldier.

GRANT
You won't. I plan to be a teacher.

Julia's smile is as big as the world. Her clutch becomes possessive.
Grant turns, kisses her. She kisses him back.

GRANT
Is that a yes?

JULIA

Yes. Now let's get to that wedding; you have learning to do.

As this is *the first time Grant has smiled*, it lights the SCREEN; he flicks the reins and...

INT. ACADEMY INDOOR RIDING ARENA—DAY

WEST POINT, GRADUATION DAY

A banner: "**Class of 1843.**" Mounted cadets perform drills to impress the YOUNG LADIES and PARENTS in the stands. Julia and her father watch Grant lead York into the arena.

YOUNG JULIA

You don't suppose Ulys presumes to ride that beast?

DRUMS ROLL. Rosecrans and a cadet jog into the arena with a bar. Rosecrans raises it as high as physically possible.

COL. DENT

Must be a foot above any record. Fool's going to kill himself.

He's delighted. Grant doesn't balk; spurs York for the bar.

GRANT (V.O.)

I made it through my final year to graduate twenty-first out of a class of thirty-nine. But, more importantly, I had secured a promise that my application for a professorship at West Point would be warmly received.

Horse and rider canter for the bar... They leap to the air.

GRANT (V.O.)
As York launched us for the bar, I believed I would land an officer of the U-S Army posted to West Point teaching algebra, calculus and trigonometry. A position from which I could honorably ask for Julia's hand in marriage.

As they clear the bar, there is the CRASH OF GUNFIRE.

GRANT (V.O.)
I didn't factor into my equation that Washington had other plans for U-S Grant and the U-S-A.

EXT. TIGHT RESIDENTIAL STREET—DAY

COMING DOWN INTO FRAME: GRANT (24) spurs a mustang, Nelly.

MONTERREY, MEXICO—September 24, 1846

Nelly gallops down a street strewn with U.S. and Mexican dead. One leg cocked over the saddle, Grant hangs alongside the horse like a circus rider, BULLETS WHIFFING all around.

EXT. AMERICAN COMMAND POST—LATER

Grant dismounts in a plaza active with GENERAL ZACHARY TAYLOR'S COMMAND. GENERAL TAYLOR (61), a tough old Indian fighter is dressed in jeans and a duster with a general's star sloppily sewn onto it. He glances from his maps as Grant approaches a staff officer: LIEUTENANT GEORGE MEADE (31). West Point Class of '35; competent, but nicknamed "Snapping Turtle" for sharp temper and rough language. Grant salutes.

[Note: the salute is the "open hand/palm out" British-style salute *which lasts through the entire Civil War.* US Army regulations of 1861 prescribe it as follows: "When a soldier without arms, or with side-arms only, meets an officer, he is to raise his hand to the right side of the visor of his cap, palm to the front, elbow raised as high as the shoulder, looking at the same time in a respectful and soldier-like manner at the officer, who will return the compliment thus offered." Similarly, if the soldier is carrying his musket, the salute is made by bringing the left hand across the body so as to strike the musket below the right shoulder.]

> GRANT
> Lieutenant Grant, 4th Infantry. Colonel Garland's brigade is pinned down in the Central Plaza, sir. We're out of ammunition.

> MEADE
> How the hell'd he get there?

> GRANT
> The ammunition we had.

> MEADE
> How'd *you* get out?

> GRANT
> *(a thumb at Nelly)*
> She volunteered.

Meade considers Grant through his goggle eyes; finds he doesn't measure up to his by-the-book standard.

> MEADE
> Lieutenant, right now I don't have a squad to escort you back into that damned hornet's nest.

Grant scowls, not liking Meade's language.

GRANT
Sir, I came for bullets, not men.

MEADE
I won't risk ammunition falling to enemy hands. Return
to your unit.

Meade moves to other business. Grant takes a case of ammunition
for himself only to be intercepted by—

GENERAL TAYLOR
(Tennessee accent)
Lieutenant Grant...may I help you?

Unable to salute due to his hands being full—

GRANT
General Taylor, sir.

MEADE
Goddammit, Grant!... General Taylor, I am sorry you
have to be bothered with this crap. Lieutenant Grant has
his orders and they don't include theft of ammunition.

GENERAL TAYLOR
As you were, Lieutenant Meade. Stealing ammunition,
Grant? Something they teach at the Point?

MEADE
Not when I was there, General.

GENERAL TAYLOR
I said, "as you were." Grant?

GRANT
General Taylor, your men are dying.

As he says this a MEXICAN SHELL EXPLODES, showering the group with dirt. Meade flinches. Taylor and Grant do not.

> GENERAL TAYLOR
>
> Hear you're good with horses. I've a horse shies from combat.

Grant gives him a funny look at the non sequitur...

> GENERAL TAYLOR
>
> Fix her...and as much ammunition as you can carry. By nightfall I'll see we've joined you. Then if Santa Anna obliges—

> GRANT
>
> We make him oblige, sir.

> GENERAL TAYLOR
>
> —it's Mexico City.

FADE OUT.

OVER BLACK: THE BOOM OF CANNON

EXT. A VALLEY BENEATH A MOUNTAIN PASS—AFTERNOON

CERRO GORDO PASS, MEXICO—April 17, 1847

Puffs of smoke ripple along a mountainside; the valley before the American Army EXPLODES with Mexican CANNONBALLS.

COMMANDING GENERAL WINFIELD SCOTT (61) scans the mountain through field glasses. Where Zachary Taylor is nicknamed "Ol' Rough and Ready," Scott is known as "Fuss 'n' Feathers;" it's said he never met an ostrich plume he didn't like. Already fat, he is nowhere near the size that will kill him.

SCOTT
(*Virginian accent*)
Santa Anna has used the winter to block our path to
Mexico City.

Scott casts his glance to Colonel JEFFERSON DAVIS (39) a tall,
aquiline-featured, aristocratic Mississippian.

SCOTT
He now has us at an advantage. As volunteer regiments
will have to do the work, I'm open to suggestions, Colonel Davis.

JEFFERSON DAVIS
General Scott, my Mississippi Rifles are eager to give
the bayonet. If you'll allow us.

Scott—who fosters rivalry among his officers, is ever amused by it,
and will one day be ruined by it—nods, considering, before turning
to a member of his staff—

CAPTAIN ROBERT E. LEE (40)

With dark hair and mustache, Lee is the picture of perfection
described at West Point.

SCOTT
Captain Lee, anything to offer?

LEE
(*soft-spoken*)
No doubt Colonel Davis's men would show themselves
well, but Santa Anna has a lot of cannon brass on that
hill aimed to keep eager men out of bayonet range.

> JEFFERSON DAVIS
>
> General, I will personally lead my men in disproving Captain Lee at your command.

> SCOTT
>
> How say you to that, Captain?

> LEE
>
> Sir, *anything* begun now cannot find success before nightfall. Let us put the men in bivouac and use the time to put our considerations to a broader solution for tomorrow.

> SCOTT
>
> As usual, Captain, you've anticipated my own inclinations.

He looks to Davis who, jealous of Lee, salutes and rides off.

INT. GENERAL WINFIELD SCOTT'S MESS TENT—EVENING

Lee places silver flatware beside china, crystal and linens. OTHER STAFF OFFICERS, including Captain Richard Ewell (30, now balding), and a handsome, brilliant, vain Lt. George McClellan (21), come to table while SLAVES enter with food.

> EWELL
>
> Your plan is audacious. You should have presented it this afternoon.

> LEE
>
> Audacious in success. Murderous should it fail.

Winfield Scott's ORDERLY stiffens to attention, signalling that their commander approaches. McClellan, who has eavesdropped on Ewell and Lee, is the first to attention as General Scott enters. The officers wait till Scott sits before taking their places.

SCOTT
This is fine silver.

LEE
George Washington's field kit while commander of the
Continental Army. A gift from his son, my wife's father,
upon joining your staff, sir.

Ewell gives Lee an encouraging nod, but Lee shakes his head.
McClellan notices. Scott notices as well; he has his glass filled from
a whiskey jug.

SCOTT
To George Washington, who won us forever the Great
State Virginia.

EXT. THE AMERICAN CAMP BEFORE CERRO GORDO—NIGHT

Tents and bonfires. Grant, who now affects Old Zack Taylor's style
of dress—blue jeans, an unadorned soldier's overcoat and slouch
hat—enjoys the company of other West Point classmates. An equal
mix of Southerners and Yankees, they are Grant's friends from the
Point: RUFUS INGALLS (25) from Maine, cheerful and full of
"quaint humor"... Thomas Jackson (now 23) still awkward in hands
and feet, but taller and filled with a passion for his country and God
beyond measure... George Pickett (22) this Virginian more dashing
than ever... And Grant's closest friend, James "Pete" Longstreet
who smokes and shuffles cards.

INGALLS
...General Pillow orders battlements built "from here,
boys, all the way down the line." No one argued. Just
put up the battlement.

PICKETT
A masterpiece of engineering. Best soldiering I ever did
in the Army.

JACKSON
First day's soldiering y'ever did.

PICKETT
Jackson, my good man, there is as much achievement in graduating last from the Academy—as I—as any man graduated first.

INGALLS
We put up the battlement. Just one problem: Pillow positioned it facing *away* from the Mexican Army.

Laughter. Ingalls throws pinon cones onto the fire.

INT. GENERAL WINFIELD SCOTT'S MESS TENT—LATER

SCOTT
Santa Anna's success will dictate American fortunes in this war.

MCCLELLAN
That needn't be, General. Captain Lee has a plan he'd like to offer he thinks might turn the tide...

LEE
Lieutenant, I don't recall sharing my thoughts with you.

MCCLELLAN
General, the plan is audacious.

SCOTT
As you are my resident genius, Lieutenant McClellan, perhaps Captain Lee would allow you to present this plan.

McClellan realizes he has overplayed his hand.

LEE
Thank you, Lieutenant McClellan, for your humbling
support, but my plan might lead to disaster and you and
I would both regret your having attached yourself to it
unwisely.

McClellan retreats to a contemplation of his wine; not tonight nor
ever in the future will McClellan best Lee.

LEE
General Scott, I propose to lead a rear envelopment of
Santa Anna's guns.

The table goes still. Lee's plan is as uncommonly simple as it is reck-
lessly bold. All eyes rest upon Scott for reaction.

The general chews thoughtfully a moment, savoring the roast beef.
Then he stares at his fork, and then at Lee, and—

SCOTT
Audacity personified. My servants—
(meaning "slaves")
will have *your* field kit polished for you by the time
you've succeeded, Colonel.

EXT. GENERAL WINFIELD SCOTT'S MESS—NIGHT

One of Scott's slaves meets with Grant's former West Point room-
mate, Southern lieutenant Simon Buckner. An exchange of coins for
a fill of Buckner's flask from Scott's whiskey jug.

EXT. THE AMERICAN CAMP BEFORE CERRO GORDO—NIGHT

Longstreet deals cards...

LONGSTREET
I swear if I were back at White Haven right now, I'd
spend a month in a tub drinking whiskey. How 'bout
you, Sam?

GRANT
I'd visit White Haven.

Ingalls pours coffee for the six of them.

LONGSTREET
Doubtless to marry my cousin. Cards?

JACKSON
Something to say to that, Sam?

GRANT
The able Lieutenant from South Carolina is not
incorrect...

Pickett, always one to find happiness in the happiness of others,
gives Grant a jaunty tip of his cap.

PICKETT
Well done, Sam.

BUCKNER
I just hope you're ready for wedding bells.

Approaching, Buckner augments their coffee from the flask.

BUCKNER
Talk around Ol' Fuss n' Feathers mess tonight is that
the remarkable Captain Robert E. Lee—

ALL OF THEM IN UNISON
West Point Class of Twenty-Nine—

BUCKNER
—is closer than y'all imagine.

LONGSTREET
The game is Brag. Three threes are top of the game.
Two bit ante...

EXT. WOODS AT BASE OF CERRO GORDO MOUNTAINS—NIGHT

Lee's column of infantry and artillery stealthily move out as
HORSEMEN burst toward them. Muskets are leveled, but—

LEE
Hold fire. They're ours.

Coming to breathless stop before Lee is a young American, Lieutenant WINFIELD SCOTT HANCOCK (23).

HANCOCK
Lieutenant Hancock, reporting, sir.

LEE
Is the path ahead clear of enemy and enemy observa-
tion, Lieutenant?

HANCOCK
It is, Captain.

Hancock looks askance at the heavy cannon...

HANCOCK
It's treacherously steep, sir.

LEE
Does that bother you, Lieutenant?

> HANCOCK
> No better place for artillery then above the enemy, sir.

> LEE
> If you're not spent, join us, Mister Hancock.

As Lee orders his troops and artillery forward, Hancock smiles to fall in with the assault mission, neither man knowing they will each use this tactic against the other—both times in the slaughter of their fellow Americans.

EXT. THE MOUNTAINS BEHIND CERRO GORDO—NIGHT

A shadow cut from a starry sky, the mountain crawls with HUN-DREDS OF MEN who use heavy ropes to pull American cannon up the cliff-face. Leading the ascent is Robert E. Lee.

EXT. BATTLEFIELD, CERRO GORDO—DAWN

ANGLE ON: GRANT—along with his brother officers from the night before—watching through a spyglass as Captain Lee's artillery OPENS FIRE on Santa Anna from above and behind.

EXT. CERRO GORDO PASS—MORNING

Santa Anna's cannon are blown to pieces from behind as the Mexicans face Lee's infantry charging down upon them.

HANCOCK

among the first Americans to clash, captures a cannon—a triumphant moment—but CRACK! a ball blasts his knee taking him down. The Mexican who shot him, comes in with bayonet, but Hancock kills him with his sidearm. The remainder of Santa Anna's soldiers flee in panic from Lee's infantry.

EXT. BATTLEFIELD, CERRO GORDO—MORNING

For the first time, Grant catches sight of the man who will be his greatest foe:

THROUGH SPYGLASS—ROBERT E. LEE—RAISING THE AMERICAN FLAG

THREE CHEERS GO UP FOR ROBERT E. LEE. With his men arrayed behind him, Jefferson Davis scowls—he detests Lee—then, drawing his saber—

> JEFFERSON DAVIS
> Mississippi Rifles: Guide center! Forward!

The CHEERS of his men increase as they move forward to meet the fleeing Mexicans on the points of their bayonets. And—

ROBERT E. LEE

stands atop the pass waving the Stars and Stripes in glory.

SMASH CUT TO:

EXT. THE GATES OF MEXICO CITY—DAY

The MEXICAN DEFENSE IS FURIOUS. American INFANTRY is held at bay by WITHERING FIRE; American ARTILLERY does its best to breach the walls, but the crews are mercilessly cut down.

MEXICO CITY—September 13, 1847

At one section of U.S. artillery, Tom Jackson's GUN CREW breaks for cover among the rocks. Jackson strides past them into an open area between his abandoned gun and the city walls from where Mexicans POUR FIRE.

Watching from the rear, Tennessean General GIDEON PILLOW (31; he of the wrong-facing battlements) motions a STAFF OFFICER.

PILLOW

Get Jackson out of there before his entire company is wiped out!

STAFFER

Yes, General Pillow.

The staffer gallops forward and is immediately cut down. Jackson sees this, sees Pillow indicating he retreat. He ignores the general, turning his back to the blizzard of ENEMY FIRE, and with remarkable cool—

JACKSON

Come on, men! This is nothing. You see they can't hurt me!

It is a display of courage that will one day earn him the name "Stonewall" in battle against other Americans as a General of the Confederacy. His men rally to their gun, two going down in the process as—

CAPTAIN JOE HOOKER (33)

The most handsome officer in the U.S. Army leads his infantry forward to the city walls.

HOOKER

God dammit! Where the hell are the ladders? We need the ladders!

As he reaches the bottom of the wall, he finds—

PILLOW

suddenly wounded in the foot.

> PILLOW
> Take over, Captain! Take over!

> HOOKER
> The ladders! Get those ladders to the top now!
> *(to Pillow)*
> Permission to storm the gates?!

> PILLOW
> Yes, do. Yes, go! Anything! Can't you see I'm *badly* wounded?!

As Hooker leads his men up the ladders and over the wall—

THE CAMERA RIPS DOWN THE AMERICAN LINE: Grant, leading his squad of privates, is pinned down by FIRE.

> A SCARED SOLDIER
> Retreat, Lieutenant!

> GRANT
> I never retrace my steps.

ARTILLERY under Longstreet in the same situation as Grant— guns poorly positioned at the corner of a wall.

> GRANT
> Pete, lend me a howitzer!

> LONGSTREET
> You got a better place for it?!

Grant points at a church. THE CAMERA ZOOMS UP AND INTO—

EXT. THE BELL-TOWER—LATER

Grant, the gun, its CREW now inside; the firing lanyard pulled, BOOM! The gun blasts barricaded rooftops below.

EXT. THE MEXICAN BUILDINGS BELOW—CONTINUOUS

Buckner and his men huddle against a wall as Mexican bodies rain from above. He leads his men, FIRING, inside.

EXT. THE GATES OF MEXICO CITY—CONTINUOUS

The GUNFIRE against Longstreet peters out and Mexicans flee.

> LONGSTREET
> Sam's done it!

Grabbing the American flag from his COLOR BEARER, Long-street waves it in broad arcs rushing forward only to—SMACK!—go down, wounded. Pickett slams down beside him.

> PICKETT
> Pete! Is it bad?

This wound is, but grabbing Pickett's sleeve.

> LONGSTREET
> Do something for me, Pickett.

> PICKETT
> Anything.

Longstreet thrusts the flag staff into Pickett's hands.

> LONGSTREET
> If you can plant our colors, I'll survive the day.

Pickett nods, clasps Longstreet's hand before shouting—

> PICKETT
> Mexico is ours, boys!

Pickett, waving the flag, rallies the infantry leading them into the plaza beyond the gates as a GROUP OF CAVALRY under the command of Richard Ewell stream inside.

EXT. MEXICO CITY PLAZA—CONTINUOUS

Ewell and his men ride in, sabers singing. The Mexican's part. Ewell reins up to see aimed directly at him: a MEXICAN CANNON. It FIRES killing Ewell's horse, but Ewell nimbly leaps free. Landing on two feet, he fights as infantry.

EXT. THE GATES OF MEXICO CITY—DAY

Longstreet, grimacing with pain, is found by STRETCHER BEARERS. They attempt to lift him onto their litter.

> LONGSTREET
> God dammit! You'll wait!

Longstreet watches the city wall where vaulting onto this parapet is George Pickett. Using the flag staff as a spear he gores one Mexican and knocks two others off before planting the flag. It unfurls in wind and gun smoke; Americans CHEER. Pickett throws Longstreet a salute before drawing saber and pistol to join the fight in earnest.

The stretcher bearers are agog.

> LONGSTREET
> His name's Pickett. Remember it. Now get me the hell out of here...

INT. THE BELL-TOWER—DAY

Grant and the gun crew FIRE their last round, then watch victory swirl in fire and death below. The day belongs to the Americans. Grant's men CHEER. Grant, seeing the dead he has directly caused, cannot find his smile.

POINT OF VIEW—A SPYGLASS—GRANT INSIDE THE BELLTOWER

> JOE JOHNSTON (O.S.)
> *(Virginia accent)*
> The field piece in the tower. Who is that officer?

EXT. A SHORT HILL OUTSIDE THE CITY—DAY

A command post where, mounted, Colonel JOSEPH E. JOHN-STON (40) observes the victory. A Virginia gentleman and West Pointer, Johnston is considered the "first and best" of the U.S. Army. The aide who answers him is a Pennsylvanian Captain by the name of JOHN C. PEMBERTON (33).

> PEMBERTON
> "Useless" Grant, sir.

Lowering his binoculars, Johnston—known as the fairest officer in the army—frowns.

> JOE JOHNSTON
> Useless?

PEMBERTON
Nickname at the Academy. Better watering horses than
leading men.

JOE JOHNSTON
He just forced the city gates.

PEMBERTON
I applaud his luck...not his tactics. Sir, you'd never find
me trapped with an artillery piece in a tower.

JOE JOHNSTON
What you call luck, Captain Pemberton, I call resource-
fulness. Write up a recommendation to General Scott;
I'll see *Useful* Grant promoted.

Pemberton scowls. Joe Johnston rides forward a few paces, following the army into the city, before looking back with—

JOE JOHNSTON
Now.

EXT. MEXICO CITY PLAZA—DAY

McClellan fights to control his horse as he hacks and slashes. His
horse is SHOT from beneath him, McClellan dashes after his SER-
GEANT into a doorway.

INT. MEXICO CITY HOUSE—CONTINUOUS

The American sergeant is bayoneted by a MEXICAN OFFICER
who swipes for McClellan's head. McClellan ducks grabbing the
fallen sergeant's musket to skewer the Mexican officer on its bayonet...behind whom are TEN MORE MEXICANS.

The first charges. McClellan frees the musket to SHOOT him and bayonet the next. Releasing the musket-turned-lance in the man's chest, McClellan draws two pistols and aims them at the remaining eight Mexicans. Weapons CLATTER to the floor as the Mexicans surrender to George McClellan. Whatever his personality flaws, McClellan is an officer who will be reckoned with today and in the future.

INT. GENERAL SCOTT'S CONVENT HEADQUARTERS—NIGHT

General Scott hands captain's shoulder straps to McClellan and shakes his hand sealing a bond and future between them. Next he promotes Tom Jackson. Where McClellan takes the honor as his due, Jackson blushes. They trade salutes then McClellan and Jackson execute an about-face and go. On their way out they pass Grant who salutes them.

GRANT
Captain McClellan, congratulations.

McClellan looks down his nose at Grant and bulls past him.

GRANT
You, too "Old Jack." We've come a long way from you
mashing my heels on the parade ground at the Point.

JACKSON
God gave me big feet.

GRANT
The better to hold your ground.

JACKSON
Only ground I care to hold is my Shenandoah Valley.

The more speaking Jackson does, the more embarrassed he becomes; Grant ends the conversation with a handshake.

GRANT
Congratulations, Captain.

Although Jackson outranks Grant he salutes him. They part, never to see each other again... Grant comes to attention before General Scott's Chief-of-Staff, Major Robert E. Lee.

GRANT
First Lieutenant Grant, reporting for General Scott, sir.

LEE
Lieutenant. General Scott received reports of your bravery and decisiveness in today's action that led to the taking of the city.

GRANT
You inspired me, Major.

LEE
For *your* action, General Scott has chosen to personally reward you a promotion to Captain.

He pauses taking in Grant's muddy, makeshift uniform.

LEE
I feel it my duty, sir, to call your attention to General Scott's order that an officer reporting at headquarters should be in full uniform.

GRANT
No discourtesy intended, Major Lee. I've been in combat—

LEE
To which you apply yourself admirably. This is not combat. This is headquarters... Only when pride in oneself
(MORE)

>   LEE (CONT'D)
> is married to ability for command does the individual
> officer open the path to personal honor.

>   GRANT
> Personal honor dies with the individual. I fight for our
> flag.

>   LEE
> Then, Captain, respect yourself as you do that flag. The
> next occasion you're invited to meet your commanding
> general, you will present yourself as equal to the honor
> bestowed.

He signs a document, hands it to Grant.

>   LEE
> Your promotion, Captain. I'll convey your apologies to
> General Scott. Dismissed.

EXT. LAKE OUTSIDE MEXICO CITY—SUNSET

Alone, Grant has retreated to this place of still water and reflection
to write his fiance...

>   GRANT (V.O.)
> Dear Julia. Since my last letter, four of the hardest bat-
> tles the world ever witnessed have taken place, and the
> most astonishing victories have crowned America... But
> dearly have we paid for it! The loss of men is frightful.

EXT. WHITE HAVEN, THE FAMILY DINING ROOM—NIGHT

By candlelight, Julia reads the letter to her family…

> JULIA
> "But Dearest Julia… I do not think there was ever a more wicked war than this waged on Mexico, I believe, for the sole purpose of providing new territories for Southern slavery."

Col. Dent SNORTS and leaves the room. JULIA'S MOTHER touches her daughter's arm—"don't worry about your father."

> JULIA
> "If only I had the moral courage to resign: but my supreme duty is to the flag…"

EXT. LAKE OUTSIDE MEXICO CITY—SUNSET

> GRANT (V.O.)
> To have been at Cerro Gordo and seen the gallant Robert E. Lee raise our national symbol above that mountain pass is something I will never forget. And so I remain… Yours devotedly, Ulys.

Grant stays a moment watching sunset's colors fade upon the water, then he mounts the little mustang, Nelly, and reluctantly rides back to join the conquerors in the city.

INT. WIIITE HAVEN, PARLOR—EVENING

ST. LOUIS—August 22, 1848

A wedding staffed by SLAVES. Grant is dressed in his finest uniform as are his groomsmen: Longstreet, Buckner, Ingalls.

BUCKNER

Your parents aren't here.

GRANT

My father won't enter the house of anyone who owns
slaves.

Julia (now 20), dressed in a white gown from Paris and wearing the
look of joy a husband treasures forever, enters.

LONGSTREET

Uncle Sam...Julia owns slaves.

GRANT

And as entirely against the practice as you know I am,
I see benefit in that I'll be short on visits from a certain
relative.

INT. WHITE HAVEN, ENTRY HALL—DAY

Grant says goodbye to his friends...

GRANT

Ingalls and I head to California—the part where Sherman hasn't started a gold rush.

To Longstreet and Buckner, respectively...

GRANT

You to Texas, you to New York.

BUCKNER

Having missed any share of glory in Mexico... I get
Commissary duty.

GRANT
You're both heroes. I'll miss you.
(shakes hands)
The Point weren't so bad.

BUCKNER
Not so bad at all.

And, with that, his friends are gone. Contemplatively, Grant wanders into the parlor where—

INT. WHITE HAVEN, PARLOR—CONTINUOUS

Julia and her family slaves have assembled luggage.

COL. DENT
Grant, I can arrange it all. After your wedding trip, you
join your regiment in California and Julia stays here.

GRANT
Colonel?

COL. DENT
You must realize, Julia could never live in the army.

Ulysses's arm goes around his wife.

GRANT
Would you like that, darling?

JULIA
I wouldn't think of it.

Col. Dent huffs.

> GRANT
>
> Since you've actually never been in the army, "Colonel,"
> we won't speak of this again, sir. She'll be coming with
> me.

EXT. FORT HUMBOLDT, CALIFORNIA—MORNING

FORT HUMBOLDT, CALIFORNIA—January 3, 1854

The harbor viewed from wooden palisades. Six skiffs filled with
SOLDIERS and their FAMILIES row for shore from a steamer.
Aboard, Grant puts the ship to the torch. Julia is nowhere to be seen.

> MCCLELLAN
>
> He's burning the steamer?

Timber fort walls enclose an armory, a quadrangle of enlisted men
tents, and a row of administration buildings and officers' houses.
Beside McClellan (now 27) is his aide de camp, Second Lieutenant
NATHAN WEXLER (25). All spit and polish and working himself
into a McClellan "disciple."

> WEXLER
>
> Sir, Captain Grant reports half the regiment and twice
> that in dependant women and children were lost to
> cholera in the mule-train crossing of Panama.

> MCCLELLAN
>
> Grant: very lackluster.

INT. MCCLELLAN'S HEADQUARTERS, FORT HUMBOLDT—DAY

Where Grant continues to affect the style of Taylor in his makeshift uniform, McClellan models Scott's vanity. A sheaf of letters
lies between them.

MCCLELLAN
Why, Captain, were these added to the mail pouch?

GRANT
They're letters from soldiers and soldier's wives who died.

MCCLELLAN
Cholera victims.

GRANT
Yes, sir.

MCCLELLAN
You fired the ship. Burn these.

GRANT
Captain, if those letters were infected, I wouldn't be here now.

MCCLELLAN
These men and their families died in Panama. Their deaths occurring before these individuals were added to my rolls; my command is not responsible for their cost.

GRANT
I'll pay the postage... Captain, about my own wife and son... I'd like to bring them overland.

MCCLELLAN
If you'd wanted them with you, they should have made the crossing.

GRANT
Sir, they would have died.

MCCLELLAN
Then you're lucky they didn't come.

EXT. FIELD OF DIRT—DAY

Blazing sun beats down on Grant who looks nothing like a soldier as he beats a hoe into the earth. Alongside him are three other men—Ingalls and twins SERGEANTS O'HARA (20s).

SGT. O'HARA #1
My family came to America to escape the damn potato!

GRANT
When everyone's complaining about rations you'll be glad to have 'em.

INGALLS
Not to mention the money you'll send your families from the surplus we sell in 'Frisco.

SGT. O'HARA #1
You all may have a wife and passel, but me and me brother's all we got.

As if this needs clarification—

SGT. O'HARA #2
We ain't married, sirs.

GRANT
Then you best enjoy hoeing.

INT. THE OFFICER'S MESS, FORT HUMBOLDT—NIGHT

A DANCE: OFFICERS and WIVES, some LOCAL COUPLES. Everyone enjoys themselves. At the punch bowl...

> MCCLELLAN
> Sitting there like the ugly girl.

Grant, alone and dirty from his field, sits against the wall. He studies a worn sheet of letter paper.

> MCCLELLAN
> Fool spends more time farming than soldiering. At the Point "Useless" Grant had trouble remembering his own name.

Wexler and other officers laugh. Ingalls does not, nor...

> INGALLS'S WIFE
> Struggling to earn money to send for his family: I think he's a noble man, *General* McClellan.

> MCCLELLAN
> You flatter me, Mrs. Ingalls. I'm yet a Captain.

> INGALLS'S WIFE
> Same as Captain Grant? My mistake.

As the WALTZ RESUMES, she detaches herself from the others.

> INGALLS'S WIFE
> Sam, you haven't asked me to dance.

> GRANT
> Music makes no sense to me, ma'am.

> INGALLS'S WIFE
> There must be some songs you know.

> GRANT
> Ma'am, there's only two songs I recognize. One's "Yankee Doodle."

> INGALLS'S WIFE
> And the other?

> GRANT
> Isn't.

Wexler sidles over to within earshot as—

> INGALLS'S WIFE
> *(re: Grant's letter)*
> Word from Mrs. Grant?

Grant shows her. It is the outline of a baby's hand.

> GRANT
> I've a second son I've never met.

Wexler sees Grant's welling eyes...

EXT. FIELD OF DIRT—DAY

POURING RAIN. Grant, Ingalls, and the O'Haras stand in a wagon as floodwaters wash away their crop.

EXT. RYAN'S GENERAL STORE, EUREKA, CALIFORNIA—DAY

MORE RAIN. Grant alone on the porch beside the whiskey barrel. He holds the dipper, stares into space. OVER THIS:

GRANT (V.O.)

Dear Wife, you do not know how forsaken I feel here. Sometimes I get so anxious to see you, and our little boys, that I'm tempted to resign and trust Providence and my own exertions, for a living.

Drunk, he refreshes from the dipper.

INT. GRANT'S HOUSE, FORT HUMBOLDT—NIGHT

Grant writing this letter...

GRANT (V.O.)

If I could see Fred, hear him talk; if I could meet baby Ulys, I'd be contented, but what then? With the failure of our crop, the young O'Hara brothers left the Army for San Francisco. Sadly, one of them fell through a rotted board on the wharf and drowned. His brother died the next day "cleaning his gun"...

Through his window, Ingalls and his wife are visible in the house next door, dining, enjoying each other's company.

GRANT (V.O.)

Captain Ingalls and I invested in hogs. After losing money shipping them, I invested my remainder in chickens to be sold in San Francisco. I've learned this morning they died on the trip. It's been abundantly proved to me that I am no businessman. When I get thinking about resigning, *poverty* stares me in the face.

Grant blows out his lamp, finds his whiskey bottle and pours a glass the measure of his pinkie.

EXT. THE QUADRANGLE, FORT HUMBOLDT—AFTERNOON

At the paymaster's table, Grant is so drunk he cannot count the troops' pay. McClellan gives him a fatal look.

MCCLELLAN

Mr. Wexler, Captain Grant has been drinking again.

For an instant, Wexler doesn't like McClellan; he knows why Grant is hurting.

MCCLELLAN

The man is drunk, Lieutenant.

WEXLER

Sergeant of the guard: arrest Grant.

As Wexler signals a SERGEANT OF THE GUARD to the job—

MCCLELLAN (V.O.)

I'm a generous man, Grant.

INT. MCCLELLAN'S HEADQUARTERS, FORT HUMBOLDT —AFTERNOON

Grant is drunk and looks like hell. McClellan slides a sheet of paper across his desk.

MCCLELLAN

Sign this resignation from the Army and there will be no trial nor will anyone need know your disgraceful personal choices which have led you to this.

Grant takes a pen. He dips it in an inkwell and signs.

INT. COMMISSARY OFFICE, NEW YORK HARBOR—DAY

NEW YORK HARBOR—

Two Months Later

Captain Simon Buckner looks up from his desk.

BUCKNER'S LIEUTENANT
Captain Sam Grant, sir.

BUCKNER
Send him in... Wait.

He quickly hides a bottle of whiskey and shot glasses. Grant enters.
Worse for his journey, he appears to be dying.

GRANT
Buck.

BUCKNER
Sweet Lord, Sam, you look the devil. I only just heard
last week from Longstreet you'd resigned. First Sherman quits, now you.

Grant purses his lips in chagrin.

BUCKNER
We'd have helped you fight those ridiculous charges.

GRANT
I was drunk on duty.

BUCKNER
Every officer out west is half the time drunk and the
other half absent without leave in recovering.

GRANT
Not McClellan.

BUCKNER
McClellan is a boy and a snob.

GRANT
I'd not have my wife know I'd been tried on such a charge.

INT. A HOTEL DINING ROOM—DAY

Buckner watches Grant finish a meal. He pays the bill.

BUCKNER
Why'd you come all the way up here 'stead of rounding the Cape and heading up the Ol' Miss'?

GRANT
I'm not sure Julia even wants me. We stopped writing. I have nothing.

Buckner lays down more money.

BUCKNER
Go home to your family.

GRANT
(embarrassed; takes cash)
As soon as I get in a crop I'll repay you.

BUCKNER
Gifts can only be reciprocated in kind. Go to your wife. Forget you were ever in this damned ol' army.

EXT. WHITE HAVEN—EVENING

Grant rides toward the plantation house. A short distance away, Col. Dent notices him from where Dent talks with his SLAVE FORE-MAN. Grant lifts a hand, but Julia's father turns away... Grant dismounts. Squaring his shoulders to the door, he KNOCKS. Julia's slave, Auntie Robinson, answers. FRED (4), at her skirts, ULYSSES "BUCK" JR. (2) in her arms...

> AUNTIE ROBINSON
> For the Lord's sake! It's the Cap'n.

> GRANT
> Auntie. Is this my new son?

> AUNTIE ROBINSON
> Yessah, Cap'n, this here's Ulysses Jr. Boys, this is your daddy.

> FRED
> *(scowling; hands on hips)*
> Mister, do you want to fight?

> GRANT
> I am a man of peace, but I will not be hectored by a person your size.

Fred's sudden grin is a mile long; he rushes his father, jumping onto him and hanging from his waist.

> JULIA (O.S.)
> Auntie, what *is* that commotion?

Julia enters. Freezes. Grant looks terrible, but to Julia he is God's grace personified. He takes a step. She doesn't move. He stops... Tears fill her eyes. She rushes his arms.

**EXT. HARDSCRABBLE FARM—SERIES OF SHOTS—MORNING/
DAY/NIGHT**

- *Grant chops trees clearing a farm from the wilderness.*
- *A log cabin rises from his hands. Fred watches in wonder.*
- *Grant behind a plow-horse pulling stumps...planting.*
- *The crops grow...and die from FROST AND SNOW.*

EXT. DOWNTOWN ST. LOUIS—DUSK

The city in winter: Grant (36) alone in a dilapidated wagon bundled
against the blowing snow in his patched army coat. He sells firewood. Grant is a failure even at this.

WILLIAM SHERMAN (39), a civilian now, exits a hotel. He looks
at Grant. Grant recognizes him, starts to smile, but Sherman sees
only a bum in a wagon and heads off... Sherman peers back.

INT. A ST. LOUIS BARROOM—EVENING

SHERMAN
Two Kentucky bourbons, bartender!

GRANT
Water for me, please... What are you doing in St. Louis?

SHERMAN
Mrs. Sherman always hated the Army. Got her wish a
few years back when I—never loving it myself—resigned
my commission to start a bank in San Francisco. I was
excellent at banking. The bank was not. You meet me
onward to Louisiana where I've been asked to head—
(grunts at the irony)
—a military academy.

He tosses back his drink.

> SHERMAN
>
> I'm a dead cock in the pit. Your prospects?

> GRANT
>
> Solving the problem of poverty.

Sherman signals another for himself; poured, he raises it.

> SHERMAN
>
> To West Point and the Regular Army: not very good schools for farmers or bankers.

INT. HARDSCRABBLE FARM—NIGHT

The boys sleep while Julia nurses a baby, Ellen "NELLIE" Grant. Grant smokes a pipe and does the family ledger.

> GRANT
>
> Fifty dollars.

> JULIA
>
> That can't be all we have left.

> GRANT
>
> It's all we made these six months.

Julia's face grows pained. What she has to say isn't easy.

> JULIA
>
> Do you remember William Jones?

> GRANT
>
> One of your father's slaves.

> JULIA
> Father is giving him to you.

Grant leans back in his chair, smiles ironically.

> GRANT
> That'd settle it for him, wouldn't it? A slave for filling
> my pipe and doing the work I've failed.

> JULIA
> It's winter. We have two children, a baby, another on
> the way: we'll be destitute before spring.

Julia finishes nursing. Grant takes his sleeping daughter and tucks
her into her cradle. Gazing at baby Nellie...

> GRANT
> We'll never be destitute as long as we have our family.

His words break the floodgates to Julia's emotions.

> JULIA
> If you didn't want him, you could sell him. Father says
> he's worth fifteen hundred dollars.

EXT. ST. LOUIS COURTHOUSE YARD—DAY

Grant and his slave, WILLIAM JONES (30s), at the auction block.
Jones is next to be sold. First in line is a used-up YARD NEGRO
(60s); the BIDDING is unmotivated. The Yard Negro is sold. His
NEW MASTER leads him past Grant faster than the old man can
handle. As the slave trips on his leg irons, Jones catches him. Jones
helps him up.

YARD NEGRO
(to Grant)
Thankee, Massa.

Jones steps to the block for Grant to sell.

INT. ST. LOUIS COURTHOUSE—DAY

ST. LOUIS, MISSOURI—March 29, 1859

Jones looks frightened as Grant raps on a CLERK'S window.

GRANT
Who do I see about transfer of ownership?

THE CLERK
The yard's where t'sell niggahs.

Grant slaps down his "Deed of Ownership."

GRANT
I'm not selling any man.

EXT. ST. LOUIS COURTHOUSE, WHARF—LATER

WILLIAM JONES
Please, Cap'n, I'm a good worker. I could git your corn
inta groun' an' offta ma'ket lickety-split.

GRANT
I couldn't afford to pay you.

WILLIAM JONES
But where'll I go?

They look at the steamboat wharf crowded with vessels and the vast Mississippi beyond. Grant puts a five dollar Half-Eagle gold piece in Jones's hand.

> GRANT
> William: anywhere you want.

EXT. MISSOURI ROAD—DAY

Winter has passed. A COMPANY of U.S. CALVARY is stretched along the spring-muddy lane. Grant, firewood wagon pulled to the side, speaks to Lieutenant GOREE (20s) who nods with a bit of embarrassment, then rides down the column to join—

MAJOR JAMES "PETE" LONGSTREET

> GOREE
> A broken down ex-Fourth Infantry captain offering services as a commissary clerk to drive beef cattle and issue rations, sir.

> LONGSTREET
> Fourth Infantry? What's his name?

> GOREE
> Grant, sir.

EXT. MISSOURI ROAD—LATER

As the column passes, Grant and Longstreet confer.

> GRANT
> Napoleon got at least one thing right: "an army travels on its stomach." Tell me where you're deploying and, with the proper authorizations, I'll see your regiment properly fed.

> LONGSTREET

Hear tell of an abolitionist fellow over Kansas way name a' John Brown?

Grant scratches his beard.

> GRANT

You know I'm not political, Pete. I just want to help feed your men.

> LONGSTREET

He massacred five pro-slavery settlers. 'Bout a hundred Missourians are armed an' achin' for a revenge we gotta put down...

Longstreet can see the desperation in his friend's face.

> LONGSTREET

Sam, the authorization I'd need to hire you'd prob'ly take more time than me gettin' my troops there an' back. This John Brown ain't no one special.

> GRANT

I only offered out of loyalty. God knows I've plenty work on my little Hardscrabble Farm... You take care, Pete.

> LONGSTREET
> You too, brother.

EXT. HARDSCRABBLE FARM—MORNING

Gray and drizzling. Grant (37) has packed Julia, Fred, Ulysses "Buck," daughter NELLIE (2) and a newborn son, JESSE, into his wagon. The NEW OWNER watches the Grants leave his property as his SLAVE chops into kindling the furniture Grant didn't have room for in his wagon.

EXT. JESSE GRANT'S HOME—AFTERNOON

Grant knocks on the door; renovation and fresh paint indicate Jesse Grant's success over the years. The door opens. Grant quickly removes his hat. His mother, Hannah Grant (50s), hardly reacts at the sight of him.

> HANNAH GRANT
> Well, well. Hiram Ulysses.

> GRANT
> I wrote I was coming.

> HANNAH GRANT
> Your father mentioned this. Your sister was here. You missed her.

> GRANT
> She and I write every week.

> HANNAH GRANT
> I s'pose you know everything, then.

> GRANT
> Everything about what?

> HANNAH GRANT
> About whatever it is you write.

Exceedingly uncomfortable, Grant enters his parents' house.

INT. JESSE GRANT'S PARLOR—EVENING

Jesse Grant (mid-60s) peers over his spectacles.

GRANT
I've never asked for anything, but as it's often customary for fathers to provide a bit of capital to sons when they start out in life, I'm prevailing upon you now for a loan to begin another farm.

JESSE GRANT
How much?

GRANT
One thousand dollars plus ten percent interest compounded over the four years of the loan.

JESSE GRANT
Hmm. Of course, you are far from "starting out in life" aren't you?
(Grant says nothing)
My gift to you was providing for your appointment to West Point and a career in the military.

GRANT
Which is why I'm proposing a loan.

JESSE GRANT
Do you actually believe after so much failure at farming you could make good of it this time?

GRANT
My bad luck has nothing to do with my abilities to work the land.

JESSE GRANT
Perhaps you should ascribe your predicament to God's justice for carrying on with slave-owning folk.

GRANT
We are starving to death.

JESSE GRANT
No one shall ever say Jesse Grant let his grandchildren starve.
(smiles blandly)
You shall disassociate yourself with the slaveholders of your wife's family and go to Galena, Illinois, where I have set up your younger brother in a store. I have given him instructions as to your salary and have asked he find a home for your family the rent to be taken from your wages.

Their handshake is awkward and they part like strangers.

EXT. "J.R. GRANT AND SONS"—MORNING

A four story and impressive leather goods store in the best part of town. A bundle of freshly tanned hides hits the icy sidewalk. Through the fancy window, Grant can be seen in the back whittling a new pipe by the stove. He pulls on a slouch hat, shoulders into his soldier's coat and heads to the door.

GALENA, ILLINOIS—October 16, 1859

Grant's strength is evident as he trudges inside with a bundle heavy enough to stagger a man much larger.

INT. "J.R. GRANT AND SONS"—CONTINUOUS

Grant's son, Fred (now 10) blocks his path.

FRED
Mister, do you want to fight?

GRANT
Not now, Fred.

Grant tries to step around him.

> FRED
>
> Mister: do you want to fight?!

> GRANT
>
> I said, not now.

> FRED
>
> Mister!

> GRANT
>
> Look you: I'm a man of peace and I'll not be hectored
> by a person your size!

Grant drops the bundle and playfully tackles Fred to the floor where they wrestle in delight. The SOUND OF THE DOOR. Fred leaps to his feet leaving Grant upon the boards. The entering customer is CONGRESSMAN ELIHU WASHBURN (45).

> WASHBURN
>
> You're the brother drummed out of the Army.

> GRANT
>
> Sam Grant. May I help you?

> WASHBURN
>
> A little early to be drinking...?

Washburn looks past Grant. Grant follows his gaze to the second floor where Grant's younger brother by fifteen years, ORVIL (23), watches, embarrassed.

> ORVIL GRANT
>
> Didn't expect a freeze overnight. What about you,
> Congressman?

Washburn steps around Grant. Grant makes a face at Fred, who old enough to understand what's happened, doesn't respond. That's what hurts Grant most.

INT. GALENA SALOON—DAY

Grant pours whiskey to the measure of his pinkie, drinks it down. Although the saloon bustles with patrons—CITY MEN in suits, TRADESMEN, LABORERS all in BOISTEROUS CONVERSA-TION—Grant keeps to himself nursing his humiliation.

> HOSTLER
>
> He beat Lincoln for the Senate, he'll beat him to President.

> HOSTLER'S BUDDY
>
> Different times. With the South threatening secession, Douglas's lick-ass of the planter class isn't going to work north of Mason-Dixon.

Grant drinks another—already halfway through the bottle.

> HOSTLER
>
> Different times don't mean nothing where that gangly railmaker's concerned. Lincoln's been a loser since the thirties.

> DRUGGIST CLERK
>
> Since thirty-two. That's the first time he lost for the legislature.

> HOSTLER
>
> There'ya go. And he got hisself beat again when he tried for Congress.

DRUGGIST CLERK
Forty-three and forty-eight. He lost for the Congress
twice.

HOSTLER'S BUDDY
All I'm saying's a vote for Democrat Douglas is a vote
for slavery.

At the back of the room, another man drinks alone. Dark-skinned,
five-eight and two-hundred pounds with massive shoulders and
chest. His name is ELY PARKER (35; Grant's future pallbearer).

BLACKSMITH
I'll give one thing for Lincoln: he'll keep us out of war.

HOSTLER
He'll be the first to get to war!

HOSTLER'S BUDDY
C'mon fellas, we can all agree on this: if it is war we'll
kick those Southern fancy boys off the tip a'Florida!

Grant speaks into his whiskey glass without looking at them.

GRANT
They'll fight hard. They have the training and the
temperament.

BLACKSMITH
Ha! All you did in the army was get shit-faced 'til your
"temperament" got you throwed the fuck out!

He laughs and the others laugh with him.

> GRANT
> Friend, I'm sure your views are quite as comprehensible if you don't try to clinch them with sulphurous language.

> BLACKSMITH
> You callin' me sul-fer-sus?

The Hostler lays a hand on Grant's shoulder.

> HOSTLER
> This ain't no lady's club, Grant.

At the back of the room, Ely Parker frowns. He doesn't appreciate the way Grant is being handled. Grant shrugs the hand from his shoulder. The Hostler doesn't like that and takes a swing, but Grant bobs out of his stool and the blow misses. Grant's blow doesn't— not his first to the Hostler's gut, nor his second to his jaw.

> HOSTLER'S BUDDY
> What the hell?!

He goes for Grant and they fight. As stools and men tumble, as glasses break, Grant finds himself the center of a BRAWL in which he is the singular opponent of everyone else. Although Grant is the shortest man in the room, he is a man who "won't be hectored." He wades into all comers with his fists...but Grant is outnumbered six to one and soon finds himself, back against the bar, in the fist-fight of his life. He'd lose this fight if it weren't that two of his attackers were hoisted into the air and thrown across the room.

ELY PARKER

loves a fight and by his own status appreciates the underdog. He joins Grant with whom he fights back to back. In a matter of moments, their opponents are laid out.

DRUGGIST CLERK
This ain't no nigger fight.

ELY PARKER
Nor am I an African.
(to the bartender)
How much?

BARTENDER
Five dollars.

Ely Parker takes his wallet from his broadcloth suit.

ELY PARKER
Here's five for the damage and one more: drinks for our friends.
(to Grant)
Another for you?

GRANT
No thanks—doesn't agree with me.

EXT. GALENA SALOON—EVENING

On the sidewalk, Grant fishes out his whittled pipe. Ely Parker lights a cigar. The two men smoke.

GRANT
I had that handled.

Parker laughs, his humor full and genuine.

GRANT
You're not Negro. You foreign?

ELY PARKER
Ely Parker.
(Ely pronounced like "freely")
Seneca Indian.

GRANT
Sam Grant.

He shakes Parker's hand.

GRANT
Parker? Did some engineering work for Army couple
years back?

ELY PARKER
Still do.

GRANT
Pay well?

ELY PARKER
Benefit of not being a citizen, Army has to pay me as a
civilian...so I stick 'em hard.

They both walk and smoke, sharing a pleasant silence.

ELY PARKER
War will come. No matter who's president. When it
does, I'll fight beside you to the end.

Grant gives his new friend a quizzical cock of the head.

ELY PARKER
However long, you, Sam, will see it to the end. I was
dreamed there.

They stop before Ely Parker's hotel. Years later Grant will remember this moment with awe, but on this night he grins not holding weight with Native American spookiness.

ELY PARKER
The Great Spirit told my mother this before I was born.

GRANT
(*chuckles*)
If there *is* a war, Ely, you might be there. Me? Doubtful.

Parker's conviction is hard. Real.

ELY PARKER
There is no doubt. I will be beside you.

EXT. A COUNTRY BRIDGE—NIGHT

HEAVY RAIN. JOHN BROWN (59), the tall, mad, messianic abolitionist addresses TWENTY-ONE ARMED MEN.

JOHN BROWN
Across this river lies Virginia and the abomination to
God known as American Slavery. We cross this bridge
to do battle against that institution; we cross this bridge
calling for uprising; we cross this bridge into history!

The men with Brown shake their muskets and—those without—pikes in the air as he leads them to destiny.

INT. REPUBLICAN PARTY CONVENTION, CHICAGO —NIGHT

A vast hall, festooned with pine boughs and bunting—

> REPUBLICAN PARTY OFFICIAL
> ...our Republican Party Candidate and next President of these United States, Abraham Lincoln!

APPLAUSE as ABRAHAM LINCOLN (51) steps forward in the "speaker's box" to address the DELEGATES. Before educating himself to the bar in Illinois, Lincoln's voice developed as the product of Kentucky poverty: shrill, nasal, somewhat southern and wholly unsettling.

> LINCOLN
> We are now far into the fifth year of a policy initiated with the confident promise of putting an end to slavery agitation.

EXT. FEDERAL ARSENAL, HARPERS FERRY—NIGHT

Brown and his raiders capture the Federal arsenal, KILLING the GUARDS on duty. Brown hands out muskets and powder.

> LINCOLN (V.O.)
> Under the operation of that policy, that agitation has not only *not* ceased, but has constantly augmented. In my opinion, it will not cease, until a crisis shall have been reached and passed. "A house divided against itself cannot stand." I believe this government cannot endure permanently half slave and half free.

FEDERAL MARINES, carrying the American flag and the flag of Virginia, arrive under the command of Colonel Robert E. Lee (52, hair and mustache still brown). Lee sends Marines, to breach the arsenal doors. A GUNFIGHT ensues.

INT. FEDERAL ARSENAL, HARPERS FERRY—LATER

Lee takes the surrender from Brown whose head bleeds from a saber cut—only adding to his maniacal look.

> LEE
> Those two dead boys—they're your sons, Mr. Brown?

> JOHN BROWN
> Forfeiting their lives for a cause greater than life itself.

> LEE
> Would that be armed treason against our nation or a father's vanity?

> JOHN BROWN
> The abolishment of slavery, sir. As God's law directs all Christian men to their duty.

As Lee stares at him before taking John Brown in arrest...

> LINCOLN (V.O.)
> I do not expect the Union to be dissolved—

INTERCUT: CLOSE ON LINCOLN'S FACE

> LINCOLN
> I do not expect the house to fall—but I do expect it will cease to be divided. It will become all one thing... Or all the other.

INT. COURT ROOM, HARPERS FERRY—DAY

The courtroom is filled with CITIZENS, STATE and MILITARY PERSONNEL. JUDGE RICHARD PARKER (34). All listen intently.

JUDGE RICHARD PARKER

I will not permit myself to give expression to any of those feelings which at once spring up in every breast when reflecting on the enormity of the guilt in which those are involved who invade by force a peaceful, unsuspecting portion of our common country, raise the standard of insurrection amongst us, and shoot down without mercy Virginia citizens defending Virginia soil against their invasion... Mr. Brown, before sentence is passed, you may speak if you so desire it.

JOHN BROWN

I have, may it please the court, a few words to say...

He is helped from the cot he lies upon, recovering from his wounds. As he speaks his words make him stronger, fill him with life...until he is standing fully erect.

JOHN BROWN

This court acknowledges, as I suppose, the validity of the law of God. I see a book kissed here which I suppose to be the Bible, or at least the New Testament. That teaches me that all things whatsoever I would that men should do to me, I should do even so to them. It teaches me, further, to "remember them that are in bonds, as bound with them." I endeavored to act up to that instruction. I say, I am yet too young to understand that God is any respecter of persons. I believe that to have interfered as I have done as I have always freely admitted I have done in behalf of His despised poor, was not wrong, but right. Now, if it is deemed necessary that I should forfeit my life for the furtherance of the ends of justice, and mingle my blood further with the blood of my children and with the blood of millions in this slave country whose rights are disregarded by wicked, cruel, and unjust enactments, I submit; so let it be done!

EXT. FEDERAL ARSENAL, HARPERS FERRY—DAY

John Brown is marched to the heavily guarded field gallows. A WOMAN in the crowd thrusts a pen and paper for Brown signature. He writes—

JOHN BROWN (V.O.)
I, John Brown, am now quite certain that the crimes of this guilty land will never be purged away but with blood...

Up the stairs and over the trapdoor, a noose around his neck.

JOHN BROWN (V.O.)
I had as I now think: vainly flattered myself that without very much bloodshed...it might be done.

Lee, representing the Federal Government, watches, Thomas (soon-to-be Stonewall) Jackson (35), beside him.

JACKSON
There'll be war, sir.

LEE
Pray not, Major. Pray to God not.

The trapdoor opens beneath John Brown's boots. He hangs.

SMASH TO BLACK.

END OF PILOT—EPISODE 101

"AMERICAN MACBETH"

BY

Michael Frost Beckner

FADE IN:

EXT. LOUISIANA MILITARY ACADEMY—EVENING

A large family house is in the process of being framed near the main, stone seminary building built the year before.

LOUISIANA MILITARY ACADEMY—
December 24, 1860

Over the entry to the seminary building the school's motto **"By the Liberality of the General Government of the United States. The Union—*Esto Perpetua.*"**

A POSTMAN makes his way inside.

INT. SUPERINTENDENT SHERMAN'S OFFICE—EVENING

Having received the mail is DAVID BOYD (30s), Sherman's professor of Ancient Languages and good Southern friend.

BOYD
Fine house they're building you.

Sherman turns from the window, agitated.

SHERMAN
If my family ever lives in it. Any news on South Carolina's vote?

Boyd hands him a rolled newspaper.

BOYD
From yesterday.

Sherman quickly opens it. Boyd stands by the fireplace where he lights his pipe. Sherman's face pales as he reads.

> SHERMAN
> They went and did it...

> BOYD
> South Carolina's seceded?

> SHERMAN
> They threatened if Lincoln were elected! He's president! Yes, they've seceded!

> BOYD
> Cump, it was inevitable.

Sherman takes on his trademark habit: pacing and talking fast.

> SHERMAN
> You people of the South—you—you believe there can be such a thing as peaceable secession?!

> BOYD
> Calm down, Louisiana isn't South Carolina.

> SHERMAN
> You'll all follow! Damn it: don't you people understand?! The North *must* fight you for its own preservation.

> BOYD
> Let me see that.
> (*grabs the paper*)
> Nothing in here says the North is planning war.

> SHERMAN
> This country will be drenched in blood.

Sherman exhibits another habit: pulling his cropped red hair.

BOYD
Sit down, Cump. Have a drink; let's talk this over.

He goes to Sherman's decanter of Madeira. Sherman is too agitated to drink.

BOYD
You need to get hold of yourself. The cadets are assembling for dismissal to Christmas break.

But Sherman can't get hold of himself and his emotions run freely in front of his friend.

SHERMAN
Boyd: if war comes it will make me fight against your people, whom I love best.
(a GROAN becomes)
I have more friends in South Carolina than Ohio.

A calculating look glimmers in Boyd's eyes.

BOYD
If there's to be war—which I don't think there will be—but if there is... Word's reached me that were you only to ask, there's a generalship waiting for you here in Louisiana.

Sherman looks at Boyd as if he were insane.

SHERMAN
This isn't a game with choosing sides! War's a terrible thing!

BOYD
Don't think we're up to the task?

> SHERMAN

You're a brave, fighting people—you'll fight like the devil—but the people of the North—

> BOYD

Shopkeepers and bankers: what do they know of a hard day's work?

> SHERMAN

Boyd, they're not going to let this country be destroyed without a mighty effort to save it! The Northern people not only outnumber the whites of the South, the North can make a steam-engine and railroads, *fleets*; hardly a yard of cloth or pair of shoes can you make. You're rushing to war with one of the most powerful, ingeniously mechanical and determined people on earth. Never in history has an agricultural people been victorious over an industrialized army.

Boyd stares hard, Sherman's words striking truth.

> BOYD

I speak for the entire faculty, Colonel Sherman: we will do anything to keep you here regardless where Louisiana falls politically in this...

INT. ASSEMBLY HALL, LOUISIANA MILITARY ACADEMY —NIGHT

CADETS, boisterous over South Carolina's announcement of secession, hardly pay attention as Boyd steps to the podium.

> BOYD
> Attention Cadets! Be seated!

They sit, but continue to fidget.

BOYD
I know how anxious all of you are what with the secession news and the Christmas holiday you-all are leaving us for... Please settle!... It is my sad, unwanted obligation to announce that, because of the political situation developing North and South, against the urging and emotion of his fellow faculty members and the Board of Directors, our Superintendent, Colonel William T. Sherman, has tendered his resignation from this institution.

Nervous energy gone, the cadets gape in shock.

BOYD
This is the worst Christmas gift I could give you as I love with a heart as open as all of yours, our dear leader.

Sherman, seated first of the rest of the faculty, holds his head. Some students VOCALIZE THEIR DISMAY.

BOYD
(*choked up*)
What more can I say? Cadets: you will now be addressed by Colonel William Tecumseh Sherman!

The APPLAUSE for Sherman is overwhelming. He removes his hands from his face. He takes a moment to gather himself to rise and step to the podium. He finds a prepared speech in his breast pocket. There is total silence in the hall. Sherman opens his speech as his eyes brim with sudden tears.

SHERMAN
Cadets—

The tears overflow his eyelids and pour down his cheeks into the red bristles of his beard. He swallows a lump...

SHERMAN
Cadets...

He can't do this.

SHERMAN
My Cadets...my dear, gallant boys. I came South to
Louisiana...

His words trail off as his tears overwhelm him. As he looks out over
these fine young men, he knows that most of them will not survive
the battlefield. Tecumseh Sherman folds his speech and pockets it.
He blinks the tears from his eyes then puts both his hands over his
heart.

SHERMAN
You are all in here.

A CADET OFFICER
(through his own tears)
Cadets, atten-tion.

The young men come to their feet as one. Sherman stops, tries to
smile bravely at them, then, shaking his head walks down the line
of his FACULTY. Each of these Southern men extend their hand to
him. He shakes a few—he wants to shake them all, but instead he
bows and with deep sadness—

SHERMAN
You are driving me and hundreds of others out of the
South who have cast our fortunes here, love your people
and want to stay.

Having regained his composure, Sherman pulls himself erect.

SHERMAN
You are all my friends... I hope that if I should go into
the army, I'll not catch you, for I should surely hang
you.

He leaves them stunned. OVER THIS: THE SCREAMING
WHISTLE—

EXT. FORT SUMTER—DAWN

—and EXPLOSION OF CONFEDERATE ARTILLERY SHOT
AND SHELLS pounding this Charleston Harbor fort to rubble.

FORT SUMTER, SOUTH CAROLINA—April 13, 1861

CLOSE ON: THE STARS AND STRIPES coming down at Fort
Sumter to be replaced by the white flag of surrender.

FADE OUT.

INT. CAILLOUX'S CIGAR SHOP—DAY

NEW ORLEANS, LOUISIANA

Two men smoke cigars. A client: Virginian JESSE DUNLAP (30s),
kind to a fault and everyone's friend; and the owner-proprietor:
Afro-Creole, ANDRE CAILLOUX (36), an athlete's build and
charismatic eyes, known to declare himself the "blackest man in all
New Orleans."

With a flourish, Jesse signs a purchase order.

JESSE DUNLAP
Deal done. Twenty barrels of Mr. Andre Cailloux's
famous hand-rolled Louisiana "perique" cigars now to
be available in Virginia.

                    CAILLOUX
          Finest hand-rolled cigars. Anywhere.

And, smiling, he gives one to Jesse and lights it for him, before lighting his own. They each savor the smoke a moment, until Jesse decides to point out the "elephant" in the room. He nods at the military uniform Cailloux wears, concerned.

                    JESSE DUNLAP
          You're a lieutenant.

                    CAILLOUX
                    (deflecting)
          Soon as we are done here, I've got to drill my men.

                    JESSE DUNLAP
          ...In the Confederate Army?

                    CAILLOUX
          1st Regiment, Louisiana Native Guard. Yes, sir, Mr.
          Dunlap.

Jesse smirks and rubs his chin not sure what one says to a friend and business colleague who is a black man in the Confederate Army. Cailloux sees his discomfort, toys with it by puffing smoke, admiring the smoldering tip of his cigar and deflecting again...

                    CAILLOUX
          Your Virginia going to follow South Carolina and the
          rest of us in secession?

This is actually a serious subject to Jesse; his smirk fades, his face grows worried.

                    JESSE DUNLAP
          A'cours't I've got no crystal ball, but, starting with
                    (MORE)

JESSE DUNLAP (CONT'D)
Washington, four of the first five presidents came from Virginia. I'd say we Virginians have more to do with building this nation than dismantling it.

CAILLOUX
Amen to that.

JESSE DUNLAP
Amen.

They smoke a moment in silence...

JESSE DUNLAP
Darn you. You're going to make me say it.

CAILLOUX
That which is..?

JESSE DUNLAP
Fifteen years ago you were a slave!

Cailloux give a slow, single nod. Jesse's cigar has gone out and Cailloux relights it.

CAILLOUX
Bought my freedom and that of my wife to marry her.

JESSE DUNLAP
Then Mr. Cailloux, for the love of God, why *that* uniform?

CAILLOUX
It allows me this.

And now Cailloux is as serious as he's ever been. He reaches below the counter and lifts his regulation musket.

                    CAILLOUX
In my hands to protect my house and my family when
N'awlins burns.

He means it and Jesse fully understands.

                    JESSE DUNLAP
You're a good man.

                    CAILLOUX
We've done business a dozen years and my sentiment is
likewise.

They shake hands. Jesse takes his paperwork.

                    CAILLOUX
That pretty wife and daughter of yours doing fine?

                    JESSE DUNLAP
Fine as frog's hair, Mr. Dunlap.

                    CAILLOUX
You keep 'em that way.

                    JESSE DUNLAP
You too. I mean that.

And as he tips his hat and goes...

INT. GALENA COURTHOUSE—EVENING

                    GALENA'S MAYOR
Peace, good citizens; peace and accommodation. Let
the erring Southern sisters depart in peace!

BOOS drive the MAYOR from the stage. A fiery lawyer, JOHN A. RAWLINS (31), of pale complexion made striking by black hair and beard, steps forward and calms the crowd.

> RAWLINS
> I have been a Democrat all my life, but this is no longer a question of politics. It is simply Union or disunion, country or no country. South Carolina! Mississippi! Florida! Alabama, Georgia, Louisiana and Texas! All seceded?! Only one course is left! We will stand by the flag of our country and appeal to the God of Battles!

The CHEERING, tremendous, is heard on the steps of—

EXT. "J. R. GRANT AND SONS"—EVENING

> GRANT
> I think I ought to go back into the service.

His brother, Orvil, takes Grant's receipt book from his hands...then gives a brush to Grant's faded captain straps. His face awash with relief—

> ORVIL GRANT
> Think so, too.

EXT. COUNTRY ROAD, ILLINOIS INTO OHIO—PRE-DAWN

As the first rays of sun lighten darkness, Grant can be seen riding alone. With purpose.

INT. DEPT. OF THE OHIO HEADQUARTERS —MORNING

Grant, in his worn-out military coat and hat, presents himself to the duty officer. It is Nathan Wexler.

GRANT
U-S Grant, Captain U-S Army retired, for the general.

WEXLER
Wait here...

He opens a door and approaches a general at his desk. The general looks up from his newspaper. It is George McClellan.

WEXLER
If you'll have a seat, General McClellan will see you presently.

Grant sits. Some civilians enter and are immediately allowed to see McClellan. Grant glances at—

THE CLOCK—9:25. DISSOLVE TO... THE CLOCK—10:00
The civilians leave. No one else enters, but...

THE CLOCK—GOES FROM 10...TO 10:30

GRANT
Is there a better time I could come back to see the general?

WEXLER
General McClellan asked you wait.

Grant resumes his seat and 10:31 BECOMES 11:30. Grant rises.

GRANT
Tell the general I'll come back tomorrow when he's less occupied.

INT. HOME OF WINFIELD SCOTT, FRONT PARLOR—DAY

Robert E. Lee (54) sits formally beside—

SCOTT

Since the fall of Fort Sumter the South is in a state of revolution.

General Scott (now 72) has become the whale his obesity promised (over 300 pounds). He sits in a wheelchair of his own design augmented by a wooden frame that rises above his head encasing him in a contraption of ropes, weights, and pulleys: the only things affording his limbs movement.

SCOTT

I'm hopeful, Colonel Lee, you are here to reverse the decision you made yesterday in rejecting President Lincoln's offer to assume command of all Federal Armies.

Scott pauses. Lee says nothing.

SCOTT

Save for your wife's grandfather, George Washington, this country has not produced a greater soldier than you, Colonel Lee.

LEE

General, you flatter me at a time when, though my cheeks are dry, my soul weeps for the nation *all* our ancestors gave so much for.

SCOTT

I expect appropriate non-violent maneuvers will bring this conflict to a speedy and peaceful end.

> LEE

I'm devoted to the Union, but if it's war—not maneuvers—that must come to Virginia? I wouldn't be able to raise my sword against my relatives, my children, my home. Sir, this is in God's hands now. As I dare not pretend to know His will, I've come only to resign my commission.

> SCOTT
> If I don't accept?

A beat. Lee rises.

> LEE

I'll return now to our native State to share in the miseries of her people. Know this, General, that save in her defense, I never desire again to draw my sword.

EXT. LONG BRIDGE, WASHINGTON CITY—MORNING

As Lee guides his horse onto the bridge over the Potomac, a NEWS-BOY thrusts a paper at him.

THE WASHINGTON *STAR*—"VIRGINIA SECEDED!"

His bleak expression grown only bleaker.

EXT. ARLINGTON HOUSE—DAY

Lee hands his horse to a SLAVE. His wife, MARY CUSTIS LEE (54), a long-time sufferer of rheumatoid arthritis, rises from her wheelchair to meet him. He hands her the newspaper. Of the two at this moment, she appears the stronger.

> MARY CUSTIS LEE
> And what of secession?

CENTER>LEE

I'm afraid I'm one of those dull creatures who can't see
good in it.

They share a sad look. He kisses her cheek. He strides in past her
and disappears up the shadowy staircase.

INT. LEE'S BEDROOM, ARLINGTON HOUSE—DAY

He removes his uniform tunic and sword. At the window, he stares
across the river toward the capitol on its hill, its uncompleted dome
appearing as nothing so much as damage from a war now coming.
Lee turns from the window and begins to pace. His troubled eyes
focus on a portrait of George Washington above a desk where he
finds his prayer book.

INT. DRAWING ROOM, ARLINGTON HOUSE—NIGHT

Mary Custis, in her wheelchair, reads from the Bible as the boards
in the floor above CREAK with the tread of her husband's PACING.
The pacing stops. There is a MUFFLED THUMP then silence.
Mary smiles softly. Knowingly.

INT. LEE'S BEDROOM, ARLINGTON HOUSE—NIGHT

Lee is illuminated by moonlight. He is a man in supplication stripped
of all: on his knees in the center of the room.

LEE

Oh God, by whom the meek are guided in judgment,
and the light riseth up in darkness for the godly: Grant
us, in all our doubts and uncertainties, the grace to
ask what thou wouldest have us to do, that the Spirit
of wisdom may save us from all false choices, and that
in thy light we may see light, and in thy straight path

(MORE)

> LEE (CONT'D)

may not stumble... Lord, there is no greater calamity for this country than a dissolution of the Union. It will be an accumulation of all the evils we complain of, and I am willing to sacrifice everything but honour for its preservation...

EXT. ARLINGTON HOUSE—MORNING

Dressed in civilian clothing, Lee stands with his wife, his THREE DAUGHTERS, and three sons: CUSTIS (29), ROONEY (24) and ROBERT JR. (17). SLAVES pack carriages with luggage.

> LEE (V.O.)

...I know, Heavenly Father, your prosperity is always given to the righteous, but in this coming fratricidal war, both parties are wrong and I see no righteousness to be found.

Moving across the Long Bridge from Washington City and heading up the single road to Arlington House, bayonets glinting, come A COMPANY OF UNION SOLDIERS.

> LEE

You will take our daughters and Robert to our "White House" on the Peninsula.

> ROBERT LEE

Father, I plan to enlist with Virginia.

> LEE

You'll do no such thing.

> CUSTIS

If it were up to me we'd use these troops to fortify Arlington House with all our guns pointing South.

ROONEY

If we free all the servants, perhaps they'll let us keep
our home.

LEE

These whom we have, having belonged to your mother's father, by his will, are to be freed next year...

The carriages are ready. Lee's horse is brought forward.

LEE

If I owned all four million slaves, I would gladly free
them to avoid war and save the Union.

Turning to a slave, SELENA GRAY (30s)—

LEE

Miss Selena, you are entrusted with preserving the heir-
looms in this home belonging to George Washington,
Madam's grandfather and the father of our country,
from marauding soldiers.

He hands her a letter. She takes it, curtsies, steps back.

LEE

Hand this to their captain with my regard.
(*mounts his horse*)
Secession is nothing but revolution. But we are Lees and
we are Virginians.

He rides off.

EXT. DEPT. OF THE OHIO HEADQUARTERS—MORNING

The civilians of the day before, now dressed in sparkling new offi-cers' uniforms, linger on the front steps. At the sight of Grant com-ing from the hotel across the street they share a joke—clearly at Grant's expense. Grant walks inside.

INT. DEPT. OF THE OHIO HEADQUARTERS—MORNING

GRANT
Captain U-S Grant, retired, for General McClellan.

WEXLER
If you'll have a seat, the General will see you when he's available.

Grant stands before Wexler a beat, then resumes his seat from the day before. He looks at—

THE CLOCK—9:18...DISSOLVE TO:...9:50

General McClellan comes to his office door. Grant rises.

MCCLELLAN
If you'd come into my office?

The request is to a LIEUTENANT waiting behind Grant. The lieu-tenant enters McClellan's office. The door closes.

THE CLOCK—9:51 BECOMES 10:30...

The Lieutenant—now a Captain—leaves. Grant waits. 10:30 BECOMES 11:25. Grant approaches Wexler. Calmer than the situ-ation actually demands—

GRANT

Tell General McClellan that I am here and I am offering my services which include my training at West Point
and my combat experience in the Mexican War. Do you
understand me, Lieutenant Wexler?

WEXLER

General McClellan asked that I only interrupt him with
Army business. You're a drunk, Grant, and when you
get thirsty enough you'll go away.

EXT. GRANT'S HOME, GALENA, ILLINOIS—EVENING

Grant, returned from Ohio, sits on his porch with Col. Dent (now
75); Julia (35) sits beside her husband, baby Jesse (2) in her lap. Grant
smokes his pipe as his three other children, Fred (11), "Buck" (9) and
Nellie (6) run across the yard, through the house, around the back
and through again.

GRANT

The fact is, Colonel, command of this volunteer army is
being given to civilians. An old regular army officer like
me isn't much in demand except for paperwork.

COL. DENT

Grant: I never intended my favorite daughter to marry
a soldier, but with this war the place for real soldiers is
the South. Yesterday, Virginia seceded and with it the
illustrious Robert E. Lee.

GRANT

Illustrious in treason.

COL. DENT

Bah. You must have some abilities he could put to use
somewhere.

JULIA
Didn't you hear Ulys, father? Bobby Lee is a traitor.

COL. DENT
Robert E. Lee, like his ancestor George Washington, understands the hard choices of duty and honor to the land of his birth.

GRANT
Washington's foremost concern was the unity of the nation.

COL. DENT
Again: bah!

GRANT
You don't see in this the doom of slavery?

COL. DENT
The Confederacy is fighting to protect the very institution.

GRANT
A fight which will force the production of cotton to other parts of the world from which the South will never recover. In the end, your Negroes will have never been worth fighting over.

COL. DENT
Daughter, it's proven: you married a fire-breathing abolitionist.

GRANT
Whatever may have been my political opinions before, there are two parties now: Traitors and Patriots and I want to be ranked with the latter and stronger party.

(MORE)

GRANT (CONT'D)
(*rising; to Julia*)
I've been asked as a civilian to accompany Galena's regiment to Springfield to help in procurement.

"A civilian?" Colonel Dent looks askance. The boys and Nellie streak past into the house.

JULIA
I'm pleased for you, Ulys. Do you think Fred might enjoy going, too?

GRANT
I'll ask.

He moves behind the door frame. The children rush up the steps only to stop, noticing their father missing.

BUCK
Where's Papa?

Grant lunges from behind the door posed like a bear. He wrestles them, laughing, into the yard and—

EXT. THE SPRINGFIELD FAIRGROUNDS—MORNING

A boisterous COMPANY OF GALENA VOLUNTEERS in all manner of uniform are led by DANDY OFFICERS on horseback who share a jug. They enter the fields where THE REGIMENT has put up a sloppy camp. In the dust at column's end ride two civilians: Ulysses Grant on a fine blooded roan and Fred on a pony.

A SERIES OF SHOTS:

- *Grant hands out uniforms from the back of a wagon.*
- *Officers failing, Grant steps in to train soldiers with broomsticks as rifles.*
- *Grant walks with some papers. A cocky soldier, PRIVATE COMBS (20), knocks off his hat, laughing, only to face with young Fred. Ashamed, Combs returns the hat. Grant thanks him. Then has Combs arrested and led to the stockade.*
- *Officers drink while Grant has the soldiers rebuild camp.*
- *Grant trains the men now armed with muskets. Private Combs performs with an alacrity Grant's discipline has produced.*

EXT. FREDERICKSBURG STREET—MORNING

FREDERICKSBURG, VIRGINIA—June 16, 1861

Light traffic, excitement among TOWNSFOLK; MILITIA MEN congregate, TEENS trying to join their circles; BOYS play army— "BANG-BANG-DEAD, BILLY YANK!"

FIND: ABBY DUNLAP (30s), local laundress and seamstress, the most beautiful woman in Fredericksburg...and, although she doesn't know it yet, its strongest citizen of heart.

Friendly eyes turn as she carries a two-handled milk pail with her husband, tobacco dealer, Jesse Dunlap. Today his usual smile is forced, distracted. Trotting alongside, their daughter, EMMA (9), is the perfect combination of both.

> EMMA
> Just because you want to come-with this morning— Daddy—carrying the pail with Mama s'my chore.

> JESSE DUNLAP
> You'll get your penny-sweet, Emma.

EXT. DAIRY, FEED AND POST STORE—CONTINUOUS

A nagging feeling something is wrong with her husband...

> ABBY
> Jesse, you all can wait here. Emma and I'll go in.

Confederate Army STAFF OFFICERS mill about Longstreet's horse at the boarding house across the street.

> ABBY
> I'd have been surprised you *wouldn't* have wanted to come out and spectate all these goings on.

Jesse smiles, handing the pail to their daughter.

> JESSE DUNLAP
> Careful placing the eggs.

> EMMA
> I'm always careful.

He tousles her hair. Strangely nervous, Abby shoots an "is everything alright?" smile over her shoulder at her husband as she and Emma go in. Jesse waits...then quickly enters.

INT. DAIRY, FEED AND POST—MORNING

Abby and Emma head out back as Jesse slips to the Postmaster window...today, a recruiting station. He leans in to a CONFEDERATE RECRUITER.

> JESSE DUNLAP
> General Longstreet's Corps?

EXT. DAIRY, FEED AND POST—MOMENTS LATER

Abby and Emma are on the front sidewalk, scanning both directions for Jesse when he emerges behind them. Stops. Abby catches her breath at his recruitment papers.

> ABBY
> You're almost forty years-old. Why would you do such a thing?

> JESSE DUNLAP
> State's Rights.

> ABBY
> I know all about State's Rights—just didn't think it would ever be used against *my rights*.

> JESSE DUNLAP
> Abby, Hanover and Prince William Counties: they're conscripting men older than me.

Off in the street, Longstreet emerges from the boarding house and mounts his horse. Begins riding in their direction.

> ABBY
> We don't live in either.

> JESSE DUNLAP
> Sure as rain, they'll come here.

Confused, Emma looks between them. Longstreet, Goree and his staff are now in earshot.

> JESSE DUNLAP
> Just saying, if I'm made to fight, it's best to *choose* who I fight with.

Goree dismounts. He goes inside.

EMMA
Are you General Longstreet?

LONGSTREET
Yes, Little Lady.

And speaking to Emma with words meant for Abby—

LONGSTREET
I'll take good care of your daddy in my army.

ABBY
General, my husband isn't like you.

LONGSTREET
No, ma'am. I 'magine he's bolder. Like you.
(to Emma)
Promise I'll have him back here in Fredericksburg by next Christmas.

A promise he will keep to the tune of 18,000 Union casualties... Goree emerges with the recruitment rolls.

INT. GRANT'S TENT, SPRINGFIELD—NIGHT

Fred, in his cot, watches his father pack their carpetbag.

FRED
Why can't we go with them, Papa?

GRANT
Because the regiment has received orders, and I gotta get you home.

As Grant speaks, Fred's eyes go to the tent flap.

> RAWLINS
> A moment, Sam?

EXT. GRANT'S TENT, SPRINGFIELD—NIGHT

Rawlins (from Galena), waits with Congressman Washburn.

> RAWLINS
> Sam Grant: the Honorable Elihu Washburn, representative from our Galena district.

Grant remembers him. He shakes his hand.

> WASHBURN
> Sam, I've been receiving complaints from the men of our regiment about their leadership.

Their first meeting an embarrassment, this cuts to the bone.

> GRANT
> It's inappropriate they bother you, sir. There is chain-of-command.

> WASHBURN
> Chain-of-command is broken. The colonel in question agrees and has resigned his commission.

Grant takes a confused beat.

> WASHBURN
> You have the unenviable quality of being a man who men above you underestimate. But in men beneath you: you instill great devotion.

GRANT

Sir, my rank and the rank of others is a system of organization—not a measure of social worth or individual
value.

WASHBURN

You're uncommon, Grant, because you believe that,
and the private soldiers of this command—my constit-
uency—see this...

Not understanding, Grant looks to Rawlins.

RAWLINS

The 21st Illinois is yours.

Grant's eyes move the to—

THE SPRAWL OF TENTS, THE STACKS OF ARMS AND
THE BONFIRES WARMING THE MEN, HIS MEN: THE
21ST ILLINOIS REGIMENT.

RAWLINS

You're back where you belong: a Colonel in Mr. Lincoln's Army.

OFF GRANT—HONOR RETURNING TO HIS FEATURES...
AND SOMETHING ELSE: THE IRON DETERMINATION TO
SUCCEED.

EXT. A MISSOURI TOWN—MORNING

WESTERN THEATER—
FLORIDA, MISSOURI—July 13, 1861

Grant rides at the head of the 21ST ILLINOIS VOLUNTEERS.

> GRANT (V.O.)
>
> Dear Julia... On July thirteenth, we commenced our
> first action.

A new private's coat has replaced the old with Grant's colonel's rank
sewn to its shoulders.

> GRANT (V.O.)
>
> In Mexico I had been led, but here I was leading and
> not just our lives were at stake but our Union and our
> reputation as men of Illinois, and they were following
> me, trusting these things to my care as I took them to
> meet the cold steel of the rebel guerilla leader, General
> Tom Harris, waiting to kill us to destroy that Union.

The soldiers rip Confederate flags from windows [**Note: this is their
national flag—the Stars and Bars—*not* the Confederate battle flag
depicting the diagonal St. Andrew's Cross**]; gaining momentum,
they move through town to A GRASSY SLOPE running, now, rifles
at right shoulder shift.

> GRANT (V.O.)
>
> As we approached the brow of the hill from which it
> was expected we could see Harris' camp, and possibly
> find his men ready formed to meet us, my heart kept
> getting higher and higher until it felt to me as though it
> was in my throat. I would have given anything to have
> been back in Illinois, but I hadn't the moral courage to
> halt and consider what to do.

Grant, leading his regiment, determined but terrified.

EXT. THE ENEMY VALLEY—DAY

—in full view. Grant halts. He slowly lowers his sword. Below are the remnants of an abandoned rebel camp; smoke curls from extinguished bonfires. Combs (now a corporal), stops, panting, beside him.

> COMBS
> Guess this fella Harris had more fear a'us then us a'him.

> GRANT
> Valuable lesson, Corporal. Secure the camp. Post pickets.

> COMBS
> Yes, sir.

Combs salutes. Grant rides down into the deserted camp.

EXT. THE CONFEDERATE WHITE HOUSE—DAY

RICHMOND, VIRGINIA—July 16, 1861

A gray stone building on a hill, the Confederate Stars and Bars flying over it.

GENERAL ROBERT E. LEE

dismounts his horse. An American Saddlebred it stands sixteen hands high and 1,100 pounds. Iron gray in color with black points, a long mane and flowing tail. Destined to become the most famous animal in American history, his name is Traveller.

> JEFFERSON DAVIS (V.O.)
> My present field commanders advise me that to win—

Handing Traveller to a SLAVE, Lee removes gloves and enters.

INT. CONFEDERATE WHITE HOUSE CABINET ROOM—DAY

President of the Confederate States of America, Jefferson Davis [now 54 and now with one damaged eye that by the end of the war will be completely covered by a gray film] faces Lee across the large cabinet table.

> JEFFERSON DAVIS
>
> —we need only stand on the defensive across the entire Confederacy and prevent the enemy from destroying us.

> LEE
>
> Mr. President: we don't have the depth of supply to hold that defense. Every day, our opponents' power grows and with it their unchristian desire to oppress us. We must meet them *here*. Virginia. And fight.

[Note: Lee's hair at the beginning of the war is brown—not white as most imagine. At this point it has begun to show iron gray. It does not go white (and then only the temples and his beard) until 1863.]

> JEFFERSON DAVIS
>
> A conclusion I've also come to... And why I have asked for you.

> LEE
>
> I will give my all to this command, Mr. President.

Lee rises and goes to a tactical wall map. He indicates—

> LEE
>
> Manassas Junction. This is where the major enemy blow falls. I will begin concentrating our forces—

> JEFFERSON DAVIS
>
> Manassas Junction? General Lee, I can't say I share that
> (MORE)

JEFFERSON DAVIS (CONT'D)
conviction. The Federals have made no move in that
direction. In any event, it is not a field command I offer
you.

Lee doesn't remember their last tactical conversation in Mexico.
Davis does and still detests Lee over it.

JEFFERSON DAVIS
As of today, you will be attached to this White House as
my personal military secretary.

LEE
I am *not* to have field command in this war? At all?

JEFFERSON DAVIS
Oh, I won't keep you too cooped up. I think you'll do a
fine job overseeing the digging of Richmond's defensive
works. And I will rely on you, in an *advisory* capacity,
as I make all strategic military decisions.

LEE
Mr. President, gladly I follow your orders.

He stands. Jefferson Davis signs and hands Lee his orders.

LEE
But the fight will be at Manassas.

Lee salutes his president and—

SMASH TO:

EXT. MANASSAS BATTLEFIELD—DAY

EASTERN THEATER—
THE BATTLE OF FIRST MANASSAS
("BULL RUN"), VIRGINIA—July 21, 1861

Colonel Sherman at the head of the Thirteenth U.S. Infantry, commanding Third Brigade, First Division, crests a ridge overlooking the stream "Bull Run." Sherman stops his horse, peering toward the SOUNDS OF A GREAT MOVEMENT OF MEN.

> SHERMAN
> I can't see a damned thing.

As if in answer, a CIVILIAN—with WIFE, OTHER GENTLE-MEN and their LADIES picnicking on the bluff—offers opera glasses. Sherman gives a quizzical look, takes the glasses.

SHERMAN'S POINT OF VIEW—OPERA GLASSES—A CONFEDERATE DIVISION

across Bull Run, wheeling its formation left in anticipation of attacking Sherman.

> SHERMAN
> Who are you, sir?

> CIVILIAN
> Name's Lovejoy; member of Congress.

> SHERMAN
> Why are you here?

> CIVILIAN
> We came to support the troops, watch them crush the rebellion.

SHERMAN
Fool politician! Get out of my lines, sir! Get out!

Affronted, Lovejoy takes his glasses and scuttles off.

Sherman leads his troops across a stone bridge and has them break
by right and left to both sides of the colors.

SHERMAN
By the Double Quick! March!

SHELLS EXPLODE, BULLETS SING, smoke roils. Sherman's brigade charges forward, flags waving, toward Confederate positions
at the crest of Henry Hill. The large percentage of men on both sides
have never seen battle before and both Union and Rebel forces break
organized ranks and turn the fight into a free for all.

[Note: For every battle, bullets that don't strike their targets do
strike something; things like trees and bushes and fences and *uniforms* quickly become bullet-riddled and destroyed. Additionally,
throughout the Civil War, "first volleys" usually are over 80% high
(looks flat, but planet is round) creating a rain of leaves, twigs and
branches on men in position. Also, Minie balls—the preferred
munition of both sides—expand when fired and make a startling
WHIZZING NOISE through the air unlike any sound normally
associated with modern gunfire. Due to slower velocity, larger size,
and a softer lead composition: when bullets hit men they make a
wet-sounding "thump;" when striking bone there is a distinctive
"crack." Men in battle, hit or not, discard items as they fight: battlefields become covered with litter; every cartridge is wrapped in
paper that, a portion of which spit from the mouth with every load,
fills the wind with scraps—and, from this, men's faces blacken over
the course of battle from the gunpowder that accumulates around
their mouth from biting open cartridges.]

Sherman rides up and down in front, urging his men on. They begin to push the Confederates back up the hill. The Henry House is turned to kindling by Union bullets and artillery shells and the Confederate morale shatters; the Rebels flee.

Sherman grimaces tasting victory. His men chase the Rebels through the bloody grass only to stall in horror as rising from the far side of Henry Hill where they have been lying—

THOMAS JACKSON'S VIRGINIANS

A WALL OF MUSKET FIRE rips into Sherman's division, breaking their charge. Sherman watches Jackson's men roll fifteen cannon forward to FIRE CANISTER. Bodies are ripped to shreds. Sherman's horse is wounded in the leg; bullets pluck Sherman's uniform without wounding him. He locks eyes with Jackson across the field. Confederate Brigadier General BARNARD ELLIOTT BEE, JR. (37), exhorts his troops—

GENERAL BEE
Form! Form! There stands Jackson like a stone wall!

Indeed, Jackson does, mounted stock-still on "Little Sorrel," the ugliest horse ever seen. Jackson is above average in height with an angular frame, muscular without a hint of fat, and in all his movements, from riding a horse to handling a pen, he is the most awkward man in the Confederate Army.

BULLETS rip into General Bee killing him. Jackson (now 38) signals his cannon to FIRE AGAIN. The Confederates, fleeing moments before, rally around Jackson shouting—

CONFEDERATE TROOPS
Stonewall! Stonewall! Stonewall!

The Federal Troops rout—among them ZOUAVES and a battalion of U.S. MARINES. Dying horses, blood pouring from their nostrils, madly fight AND SCREAM at each other on the ground to break free of destroyed artillery wagons that trap them in their traces.

Sherman holds his pistol as the smoke and chaos of a losing battle swirl around him. He watches in horror as U.S. Marine Corps LIEUTENANT is decapitated by an artillery shell an instant before a second shell cuts him in half taking the arm of another Marine who has reached out to catch him. All around, men of Sherman's division flee from GUNFIRE coming at them from every direction.

SHERMAN

Get into line, you pack of loafers and thieves!

But no one listens, and, soon, Sherman is impelled to disgracefully follow his dispirited men.

EXT. A VIRGINIA ROAD—EVENING

EASTERN THEATER—
RETREAT FROM THE BATTLE OF
FIRST "BULL RUN", VIRGINIA—July 21, 1861

The retreat from the battle is the worst panic the U.S. Army has ever seen. There is no order whatsoever and those PICNICKERS from Maryland who came to "watch the show," scramble, terrorized, through the tangled confusion of THE DEMORALIZED ARMY IN CHAOS. RAIN falls.

EXT. A FARM—NIGHT

The RAIN FALLS as the retreat continues throughout the night. Sherman has encamped his division in and around a farm. He gazes at a farmer, WILMER MCLEAN (47), and his miserable FAMILY, possessions loaded in a wagon. SERGEANT BANCROFT (22), Sherman's Orderly Sergeant, shows the man's identity papers.

SHERMAN

Mr. McLean, sir, I'm Colonel Sherman. Sergeant Bancroft informs me you were stopped headed for enemy lines.

MCLEAN

I'm no spy—no sesch, either—Colonel, sir.

SHERMAN

You realize any property left behind can be seized by the Federal Government.

MCLEAN

Welcome to it! First cannon shot of this war came down my chimney.

Sherman returns McLean's papers.

MCLEAN

Sir, we don't mean any trouble. We just want to go somewhere to live safe and quiet.

SHERMAN

I don't blame you, sir... Sergeant Bancroft, escort Mr. McLean outside our lines.

As Bancroft mounts his horse—

SHERMAN

If you don't mind my asking, where do you plan to move?

MCLEAN

To Appomattox—Appomattox Courthouse, sir.

SHERMAN
Never heard of it. Safe choice.

He tips his hat to Mrs. McLean—

SHERMAN
Take care, ma'am.

Sherman beds down out of the rain beneath a broad-branched tree.
Presently, he awakens at the approach of some of his men. Although
still in uniform, they have the appearance of a rabble bent on vio-
lence. Sherman comes to his feet.

SHERMAN
What can I do for you, Captain?

CAPTAIN
Wanted to tell you. I'm going to New York.

SHERMAN
And your men?

CAPTAIN
They're coming too, sir.

Sherman slips his hand into his coat.

SHERMAN
I've no recollection of signing any pass.

CAPTAIN
Don't need a pass. We fought our fight. We're done with
this.

Sherman removes his hand enough to reveal his pistol.

SHERMAN
Captain, if you attempt to leave without orders, it will
be mutiny and I will shoot you like a dog.

CAPTAIN
Shoot me, sir. My men'll tear you limb from limb.

SHERMAN
How?
Sherman nods him in the direction of a campfire down the road.
Firelight flickers off the barrels of three cannon.

SHERMAN
Those cannon are loaded with canister. After today, I
imagine your boys know exactly what clusters of iron
balls do to flesh and bone... If the men on those guns
hear me fire, I'll sleep the rest of the night in a scatter of
your heads and limbs.

The Captain's resolve fails. He stomps away and goes among his
men. They filter back to the shelter of corn cribs.

Sherman eases down the hammer on his pistol. He turns to Sergeant
Bancroft who has returned from escorting McLean.

SHERMAN
Sergeant, get over to those cannon and wake whoever's
watching 'em. Tell them to load cannister and if they
hear my pistol fired they are to open on any deserters.

BANCROFT
You were bluffing, Colonel?

Sherman gives him a hard look.

SHERMAN
They'll serve or die... Damn, the Rebs whipped us
soundly today.

Cold fear has also crept into his features...

SHERMAN
They're wrong, you know.

BANCROFT
Who's wrong, General?

An all encompassing, slightly crazy, gesture—

SHERMAN
Everyone. Both sides. This isn't a few months work. This is years we're facing and at least a million dead before we eat each other up.

TO BLACK.

EXT./INT. WINFIELD SCOTT'S CARRIAGE—DAY

PULL BACK FROM THE BLACK CARRIAGE DOOR and THROUGH THE WINDOW to where the obese and opulent, elderly General-in-Chief of the Armies, Winfield Scott, resplendent in epaulets of solid gold, and wearing an aura of victory through two wars, rides with the young and commanding, George McClellan.

SCOTT
Bull Run is our nation's greatest embarrassment. The President has called you here in order for you to make a swift, brilliant victory.

MCCLELLAN
Clearly. But the prospect of brilliant victory can't induce me to depart from my intentions.

SCOTT
That is the question, isn't it: your intentions?

                         MCCLELLAN
My intentions are success by maneuver rather than by
fighting.

Scott nods. He has so much faith in McClellan.

                         MCCLELLAN
General, you know there is no man I hold in higher
esteem than you.

Scott's face fills with pride.

                          SCOTT
I have fathered your career since Mexico. I'm telling
you, George: if you want to hold this post longer than
McDowell—humiliatingly fired after Bull Run—tell
the President you will cross into Virginia and *begin*
those maneuvers... Now, help an old man from his
carriage.

EXT. WINFIELD SCOTT'S CARRIAGE—DAY

THE EXECUTIVE MANSION,
WASHINGTON CITY—July 27, 1861

1600 Pennsylvania Avenue. [**Note: Theodore Roosevelt changes
the official name of the structure to the White House in 1901. The
"White House" is a nickname at this time and only used informally.
It's color isn't true white but an off-white "whitewash"—it must
look garishly different from what we know. Additionally, the Oval
Office is not visible as it won't be built until 1909.**] As the COACH-
MAN unstraps General Scott's wheelchair from the back, McClel-
lan straightens his tunic, cocks his hat, and gripping his map-case,
doesn't help the old general. McClellan heads to the front door.
General Scott watches, disturbed, McClellan ushered inside.

INT. LINCOLN'S OFFICE—DAY

A large room overlooking the UNFINISHED WASHINGTON MONUMENT and soldier encampments this side of the Potomac River. A large desk near the window wall, a smaller desk against it; there is a large table with enough chairs to seat his cabinet; over the fireplace an engraved portrait of Andrew Jackson; two horsehair sofas and some chairs; everywhere maps, books, military documents spread out or in cases and folios against the walls, tucked into corners, behind furniture. The clutter, like its maker, large and un-presidential. It's just how it was.

Lincoln and War Secretary EDWIN STANTON (48), a humorless, secretive and self-possessed, hard-bitten abolitionist, rise. Handshakes all around. [**Note: At this period, etiquette is such that a handshake is accompanied by a slight bow.**]

> LINCOLN
> And where is General Scott..?

> MCCLELLAN
> Mr. President, he urged me ahead to begin as quickly
> as possible.

Lincoln nods. He sits, motions for McClellan to do likewise. McClellan sits at the cabinet table and regards Lincoln. The president's knees jut awkwardly in a chair too small for him.

> MCCLELLAN
> Mr. President, may I say there is no man in this great
> nation I hold in higher esteem than you, sir.

Lincoln smiles—no idea McClellan just paid Scott the very same compliment.

LINCOLN
Thanks, General. The esteem in which I hold you can
be measured by the task I've called you to undertake.

MCCLELLAN
What I've come to tell you, Mr. President will more
than equal your faith.

As McClellan speaks, Lincoln and Stanton look to the door where
General Scott is wheeled into the room. Scott's expression shows
clear annoyance at McClellan's abandoning him. Of course he did;
McClellan ignores the old hero.

MCCLELLAN
I pledge today that with a single, crushing battle I'll give
you the victory you have entrusted me.

LINCOLN
That would do nicely.

MCCLELLAN
Consider it won.

McClellan's total and charismatic conviction of his own words
always take the breath from others. Lincoln and Stanton are
impressed; General Scott—the earlier ruffling of his feathers
smoothed—swells with pride for his protege. Then, as if a minor
afterthought...

MCCLELLAN
There is the getting to the battlefield. Without total
support, *that* may be beyond my power.

He's hooked them and he knows it. McClellan deliberately opens
his map case and removes three copies of a report.

MCCLELLAN

This report is based on findings of my spies operating
in Richmond.

Like most people, Lincoln and Stanton are not immune to the almost
preternatural powers people tend to ascribe to spies.

MCCLELLAN

(re: the documents)

Troop strengths of Joe Johnston's rebel armies arrayed
against us—some, as you know, directly across the river
this very moment.

STANTON

Dear God! These figures are twice what we've been led
to believe!

LINCOLN

General Scott?

Scott lifts doubtful eyes from the document to McClellan.

SCOTT

I'm surprised to see this since my own estimates put
Johnston's army at less than 50,000 men.

MCCLELLAN

And yet, General, as I now learn, the enemy have a
force on the Potomac not less than 100,000 strong, well
drilled and equipped, ably commanded, and strongly
entrenched. And what of my force? I visited their camps
yesterday.

LINCOLN

And?

MCCLELLAN

Mr. President, I found no army to command; a mere collection of regiments cowering on the banks of the Potomac, some perfectly raw, others dispirited by their recent defeats.

Stanton, put in a panic, goes to the curtains and peers out.

LINCOLN

Edwin, please set. We'd know if the Rebels were in the garden.

MCCLELLAN

This city is almost in a condition to be taken by a clash of a single regiment of cavalry.

Stanton returns to the table but does not sit. Lincoln sobered, indeed a bit frightened by this report...

LINCOLN

General McClellan, tell me what you require and I'll give it to you.

MCCLELLAN

Twenty-five more regiments.

STANTON

30,000 new men, sir?!

MCCLELLAN

I will also require the best rifles, equipment, uniforms, horses and artillery available. I will personally see to the training and, when I am finished, I will deliver to you the finest army this world has put afield.
(*chuckles*)
I actually feel sorry for the enemy. Honestly. I do.

Lincoln and Stanton regard him with feelings close to awe.

> LINCOLN
> General: you shall have it.

INT. MCCLELLAN HOME—NIGHT

The gaslights are dim; a SERVANT dozes in a chair. From upstairs comes the sound of FEMALE GIGGLING.

> MCCLELLAN (O.S.)
> ...It's true—I'm telling you—the President, Stanton, General Scott: all deferring to me.

INT. MCCLELLAN BEDROOM—CONTINUOUS

In a diaphanous dressing gown and in bed, the attractive ELLEN MCCLELLAN (33) allows her husband, embracing her from behind, to feed her an oyster.

> MCCLELLAN
> By some strange operation of magic I seem to have become *the* power of the land. I almost think were I to win some small success now I could become Dictator.

Ellen follows the oyster with champagne.

> ELLEN
> I like the sound of that, "*Dict*ator," mmmm...

As she says this she reaches between her legs to find him.

> MCCLELLAN
> No, darling, this Republic is ruled by a president— therefore I *won't* be Dictator.

On the last word he enters her. She SQUEALS.

ELLEN
Admirable self denial!

MCCLELLAN
I'll be president.

EXT. ARMY OF THE POTOMAC ENCAMPMENT—MORNING

*THE ARMY OF THE POTOMAC,
BAILEY'S CROSSROADS*

Outside Washington City—July 29, 1861

Over ONE HUNDRED THOUSAND UNION SOLDIERS assembled on a parade ground. To give McClellan his due, they are as he described: motley, lax and lazy, dispirited men and boys.

MCCLELLAN

sits upon his charger, Dan Webster (a dark bay about seventeen hands, pure bred), looking glorious in his uniform.

[Note: Every general North and South will, unless otherwise noted, at all times have his CHIEF OF STAFF (always closest physically to their general); STAFF OFFICERS (who act, primarily, as clerks writing down every word spoken by their general including copying orders written by the general into calligraphy for distribution and/ or telegraph); his AIDE-DE-CAMP (always second closest in proximity to take care of personal needs); GUARDS and ORDERLIES (the former not "bodyguards" but to keep private soldiers and junior officers from bothering their commander, the latter to deliver messages, organize material and equipment). In the field there is also a FLAG BEARER who carries the general's standard (flag); when at headquarters the standard is displayed at tent flap or door. The size of these retinue expands as the general climbs in rank.]

McClellan addresses his army in a loud clear voice.

MCCLELLAN

I have heard there was a danger here! I have come to place myself at your head and share it with you!

At the head of each regiment McClellan's GENERAL OFFICERS READ ALOUD the same text from printed broadsheets. Among them: George Meade (45), and Joe Hooker (46) the blond and blue-eyed Massachusetts Yankee, the most handsome officer of his generation also known for his fondness of women of a certain repute ("Hooker's Brigade" the name given the prostitutes who frequent his camps), and AMBROSE BURNSIDE (37). McClellan's classmate at the Point and close friend, the thing need mentioning about Burnside is that the top of his head is bald while wreathing the sides of his skull ending upon his cheeks is a thick profusion of facial hair that will give the English language: "sideburns."

MCCLELLAN/MEADE/HOOKER/BURNSIDE

We have all heard of the victories gained by our fellow soldiers skirmishing in the west and none can rejoice in these successes, my comrades, more than we do; but, if I judge aright by taking my feelings as yours there is awakened in your minds another sentiment—

WITH MCCLELLAN

MCCLELLAN

The desire to eclipse these noble deeds of our brethren.

A SOFT RIPPLE OF CHEERS.

MCCLELLAN

You wish to strike *your* blow and to show that the Army of the Potomac strikes hard and true; that it is equal to the great hopes reposed in it by the nation!

The CHEERING GROWS.

> MCCLELLAN
>
> I hold you back now only to cement you into an Army equal to this task. The task of discipline is upon us. It will not be easy, but your sweat will be my sweat: when you drill I will march beside you; the food you eat will be the food that sustains me, your general, through every minute of every hard day...

The idea of discipline gets some CATCALLS, but most of these men look upon their general with growing affection.

> MCCLELLAN
>
> When I do place you in front of the rebels, remember that the great God of Battles ever favors the just cause, remember that you are fighting for all that men hold dearest! You have battles to win, fatigues to endure, sufferings to encounter, but remember that they will conduct you to a goal from which you *will* return, covered with glory to your homes—

The CHEERING begins again, and this time it is SUSTAINED AND GROWS through the rest of McClellan's speech.

> MCCLELLAN
>
> —and that each one of you will bear through life the proud honor of being one of the men who crushed the most wicked rebellion that ever threatened freedom!

Finished, McClellan spurs his horse. It leaps forward into a gallop. McClellan is a superb rider, his body completely still and turned in his saddle to face his men who respond by waving and throwing their hats. McClellan grins fiercely; removing his own hat, he twirls it in his hand. The CHEERS of the Army of the Potomac are THUNDEROUS.

EXT. ARMY OF THE POTOMAC ENCAMPMENT—A SERIES OF SHOTS—DAY

McClellan's army equipped as Lincoln promised, drills. McClellan—as he promised—is among them: encouraging, working with them, or riding past in review. And everywhere he is CHEERED. His men love him and he, them. OVER THIS:

> MCCLELLAN (V.O.)
> Ellen, I have restored order completely.

INT. MCCLELLAN BEDROOM—EVENING

The couple sit beside one another. Champagne and oysters. McClellan smiles, but Ellen does not.

> ELLEN
> That isn't what troubles me...

He kisses her neck.

> MCCLELLAN
> What troubles my darling?

> ELLEN
> There is...talk... Among the wives, that—as General-in-Chief—credit belongs more to General Scott than to you.

> MCCLELLAN
> As McClellan's we're above gossip.

> ELLEN
> Above newspapers as well, I s'pose.

From another room comes the sound of a CRYING BABY.

MCCLELLAN
What papers?

ELLEN
(weary look)
Our daughter needs her daddy.

MCCLELLAN
What papers?

Ellen wipes her lips and rises from dinner.

ELLEN
I'll wait for you. Be quick.

MCCLELLAN
I owe my career—everything we have—to that old dotard.

ELLEN
General Scott is the most dangerous antagonist you have! Goodnight.

INT. LINCOLN'S OFFICE—NIGHT

LINCOLN
Mac, I've given you everything you asked for. You've been drilling your men for weeks and have turned them into an army. Surely, it's time now to move.

Lincoln stands behind his desk while McClellan sits, confidently, before him.

MCCLELLAN
You have delivered on your every promise...as I have fulfilled my word to you, sir.

Silence.

LINCOLN
And?

MCCLELLAN
And, sadly, as I prepare your army for war, I'm left to
read in the papers that General Scott has submitted to
you his own plan for the dismantling of the rebellion.

Lincoln blanches.

MCCLELLAN
His "Anaconda Plan?"

LINCOLN
Winfield Scott is a national treasure. He *is* my
General-in-Chief.

MCCLELLAN
Treasures belong in museums.

LINCOLN
General, please, if you read his plan you'd see that it calls
for a blockade of the southern seaboard and maneuvers
in the west to control the Mississippi.

MCCLELLAN
Dangerous distractions, sir. That, if implemented, will
draw away from me the Rebel forces I plan soon to
crush on my sweep to Richmond.

LINCOLN
Soon, soon, soon. A bird-song is all I ever hear from
you. General McClellan, do you have a plan?

MCCLELLAN

I do, Mr. President. For it to work, I would need 30,000 <u>more</u> men. Which is why I wait. Without the authority that now belongs to General Scott—

LINCOLN

That old man loves you like a son.

MCCLELLAN

And my filial piety toward him is pure of heart. But he does not see the urgency of things as you and I see them. And, like an anaconda, his plan will take longer to crush our enemies than he has years left.

LINCOLN

You ask too much.

McClellan nods, thoughtfully.

MCCLELLAN

I understand completely and your honor toward our hero humbles me.

McClellan opens his map case.

MCCLELLAN

Mr. President, my plan will give you Richmond and deliver Jeff Davis to your justice in two weeks...

He puts the plan back into his case.

MCCLELLAN

But perhaps it's better we wait on the General-in-Chief.

Lincoln studies McClellan's face. He sees what he wants to: the deliverance he so desperately seeks.

INT. GENERAL SHERMAN'S HEADQUARTERS—DAWN

WESTERN THEATER—
SHERMAN'S HEADQUARTERS—
LOUISVILLE, KENTUCKY, October 17, 1861

Sherman (now Brigadier General) paces. Has the entire night. On the verge of a breakdown. Stops quickly. Writes an order.

SHERMAN
Bancroft! Get this out immediately!

BANCROFT
You get any sleep last night, sir?

SHERMAN
How can anyone sleep with what I'm facing?

BANCROFT
I meant from what the doc gave you.

Sherman glances at a brown bottle on his washstand.

SHERMAN
Laudanum works just as bad as whiskey. Get out of here!
(Bancroft shuts the door)
And get back quickly! I have more orders to get out!

Sherman paces...to the laudanum bottle. He uncorks it. Takes a swig. He waits. Begins to calm. He sighs and his shoulders relax... Then he tenses; resumes his pacing. The door opens.

SHERMAN
Sergeant Bancroft?!

It isn't Bancroft, but bug-eyed Henry Halleck (now 46). Last seen berating Grant at West Point, more portly now, he's added mutton chop sideburns, and been promoted to general.

> HALLECK
> General Sherman...

They exchange salutes. Halleck is unnerved at his appearance.

> SHERMAN
> Did the president send you?

> HALLECK
> The president... No...

> SHERMAN
> I telegraphed him yesterday. How is it McClellan has one hundred thousand men, Fremont sixty thousand—each with only one hundred miles of front?
> *(resumes pacing)*
> While here I am in the heart of the insurrection with three hundred miles and only eighteen-thousand poorly equipped Kentuckians, half of whom are spies for the enemy?!

As Sherman rails, General Halleck sniffs the laudanum bottle.

> SHERMAN
> Doctor gave it to me to help me sleep. Damn poison doesn't work.

Halleck scratches his elbows.

> SHERMAN
> To defend Kentucky I told the president I need sixty thousand more men. Sixty thousand at least.

HALLECK
Good God, Sherman! Look at you! You're on the verge
of lunacy!

Sherman's eyes flash with anger, then he abruptly sits, gripping the
back of his neck and lowering his head until it is almost between his
knees. To the floor...

SHERMAN
Who wouldn't..? Who wouldn't be?!
(back to pacing)
Hell, I'm damn fine, considering. I visited General Pope
tonight—

HALLECK
It's morning.

SHERMAN
Last night! He's spread his units so thinly, the damn
rebel Sterling Price could bowl him over in two hours of
concerted attack.

HALLECK
Pope's confident he could meet and not only repel Price
but capture that entire army.

SHERMAN
General Pope's a notorious liar!

Halleck says nothing. Sherman stops moving. He's heard himself.
From a deep inside comes a look that begs for help.

HALLECK
William, I've brought someone anxious to see you.

Ice flows through Sherman's veins. Halleck pokes his head through the door...then opens it wide. ELLEN SHERMAN (his foster sister, now his wife and 35) enters.

SHERMAN
Ellen..?

ELLEN SHERMAN
William we're concerned.

SHERMAN
What?!

ELLEN SHERMAN
(patient; loving)

Father received your letter. It's caused us great pain and anxiety.

Behind her come two of their children, WILLY (6) and TOM (5). In modern terms this is an intervention. Humiliated to have his sons see him like this—

SHERMAN
Why'd you bring them?

ELLEN SHERMAN

They couldn't be left. Boys, greet your father.

WILLY
Father.

TOM

You missed my birthday. I'm five now, can you tell?

Sherman, always emotional, begins to tear. He goes to them and hugs them both in turn.

SHERMAN
Willy... Tom, I have something for your birthday.

TOM
Where?

SHERMAN
I'm...sending it.

He rises before his wife. A cross hangs over her heart. Sherman's gaze lifts from the cross to his wife's face.

ELLEN SHERMAN
I've come to bring you home.

CUT TO:

INT. MCCLELLAN BEDROOM—NIGHT

RAIN POUNDS outside a window under which a tray table holds the remains of the McClellan bedtime oysters and champagne.

McClellan moves quietly about the room dressing in his parade uniform over which he puts a rubberized rain cloak. Ellen sleeps as he leaves the room and, with the sound of the CLOSING FRONT DOOR, leaves the house for the night.

EXT. MCCLELLAN HOME—NIGHT

WASHINGTON CITY—November 1, 1861

Dan Webster saddled and waiting along with McClellan's entire STAFF, as resplendent beneath their glistening rain gear as their commander. A distant CLOCK CHIMES FOUR.

> MCCLELLAN

Let us do nothing that can cause him to blush for us; let no defeat of the army he has so long commanded embitter his last years, but let our victories illuminate the close of a life so grand.

With that, McClellan rides forth.

EXT. WASHINGTON STREETS—NIGHT

The RAIN POURS as McClellan, at the head of his officers, escorts Winfield Scott's carriage to the railroad depot.

EXT. RAILROAD PLATFORM, WASHINGTON CITY—NIGHT

On the depot platform, gaslights glitter in reflection on McClellan's and his officers rain-suits. As Winfield Scott is wheeled to the train, McClellan and his officers draw sabers and salute: hilt to eye level, dropping the blade to their sides, then bringing it up to shoulders where sabers rest. Touched by this show of respect, Scott addresses McClellan.

> SCOTT

You were called here by my advice. The times require vigilance and activity. I am not active and never shall be again. When I proposed that you should come here to aid, not supersede me, you had my friendship and confidence.

McClellan nods once.

> SCOTT

You still have my confidence... Give my best regards to your wife and baby...my sensations are very peculiar on leaving active duty.

He is wheeled onto the train.

INT. MCCLELLAN BEDROOM—NIGHT

McClellan sits on the side of the bed undressing.

MCCLELLAN

...and asked I pass on his regards to you and the baby.

Ellen helps him out of his shirt and strokes his back.

ELLEN

Thoughtful of the general.

MCCLELLAN

Yes.

He lies on his back across her, looking up into her eyes.

MCCLELLAN

The sight of him this morning was a lesson I hope I don't soon forget. The end of a long and industrious life, the end of the career of the first soldier of his nation... And it was a feeble old man scarce able to walk; hardly anyone there to see him off but his successor.

He leans up to kiss Ellen's neckline, working his lips towards her breasts, stopping only once to finish—

MCCLELLAN

Should I ever become vainglorious and ambitious, remind me of that pathetic spectacle.

INT. MCCLELLAN HEADQUARTERS TENT—MORNING

As McClellan works industriously at some papers, Lincoln ducks into his tent. McClellan notices how ridiculous he looks with his head practically touching the ceiling.

> MCCLELLAN
> Mr. President.

> LINCOLN
> General-in-Chief McClellan.

McClellan smiles politely, but doesn't offer a word of thanks. Instead, he signs the document before him.

> LINCOLN
> I should be perfectly satisfied if I thought this vast increase of responsibility would not embarrass you.

> MCCLELLAN
> It is a great relief, sir. I feel as if several tons were taken from my shoulders today. I am not embarrassed by intervention.

> LINCOLN
> Well, draw on me for all the sense I have... The supreme command of the entire Army east and west will entail a vast labor upon you.

McClellan has come to his feet during this, chest swelling, facial features drawing into his most charismatic smile.

> MCCLELLAN
> Assuredly, I can do it all. And when I am soon in Richmond we will remember this day with pride.

A smile creases Lincoln's careworn face.

LINCOLN
I'm mightily pleased by this, George... Mind if I set?

Having thought they were finished, McClellan gives an annoyed gesture to a chair. He stands while Lincoln sits.

LINCOLN
There is another matter you need to be aware of... You're familiar with the Joint Committee on the Conduct of the War?

MCCLELLAN
That abolitionist star chamber?

LINCOLN
I refer to them as a cabal, but, yes: them. Though their proceedings are secret, word has reached me that Senators Wade and Chandler have begun investigating you and me under the bent belief that time we've put into building your army has been nothing but stalling in concert with the enemy to allow them to grow stronger.

MCCLELLAN
Outrageous, piffle.

Lincoln probes McClellan with his eyes.

LINCOLN
General McClellan, this is serious. You may be called to testify.

MCCLELLAN
I intend to be careful with them and do as well as possible. Don't let them hurry me, is all I ask.

> LINCOLN
> I have studied and believe in your Peninsula Plan; you
> shall have your own way in the prosecution of this cam-
> paign: I assure you.

INT. SHERMAN HOME, LANCASTER, OHIO—NIGHT

THE CINCINNATI COMMERCIAL (A NEWSPAPER DATED
DECEMBER 11, 1861)—"GEN. WILLIAM T. SHERMAN
INSANE!"

A POCKET COLT PISTOL AND A BULLET—PLACED
UPON THE PAPER; THE BULLET SPUN BY A FINGER AND
PULLING BACK REVEALS...

Sherman in his study. The newspaper upon his desk. The bullet
(with its paper cartridge) stops spinning. It points at the handgun.
Sherman loads the bullet into the empty pistol. He sets the cylinder
so it will be fired at first pull, then like Sherman empty. Safe. Sherman raises the weapon upside down to his forehead so that the slug
will travel downward through his brain to the cortex rather than
out the top.

From upstairs, faint sound of a CHILD CRYING. Sherman cocks
the gun. He tightens his finger on the trigger. The CRYING CON-
TINUES and Sherman looks at the ceiling. His hands are shaking.
He turns the chamber making the gun safe.

INT. BOYS' ROOM, SHERMAN HOME—NIGHT

Sherman finds Willy standing over Tom's bed. Tom sobs softly, having returned to sleep in the passing moments. On his head he wears
a Union private's kepi.

WILLY
(re: the cap)
Your birthday present fell off and he couldn't find it. It
was under the bed.

Sherman's face twists with conflicting emotions as he realizes that
had he shot himself he'd have missed this moment... Sherman strokes
Willy's hair, then hugs him.

SHERMAN
Ready to go back to bed?

WILLY
I can't.

SHERMAN
It's only four.

WILLY
I can't sleep.

Sherman thinks for a moment. He tosses Willy his bathrobe.

SHERMAN
I'll boil some army coffee and we'll do Ol' Mr. Johnson
a favor and feed the horses.

The idea overwhelms Willy. He smiles and nods as he wiggles his
little shoulders into the bathrobe.

WILLY
You think for my birthday I could get a hat like Tom's?

Sherman notices his wife, Ellen, in the doorway behind him holding
the cross hung over her heart, her prayers answered.

ELLEN SHERMAN
You'll have your very own uniform.

Sherman gives Ellen a grateful smile. They leave Tom in his hat to sleep and, whatever the boy dreams now, he smiles.

INT. THE U.S. CAPITOL—MORNING

THE CAPITOL BUILDING, WASHINGTON CITY—January 15, 1862

A U.S. Congress SERGEANT AT ARMS escorts McClellan down the first floor "Brumidi" corridor to the chambers of—

INT. JOINT COMMITTEE ON THE CONDUCT OF WAR—MORNING

McClellan sits in a single chair illuminated by gaslights behind him, while the COMMITTEE sits at a crescent of tables in the shadows across the otherwise dark room. Chaired by "Radical Republican" Senator BEN WADE (62) of Ohio, and SENATOR CHANDLER (49) of Michigan—a pair of abolitionists who use this committee for personal and political vendetta.

CHAIRMAN WADE
General, please explain to this why the army, after five long months of training, is not marching out to meet the enemy again at Manassas.

MCCLELLAN
Mr. Chairman, Committee members: there are only two bridges to Alexandria which do not satisfy the requirement that a commander must safeguard his lines of retreat in the event his men are repulsed...as they have been before.

CHAIRMAN WADE
General McClellan, do I understand you correctly?
Before you strike at the rebels you want to be sure of
plenty of room so you can run in case they strike back?

SENATOR CHANDLER
Or in case you get scared.

MCCLELLAN
In military practice—how battles are actually fought—
lines of retirement are sometimes as necessary to an
army's survival as lines of communication and supply.

CHAIRMAN WADE
General McClellan, this is *not* what we have called you
in to tell us! You have all the troops you have asked for.
They are well organized and equipped. The loyal people of this country expect that you make a short and
decisive campaign. Is it really necessary for you to have
more bridges over the Potomac before you move?

MCCLELLAN
No. Because I do not plan to take my army over the
Potomac.

SENATOR CHANDLER
I beg your pardon, General?

MCCLELLAN
I have another plan for taking Richmond in a single
campaign.

HUSHED DISCUSSION in the shadows.

CHAIRMAN WADE
Reveal this plan, General...

MCCLELLAN

I will not. No general fit to command an army will ever submit his plans to such an assembly. There are men here entirely incompetent to pass judgment upon them; no plan made known to such persons can be kept secret an hour.

The committee is stunned. McClellan rises.

SENATOR CHANDLER

Sit down, General McClellan.

MCCLELLAN

That would defeat my purpose of leaving.

CHAIRMAN WADE

You are aware we can put you under arrest if we so choose?

MCCLELLAN

Yes. As you have already done, without evidence or trial, to lesser—innocent I might add—of my military brethren.

He looks over the shadowy figures with dangerous eyes.

MCCLELLAN

I am General-in-Chief of the Armies of the United States of America. I have the support, not only of the President, but the support—nay, the unquestioning devotion, the *love*—of every man in my entire "well-equipped" army.

(*soft*)

I dare you: arrest me.

INT. MCCLELLAN BEDROOM—NIGHT

McClellan paces while his wife readies their evening oysters and champagne. But McClellan is in no mood.

> MCCLELLAN
>
> I can't tell you how disgusted I am with this Administration—perfectly sick of it! It is sickening in the extreme when I see the weakness and unfitness of the poor beings who control the destinies of this great country led as they are by that original gorilla! *He* deceived me! *He* sent me into this knowing full well what they were about and hoping that they would achieve it!

> ELLEN
>
> George, we knew the weakness of this government long before we arrived in Washington. But we have arrived. We are here. We have the army and you have victory waiting for your pluck. Seize it now, and with it your rightful glory, and I will be at your side as you ascend to your rightful place in that white house now inhabited by the idiot baboon, where I will watch you rebuild this nation and its government to your inclination.

It is the very thing both of them dream of: the presidency.

> MCCLELLAN
> Champagne?

INT. LONGSTREET'S HEADQUARTERS—NIGHT

CENTREVILLE, VIRGINIA—January 19, 1862

Confederate winter quarters are a canvas and wooden structure with a warm stove and furniture slightly more comfortable than folding camp tables and chairs. The air is hazy with smoke from cigars and pipes while the beverage of choice is whiskey, the game brag, and Longstreet is raking in the pot.

> GOREE
>
> General, you can't think after our victories at Manassas and Ball's Bluff your boys outside won't stay in to see this struggle through.

Fresh cards dealt, Longstreet throws back some whiskey.

> LONGSTREET
>
> My boys outside are freezin' their asses off in the snow.
> *(check his cards)*
> Jus' the same as they did last week and'll be doing next week on till the spring rains when their one-year enlistments end.
> *(he bets)*
> Every one of 'em wants one thing: to be home by a warm fireplace, preferably with a warm, plump little gal. So unless there's a policy change in Richmond...

> GOREE
>
> A draft?

> LONGSTREET
>
> We may have McClellan fooled, but our 48,000 men are outnumbered three-to-two on this line, and—

The door opens and a MESSENGER arrives in a swirl of snow.

> LONGSTREET
>
> Close the damn door, soldier.

The messenger offers a telegram.

MESSENGER
From Richmond, General Longstreet.

LONGSTREET
Lieutenant Goree, give the boy a snort and make room
by the stove.

Goree sees to the drink. Longstreet finishes his whiskey, puffs his
cigar and increases his bet before opening the telegram. He grows
alarmed. Grabs hat and overcoat. To Goree—

LONGSTREET
T.J.: my horse!

GOREE
Yanks on the move?

LONGSTREET
Richmond's been hit by the scarlet fever.

EXT. LONGSTREET'S RICHMOND HOME—DAWN

Longstreet rides up fast, leaping from his horse and tossing the reins
to a bundled, waiting SLAVE. One look at his red, cried-out eyes
tells Longstreet the worst. He rushes inside.

INT. LONGSTREET'S FRONT PARLOR—CONTINUOUS

General George Pickett (now 37) rises from the chair he's waited in
the entire night. Usually charming and dapper, he is, this morning,
haggard and frightened.

LONGSTREET
George, is it Louise?

> PICKETT
> Louise is fine. It's your children.

> LONGSTREET
> Which?

> PICKETT
> All of them. Mary Anne is almost gone, Pete.

Longstreet dashes up the stairs.

INT. LONGSTREET NURSERY—MORNING

The tears streaming down Longstreet's cheeks and into his heavy beard match the tears of the stunningly gorgeous SALLIE CORBELL (19; Pickett's fiancee) who turns from the cradle.

> SALLIE CORBELL
> She's gone James, just this hour.

> LONGSTREET
> Where's Louise?

> SALLIE CORBELL
> With the boys and Doctor Emile. Miss Lucy and I will tend to your baby.

MISS LUCY (40s), another slave, throws her arms around Longstreet and WAILS.

> MISS LUCY
> Oh, Gen'ral, my little lamb's gone to Jesus and I could'n' stop it!

Longstreet strokes her hair and WHISPERS COMFORTING WORDS.

SALLIE CORBELL
General, your wife needs you, sir. She needs you now.

Longstreet gently releases Miss Lucy. He pauses to look at his dead baby daughter. It breaks his heart.

INT. LONGSTREET BOYS' ROOM—MORNING

Three beds for three sick boys: JAMES (4), AUGUSTUS (6), GARLAND (13). Longstreet holds James's little hand in one of his massive palms as DOCTOR EMILE (50s) takes the boy's temperature. Beside him, his wife, LOUISE (35) does the same for Augustus until WHIMPERING from Garland draws them both to the eldest boy's bedside.

LONGSTREET
I should have been here earlier.

LOUISE
I know how busy you are.

Playing cards, drinking whiskey: Longstreet feels these words like bullets to his heart.

LOUISE
It crept up on us so quickly.
(sobs)
My baby-girl is gone!

She breaks down in her husband's arms.

DOCTOR EMILE
(re: James)
His fever's climbing. We must cool him down. Is the bath prepared?

Louise pulls her face from her husband's chest and nods.

INT. LONGSTREET CHILDREN'S BATHROOM—MORNING

The bath is filled with freezing water thick with ice. James is awake and naked and CRYING DELIRIOUSLY at the sight of the freezing tub. He fights his mother not to be put into it.

> LOUISE
> Help me.

She turns. Longstreet is already half out of his uniform. He pulls a nightshirt over his head before removing his boots and trousers. He holds his arms open to his son.

> LONGSTREET
> Daddy's going in, too. I'll holdja.

Little James nestles into his father's strong arms.

> DOCTOR EMILE
> General, we do not need you suffering from exposure.

> LONGSTREET
> You think, this moment, I care for my own life more than my child's?

And, holding his son to his chest, Longstreet climbs into the freezing bath. The boy WAILS and Longstreet's teeth chatter, but the general strokes his son's hair with handfuls of cold water while making SOOTHING NOISES in his ear and, cooling...

> JAMES
> ...papa..?

> LONGSTREET
> Papa's here.

The boy's CRYING changes from fear to release.

> LONGSTREET
> Shhh... Papa's here, Papa's here.

INT. LONGSTREET'S FRONT PARLOR—DAY

Three coffins for three children: Mary Anne, James, Augustus. Sallie Corbell holds Louise as she weeps. George Pickett stands with a bracing hand on Longstreet's shoulder. In Longstreet's hand is a brand new bible, the spine un-cracked.

> LONGSTREET
> George, it isn't five years since Louise and I buried our first two... When I was wounded in Mexico you carried the colors for me.

Pickett nods, remembering.

> LONGSTREET
> We'll say our good-byes to the children here. Louise shall stay home to nurse Garland, I'll return to our army... Will you and Sallie stand for us at the funeral?
> *(losing composure)*
> Don't let this be too much to ask.

> PICKETT
> Nothing you would ask could ever be too much.

Longstreet nods thanks, neither man knowing that soon, a place called Gettysburg, Longstreet will ask so much more...

INT. ST. LOUIS COURTHOUSE—DAY

GENERAL HALLECK'S UNION ARMY OF THE WEST HEADQUARTERS—February 1, 1862

The place where Grant freed William Jones now headquarters of General Halleck. Across from Halleck is LT. COL. JAMES B. MCPHERSON (34): a handsome West Pointer, confident, magnetic.

> HALLECK
>
> Having served in California, you've doubtless heard the claims surrounding Grant?

> MCPHERSON
>
> I've never met the man, sir.

> HALLECK
>
> You will. I'm assigning you to Grant's command as his Chief of Engineers and my observer.

> MCPHERSON
>
> Observing his "behavior?"

> HALLECK
> *(scratches his elbows)*
> As concerned as I am with his intemperate behavior, I'm equally concerned with his lack of military acumen— Grant's strategy is not good. If he fights, he will lose.

Halleck hand McPherson his orders. Off McPherson's salute—

INT. GRANT'S HEADQUARTERS, FORT HENRY—DAY

A CAMPAIGN MAP

Grant's index finger—his whittled pipe smouldering between it and the next—traces a path as he speaks...

GRANT

The Confederacy is a rectangle. Its top western corner secured by Fort Donelson, here on the Cumberland River. Stretch that line south...there's Vicksburg, Mississippi—its western foot; moving east gives you Savannah, Georgia; then back up to complete the geometry we find their capital: Richmond, Virginia.

WESTERN THEATER—FORT HENRY, TENNESSEE—*February* 11, 1862

Weak sunlight swimming with smoke frames a table covered with maps. Around it: Grant and his Assistant Adjutant General, Captain John Rawlins; General C. F. Smith (55, Grant's first instructor at West Point, now adorned with a white mustache past his chin); and Lt. Colonel McPherson—Halleck's spy. STAFF OFFICERS for each general officer are on hand.

GRANT

That makes Donelson a position so important to the enemy that once we move against it reinforcements will pour from every quarter. They're already 12,000 rebels entrenched. We can't let it get to more.

He regards each of the men in a sweep of his eyes.

GRANT

Smith: take your division in column along this line of march. I'll do the same with the rest of the army just south of you. Together we'll form a semi-circle around the fort with the river at its back.

MCPHERSON

Sir, I'm not sure General Halleck feels comfortable with you moving the army deeper into enemy lines.

GRANT

Colonel McPherson: our 10,000 men will be more effective moving out tomorrow than doing nothing from now until a month from tomorrow.

MCPHERSON

General: you are splitting your army. We're already outnumbered, but two groups of 5,000 against a single mass of twelve? Not to mention the strength of an enemy entrenched: it's four-fold what it would be in the field... General Smith, would you not concur, sir?

SMITH

I do have something to say. General Grant violate every maxim of our profession. Personally, I'd pay attention to the tactics taught at West Point.

McPherson gives Grant a glance to see if he's getting this.

SMITH

That said, Colonel, his plan is wholly original and that's why he'll win. The general's boldness humbles me while yours, sir, rankles of insubordination.
(*picks up his gloves*)
Excuse me, General Grant. Much to prepare.

Smith salutes and goes. To Rawlins—

GRANT

I'll have a word with Colonel McPherson.

Rawlins salutes, departs with Grant's staff.

GRANT

You're an Ohio man.

MCPHERSON
I am, General.

GRANT
I was born in Ohio. Sherman, too... Colonel McPherson: your rise in rank will be steady, but only once you're no longer pulled in two directions.

MCPHERSON
I can pack my bags as soon as necessary, General.

GRANT
Good. This army needs good officers in the field, not behind desks. With your permission, I'll request of General Halleck your permanent transfer to my staff.

Field command being every officer's dream—

MCPHERSON
Yes, sir!

Grant writes in his order book, hands the order to a staffer.

GRANT
Your warning about the strength of fortifications is valid. I'd forgotten that. Before I take you from Halleck, get Sherman.

MCPHERSON
Surely you saw the headlines? General Sherman had a mental breakdown in Kentucky. He makes the claim that this war will last five years and cost one million lives.

GRANT
Don't be so sure it won't.

MCPHERSON
General Halleck's put him on indefinite leave, sir.

Grant rips the order from his book.

GRANT
Sherman.

INT. SHERMAN'S OFFICE—DAY

SAINT LOUIS—February 12, 1862

A PISTOL AND A SINGLE BULLET. As before, Sherman spins the bullet. THE NEWSPAPER—"GENERAL WILLIAM T. SHERMAN: INSANE!" The bullet points away from the gun. A KNOCK on the door.

SHERMAN
Enter.

Sergeant Bancroft enters. He hands Sherman a dispatch. As Sherman reads, Bancroft blanches at the pistol and bullet.

SHERMAN
Think I'm insane, too?

BANCROFT
No, sir.

SHERMAN
Including Sam Grant, then, I'm showing a pair... At any rate.

Sherman steps to a window overlooking a warehouse: UNION QUARTERMASTER TROOPS busily load train cars with supplies.

SHERMAN
Where's that train headed?

BANCROFT
Army of the Potomac, sir.

SHERMAN
No more. That train goes to General Grant.

BANCROFT
It carries the rest of General McClellan's personal belongings.

SHERMAN
Paper-doll clothes.

BANCROFT
Sir, President Lincoln has appointed McClellan commander of the entire Union Army.

SHERMAN
(*dark scowl*)
Fill that train with ammunition and two divisions and send it to Grant.

Sherman waves Bancroft from the room. Finding the bullet, he drops it into the wastebasket. As it lands—

EXT. THE WESTERN SLOPES BEFORE FORT DONELSON—DAY

BOOM! CANNON FIRE. DEAD AND DYING UNION SOL-
DIERS litter a ravine. McPherson, on horseback, fights valiantly
with his men against overwhelming odds.

FORT DONELSON, TENNESSEE—February 16, 1862

Grant spurs his horse to Smith.

GRANT
All's failed to our right. You must take Fort Donelson.

Smith salutes and wheels his mount to his lead division.

SMITH
Firing caps off your guns! Fix—!

SMITH'S COLONELS
Battalion!

SMITH'S COMPANY OFFICERS
Company!

SMITH'S COLONELS
Bayonets!

MCPHERSON
Fix bayonets!

The command "Bayonets" ripples among the Company Officers.
Ominous METAL CLICKS break the cold winter air as the young
soldiers respond, the silver of their bayonets flash, their guns now
deadly lances. IT BEGINS TO SNOW.

SMITH
—BAYONETS!

TRACKING WITH SMITH—high on his horse, keeping pace with the man who carries the flag.

> SMITH
>
> Come on! This is your chance! You volunteered to be killed: now you can be!

Confederates RAIN LEAD. Union troops fall, but their line keeps coming. More drop, including the man with—

THE REGIMENTAL FLAG WITH 34 STARS IN TWO ROWS IN AN ARC OVER A SPREAD EAGLE HOLDING AN ARROW IN ITS TALONS

Another soldier picks it up and is killed. Another grabs it.

> SMITH
>
> No flinching, my lads! Come on!

EXT. THE CONFEDERATE EARTHWORKS—CONTINUOUS

Colonel JOHN GREGG (33) commanding the 7th TEXANS is a tall man with thick dark hair, high forward, caring eyes, a long narrow beard and aggressive nature.

> GREGG
>
> We are the far right, Texans! We must hold firm! Boys, aim low and keep pouring it on!

The Confederates FIRE, killing the third man with the flag.

CORPORAL COMBS

drops his rifle and picks up the regimental flag. He is HIT. HIT again. As he falls backwards, his bedroll over his shoulder smoulders from seven bullets. Clawing at it—

COMBS
Aw hell! I'm shot, fellas! Shit! I'm damn belly shot!

But tearing off the blanket, the balls harmlessly embedded in the blanketing, drop to SIZZLE in the snow. Realizing he *isn't* shot, with a FEROCIOUS YELL, Combs grabs the flag before another soldier can take it—

COMBS
That's mine, private. Fall in behind me and use your bayonet!

—and charges the top. Smith spurs his horse; mustache flowing over his shoulders, saber flashing red, he bounds over barricades and plows into the enemy. The fighting is furious between the two sides. Combs plants the flag, picks up a rifle and joins the fight inside the fort.

[Note: Color guards—the men carrying and guarding the flag—are the most important men on the battlefield as what they carry is the visual standard for organization during battle. As the men of the color guard go first, are unarmed and are primary targets—more so than generals—it is a battlefield role given only to the bravest most honorable of soldiers. The vast majority of the 1,522 Medals of Honor awarded in the Civil War were to color bearers. The "colors" is the mark of an army's advance and the rallying point in retreat. For the Federal Army: each company carries a swallow tailed flag called a "guidon" (guide-on) that is half red and half white divided at the fork. The letters U.S. are in white overlaying the red; the letter of the company is in red overlaying the white. Each regiment carries a regimental flag (of regimental art/design) identifying the regiment; each brigade, division, and corps all have their flags identifying their commands. Additionally, from company on up flags are positioned in descending order on the right of the national flag. They are Left to Right: National Flag/Corps Flag/Division Flag/Brigade Flag/Regimental Flag/Battalion flag/Company flag. For the Confederate Army: flag regulations/exhibition are much the same except in place of company guidons there is the (much maligned) Confederate battle flag. And in lieu of Corps flags, they carry the St. Andrew's battle flag to the left of the national flag and then their State battle flag—e.g. Commonwealth of Virginia, etc. Depicting the St. Andrew's Cross *it is not a political flag and therefore has nothing to specifically do with slavery (as does the Confederate national flag).* Finally, every general is accompanied by the national flag, his own flag, and the flag of the corps or army he is with at any given moment. All told, battlefields are visually resplendent in streaming banners.]

INT. FORT DONELSON—EVENING

The SOUND OF BATTLE BLASTS AND ECHOES AROUND. Confederate General JOHN FLOYD's (55) face flush with rage.

FLOYD
The fact is we're surrounded. We must turn this fight!

A FAMILIAR SOUTHERN VOICE (O.S.)
General Floyd: if we attempt to fight our way out it will cost three quarters of your command.

ANOTHER ANGLE REVEALS THE SPEAKER:

BUCKNER
No man has the right to make such sacrifice of human life.

Most junior in command, Buckner (now 39)—Grant's true and close friend—is the voice of authority.

FLOYD
General Buckner, under no circumstances will I allow myself to be taken alive.

He regards Buckner with pompous gravitas.

                    FLOYD
But I won't subject the men to the massacre which
would result from a useless defense; I therefore see it
my duty to cut out.
                (to *General Pillow*)
I turn the command over, sir.

Buckner's gaze fastens on Pillow (backwards lines in Mexico).

                    PILLOW
It would be far pleasanter to be in a comfortable bed
than sent to a Yankee prison. General Floyd, I will
escape with you.

Buckner looks at his cowardly companions with contempt.

                    BUCKNER
Go. I'll remain with my men and share their fate.

INT. GRANT'S HEADQUARTERS, A FARMHOUSE—NIGHT

                    SMITH
A note from a classmate...
                (*shivering*)
Anything to drink 'round here?

McPherson hands Smith a flask. Smith drinks, offers Grant the
flask...McPherson watches...Grant declines, reads instead.

                    GRANT
So Buck's assumed command...What answer shall I
send?

SMITH
No terms with the damned rebels.

Smith moves to the fireplace. Grant chuckles. He writes.

GRANT
Sir: No terms except complete and Unconditional Surrender can be accepted. I propose to move immediately upon your works. I am sir, very respectfully, your obedient servant, U-S Grant, Brigadier General.

EXT. FORT DONELSON—MORNING

Grant enters the fort at the head of his troops. Buckner and his OFFICERS—including Colonel Gregg—sit at a long table beside a bonfire eating a meager breakfast of corn bread and coffee. Buckner is not happy to see his friend, but he stands and salutes Grant.

BUCKNER
Due to the hasty departure of General's Floyd and Pillow I am unsure of the number of men I surrender to you. I believe them to be near 15,000.

Grant's staff gapes: it's the biggest victory yet in the war.

BUCKNER
If I'd been in command from the beginning, you'd have not been able to get here as easily as you did.

GRANT
If you'd been in command I'd not have tried it the way I did.

Buckner frowns, unsure how to take this. Union cooks augment the Confederate breakfast with pork and beans that officers—South and North—now sit down to share.

GRANT
So where's old Pillow?

BUCKNER
Gone. Thought you'd rather get hold of him more than
any other man in the Southern Confederacy.

GRANT
Oh, if I'd got Pillow I'd let him go again. He'll do us
more good commanding you fellows.

EXT. FORT DONELSON, RIVER LANDING—EVENING

Transports line the banks filled with Confederate prisoners. Buckner is the last to board. His fond feelings for Grant have returned
and a handshake becomes an embrace.

GRANT
Buck, you're separated from your people. My purse is
at your disposal.

BUCKNER
Very thoughtful of you, Sam, but unnecessary, though
I do wish you'd taken my advice and stayed out of the
damned army.

Buckner boards. The transports cast off. Grant steps from the dock
as a QUARTERMASTER NCO approaches with a full wagon.

GRANT
What's this?

Before the Quartermaster NCO can answer, approaching, a jaunt in
his step, a familiar voice answers—

SHERMAN
Been coming in all day from admirers of "Unconditional Surrender" Grant.

Grant gives him a dubious look.

SHERMAN
(mocking Halleck)
The "U.S." in your name has to stand for something.

Grant laughs, remembering West Point and happy to see his friend back to his old self.

SHERMAN
You've done what no one's thought possible—especially from you: you've captured an entire Rebel Army. How, Sam?

Sherman wants a real answer; wants to see the light at the end of his terrible war-dark tunnel.

GRANT
Took your advice. Algebra, geometry, calculus, trigonometry: made mathematics my own.

Sherman throws back the wagon's tarpaulin revealing barrels and boxes-upon-boxes of cigars. Grant opens a box, offers a cigar to Sherman and then selects one of what will kill him: he lights his cigar and savors it, and to the Quartermaster—

GRANT
General Sherman will take this to my headquarters tent. See to it the rest get to the men.

Grant puffs as he and Sherman watch the transports cast off into the Cumberland. He savors the smoke almost as much as his savors his first major victory. The first Union victory of the war.

Night falling, Grant and Sherman head for Grant's headquarters tent. [**Note: From here on, Grant will always have a lit cigar.**]

FADE OUT.

END OF EPISODE 102

"A NATION DIVIDED"

EPISODE 103

"FOOT CAVALRY"

BY

Michael Frost Beckner

FADE IN:

EXT. THE SHENANDOAH VALLEY—MORNING—A SERIES OF SHOTS

- *Winter wheat poking golden through rich earth; fruit trees dewy in first leaf; cornfields rising new...*
- *The Valley Pike, a macadamized road, is the main transportation artery of the Valley linking...*
- *Picturesque farming villages of varying sizes along...*
- *The deep blue waters of the Shenandoah River and its tributaries, all of this bracketed by...*
- *The Blue Ridge Mountains on one side of the Valley richly green with pines, chestnut trees, maple and birch, while on the Valley's opposite side are the rolling hills and granite crowns of the Alleghenies... OVER THIS comes the VOICE OF TOM ASHBY (13).*

TOM (V.O.)

In February of 1862, General Banks—once Governor of Massachusetts—crossed the Potomac with a Federal Army and began the invasion of our Shenandoah Valley. The "Breadbasket of the Confederacy," what was grown here and who controlled that, would either see fed or see starved the entire Southern Cause.

In the distance, lies—

KERNSTOWN

For many settlers to this region, Kernstown was the end of the rainbow. Today, however, it isn't a rainbow that rises from this town to the sky. It is a plume of thick black smoke. The CAMERA MOVES TOWARD IT.

TOM (V.O.)

On March twenty-third, Stonewall Jackson's army of thirty-four hundred attacked the Union position at Kernstown. Led to believe he was facing only 3,000 opponents, the town turned out to be occupied by 9,000 of Banks's best men.

EXT. KERNSTOWN—MORNING

UNION INFANTRY supported by BOOMING ARTILLERY, have invested the farming town. Vastly outnumbered CONFEDER-ATES flee between farm buildings and over fences onto the road and into the fields and thickets in a perfect rout.

EXT. HILL ABOVE KERNSTOWN—MORNING

Seeing this below, the line of graybacks on this hill show signs of growing panic. As the horde of Union soldiers advance, MUSKET BALLS SLAP into Confederate flesh. As men go down with GASPS and CRIES, to their forefront gallops—

THOMAS "STONEWALL" JACKSON

Last seen braving gunfire at First Manassas he is unperturbed by the bullets WHIZZING around him. Jackson leaps from Little Sorrel seizes A DRUMMER BOY (15). Dragging the boy to a rise where all the troops—breaking Confederate *and* charging Union—can see them, he cries above the din—

STONEWALL JACKSON
Beat the rally, boy!

The DRUM ROLLS at his order and with his hand on the fright-ened boy's shoulder, amidst a STORM OF BALLS, he tries to check the flight of his defeated troops. His efforts are useless. This fighting line is as shattered as the one below. As CHEERS rise from the Union soldiers moving up from the village, Jackson sends the drummer after his retreating infantry and mounts his horse.

Riding down the backside of the rise, Jackson is met by COLONEL ELISHA FRANK "BULL" PAXTON (30s) coming up with a nervous company of reserves. Where Paxton's uniform is double-breasted, tailored gray and gleams with gold buttons, Jackson wears a rough homespun single-breasted coat and a ratty private's cap. He still prefers homespun.

> STONEWALL JACKSON
> Colonel Paxton: you will set the rear-guard and protect the pike until our artillery and ambulances have passed.

> PAXTON
> *(doubtful)*
> Yes, General.

> STONEWALL JACKSON
> Be not troubled by this—

> PAXTON
> Defeat?

> STONEWALL JACKSON
> Success. As we fight for the Lord, so by His choice for how this day must end does He communicate to Richmond—more eloquently than I—our need for reinforcements.

Jackson's conviction steadies the handsome young colonel. He salutes his "Stonewall" and moves to his task. As cannon are rolled forward to hold back the victorious Federals…

TOM (V.O.)
Such was the battle of Kernstown in which over twelve hundred men were killed and wounded, more than the half of them Confederates.

EXT. KERNSTOWN—DAY—VARIOUS SHOTS

Corresponding to Tom's narration: THE DEAD AND THE WOUNDED... CONFEDERATE CAPTURED... THE ABANDONED REBEL STORES AND WEAPONS...

TOM (V.O.)
Two or three hundred prisoners fell into the hands of the Federals; nearly one fourth of Jackson's infantry was out of action; and of the four cannons he'd fought with, he lost two that could not be replaced...

EXT. JACKSON'S CAMP ALONG THE VALLEY PIKE—NIGHT

[Note: Regarding the presence of blacks attending to the Confederate Army, in 1862, for every twenty white Confederate soldiers, there is one slave or freed black attending in camp/behind the lines as servant or laborer. By the start of 1864, it will be up to one in twelve. For specific labors such as digging defensive fortifications (behind the lines), railroad repair, burial details, wagon train/supply work, crews are entirely slaves or free men of color.]

SERVANTS (slaves) rip apart a fence to feed a fire as Jackson stands wrapped in a long coat hands behind his back, stirring the embers with the toe of his boot. JACKSON'S STAFF and OTHER OFFICERS sit, depressed. A YOUNG CAVALRY OFFICER can't hold back his frustration.

YOUNG CAVALRY OFFICER
The Yankees just won't quit!

STONEWALL JACKSON
(*shrugs*)

The Valley is a pleasant place to stay in this time of year.

YOUNG CAVALRY OFFICER

It was reported they were retreating, sir...Guess they're retreating after us *retreating*.

Eyes fixed on the burning logs—

STONEWALL JACKSON

The Valley runs in two directions, all of it ours and everything in it. Be satisfied that no movement we make here can ever be retreat, sir.
(*addressing all*)
Prepare to resume the march at four ayem.

Jackson's beard bobs as he nods once with finality. One of his generals at the fire, General WILLIAM LORING (44), is clearly uncomfortable with this.

GENERAL LORING

We've fought a hard day, General, marched an even harder night.

STONEWALL JACKSON

Do not think I expect more of my men than I expect of myself.

Looks are exchanged among the others: they all think that. But Jackson is uncomprehending of sarcasm or cynicism.

PAXTON

Perhaps if we knew our objective, General..?

Jackson gives him a closed look. A beat, and Paxton, uncomfortable having to explain why he asked...

> PAXTON
>
> To prepare and incentivize the men as to what to expect next?

> STONEWALL JACKSON
>
> The men need only expect that as the Lord provides and I am serving as His humble instrument, His objectives and mine must be taken upon faith.

> GENERAL LORING
> *(annoyed)*
>
> Least you might let us know the direction you want us faced?

> STONEWALL JACKSON
>
> General Loring: when I begin the march you'll surely know which way to follow.

Leaving his staff dumbfounded, Jackson strides into the darkness. A SLAVE comes forward with coffee. Cups are held out for filling.

> TOM (V.O.)
>
> From Colonial Days to the middle of the nineteenth century the Southern States had grown in wealth, population and civic pride. A civilization of rare culture and refinement it represented the high spirit and virtue of the Anglo-Saxon race in the South. One of the foundation stones upon which this civilization rested was the institution of slavery.

PUSH INTO THE FIRE UNTIL IT FILLS THE SCREEN and—

MATCH CUT TO:

A HOODED LANTERN

its small circle of veiled flame surrounded by darkness and moving figures as spied from—

INT. THE ASHBY BARN, HAYLOFT / FLOOR—NIGHT

—where TOM ASHBY (13) and his companion GEORGIE (10 and a slave) lie hidden, spying down on Georgie's father, MARCUS (20s), and two other slaves gathered around a horse...

> MARCUS
> If you ain't comin' you ain't comin'.

THE BARN FLOOR

> MARCUS
> Your excuses just waste our time.

> LAWS
> Listen, Marcus: the talk in da house is Jackson's done whupped. Yanks'll be rollin' up these parts any day. Tomorrow, pos'bly.

THOMAS LAWS (40s) with a heart as true as his arms are strong, looks to Marcus's mentally handicapped brother, ANTHONY (18)—"feeble-minded" to use the day's vernacular.

> LAWS
> Anthony, we could jes walk upta dem tomorrow and we's free wit'out havin' done no stealin' or runnin' or nothin' else to get lashed or wo'se.

Anthony grins and nervously scuffs his shoes on the floor.

THE HAYLOFT

Tom and Georgie exchange wide-eyed looks.

> TOM
> (whispered)
> Your daddy's running away.

> GEORGIE
> Is not.

> TOM
> Is so.

> GEORGIE
> My daddy wouldn't leave me.

But his tone reveals he's not so sure about that.

THE BARN FLOOR

Marcus finishes saddling the horse.

> MARCUS
> Where I go Anth'ny goes. Right brother?

> ANTHONY
> I'm goin' with Marcus cross't the 'tomac—*Pah*-tomac.

Laws shakes his head, but doesn't press the issue. Marcus swings himself into the saddle.

> MARCUS
> (re: Anthony)
> Help him up behind me?

Laws stirrups his hands and does, while—

THE HAYLOFT

> TOM
> Come on. We needta tell Aunt Susan.

As the three men extinguish their lantern and slip through the doors, the boys crawl to the ladder that takes them out the back.

EXT. SLAVE CABINS, ASHBY FARM—NIGHT

AUNT SUSAN (40s), the "Mammie" of the house, a disciplined, responsible woman whose no-nonsense exterior belies deep kindness and affection, holds Georgie to her breast quieting his tears while to Tom—

> AUNT SUSAN
> You think anything goes on around here I *don't* know about?

> TOM
> But what'll we do?

> AUNT SUSAN
> Your brother Ben's master since your Papa passed. He'll do what's right.

> TOM
> Ben knows—how?

> AUNT SUSAN
> I told him, a'course.

This only increases Georgie's sobs.

> AUNT SUSAN
> Get a'hold a'yourself, boy.

GEORGIE
Daddy stole old Clover—they'll hang him!

AUNT SUSAN
What do you know about hangin'? Hear you babbling
make it sound like we some kind of plantation niggers
from Natchez. No one ever been hanged 'round here.
Ever.
(growing harsh)
And that loaf-around, Marcus, ain't your daddy no
more 'cause I done this day give him up as my son. So
you ain't never gonna call him such 'round my hearin' if
you know what's good for you.

GEORGIE
But I don't got no ma!

AUNT SUSAN
You got me—your grandma—like you always have 'n
always will, Georgie, now hush up.

Her words have a bracing effect on Georgie who immediately forces
himself to stop crying.

AUNT SUSAN
But you, young Tom: your mama and I didn't rear you
to be sneakin' 'round nights like a mangy fox huntin'
chickens. Now you get right back to the house and get
yourself in bed where you're s'posed to be. You hear
me?

Tom bows his head obediently.

TOM
Yes, Mammie.

She pinches his ear and propels him from her porch.

EXT. THE VALLEY PIKE, A COVERED BRIDGE—NIGHT

Marcus and Anthony cautiously approach a bridge. The WATER of
the North Fork of the Shenandoah burbles below.

> ANTHONY
> That the 'tomac, Marcus?

> MARCUS
> Shh!

He's heard something else—a CLINK OF METAL—but before he
can turn the horse, stepping from the darkness comes their father,
UNCLE LEWIS (50s), and the eldest son of their passed master,
BEN ASHBY (19). Ben, tall, gallant, handsome—the very picture of
white Southern youth—holds a shotgun.

> UNCLE LEWIS
> Evening, boys. That your horse?

> MARCUS
> You know it's not.

> UNCLE LEWIS
> Get off it.

> MARCUS
> So he can shoot us?

> ANTHONY
> Jackson's whupped. We're going North, Daddy.

> BEN
> Get off the horse. It doesn't belong to you.

MARCUS
No, it belongs t'you. Like me an' Anth'ny an' Uncle Lewis here.

UNCLE LEWIS
Wrong, boy. You're my property now.

Uncle Lewis holds up the papers. Marcus stares, stunned a beat, before giving Anthony a nod. Both young men climb down from the horse.

MARCUS
Where'd you git money for that?

Uncle Lewis takes the horses reins and leads it aside. Ben lowers his shotgun.

UNCLE LEWIS
None yo' business. Git goin'!

Anthony turns to go back the way they came, Marcus is about to, but—

UNCLE LEWIS
Not that way.

There's deep fury in his words. Marcus understands. He takes a breath, swelling his chest. Uncle Lewis hands him the ownership papers.

UNCLE LEWIS
You're not welcome in this Valley. Ever again.

Then he turns his back on his two sons.

ANTHONY

We're goin' North to be free. We're going to see the Lincoln and buy some sweets and I'll bring some back for Mama, too.

But Uncle Lewis ignores him.

MARCUS

Come on, Anth'ny, we's free already.

He takes his feebleminded brother's hand and leads him into the darkness of the bridge only to stop. Feeling guilty—

MARCUS

I'll send you money, Daddy. I know this is what you save for a mill a'your own. I'll pay you back for what you done. How much you pay?

Ben looks from the two slaves, now freemen, then to Uncle Lewis who remains with his back to his sons, his face clenched and quivering.

UNCLE LEWIS

Trash don't cost nothing and you could never buy back my shame. Now get the hell outta here—

He wrenches the shotgun from Ben's grip.

UNCLE LEWIS

Or, by God, I will take this gun and use it!

CUT TO:

EXT. MASSANUTTON MOUNTAIN—DAWN

THE NEW MARKET GAP, MASSANUTTON MOUNTAIN—March 24, 1862

Massanutton Mountain is a narrow, fifty mile mountain range that splits the center of the Shenandoah Valley. A single, mountain road cuts across it and it is here that in disarray Jackson's small army slogs through rain and places of knee-deep mud to get to the Valley's opposite side. Because of the weather, the conditions of the road and the conditions of these men, there is much straggling and little enthusiasm. Many men have collapsed along the sides of the road.

Jackson rides up the length of this sorry force. Coming upon Colonel "BALDY" JOHNSON (40s)—

> STONEWALL JACKSON
> Colonel, who are these men loafing along the roadside?

> "BALDY" JOHNSON
> These men are mine of the 1st Maryland Confederate. And they aren't loafing, General. They're weary, broken down and—
> (disgusted)
> —refuse to continue.

Jackson stiffens taking personal offense.

> STONEWALL JACKSON
> You will let them know, and be advised yourself, sir, that a broken down man and a straggler are two of a kind. Men who are weak and weary, who faint by the wayside, are men who are lacking patriotism... Take their weapons and arrest these men and their entire regiment for treason.

"BALDY" JOHNSON
General?!

STONEWALL JACKSON
In that it's your regiment: arrest yourself as well.

Leaving the Colonel mortified, Jackson spurs his horse onward.

INT. CONFEDERATE WHITE HOUSE, JEFFERSON DAVIS'S OFFICE—DAY

Robert E. Lee stands before his president as Jefferson Davis, behind his desk, reads reports.

LEE
The Court of Inquiry has returned guilty verdicts on Generals Floyd and Pillow for abandoning Fort Donelson.

JEFFERSON DAVIS
I'll remove them from command... This General Grant who captured Donelson, continues to advance.

LEE
As the cowardly behavior of Floyd and Pillow proves, Donelson was our defeat not that man's victory.

From outside the shuttered doors there comes the SOUND OF CHILDREN PLAYING WAR in the street below.

JEFFERSON DAVIS
And our defeat yesterday at Kernstown, how do you propose I rectify that, General?

LEE
Jackson will be victorious over General Banks in the Valley.

JEFFERSON DAVIS
(frustrated)

Jackson's outnumbered ten to one! His men are exhausted.

LEE

General Jackson knows the stakes. He's telegraphed me that with only a small reinforcement he can secure the Valley.

Jefferson Davis takes a long, troubled moment with this as the sound of the CHILDREN OUTSIDE increases.

JEFFERSON DAVIS

General Loring believes Jackson's insane. Do you think he's insane?

LEE
I think he's a believer.

JEFFERSON DAVIS
In?

LEE
God, his country, his cause. Himself.

JEFFERSON DAVIS
The men don't like him.

LEE

He doesn't want their affection. He wants their fight. They'll love him when he wins.

JEFFERSON DAVIS
Who will you send?

> LEE
General Taylor in advance of Ewell's army.

> JEFFERSON DAVIS
Very well. Do so.

And Lee goes. Davis turns to his paperwork, but soon the sound of FIGHTING CHILDREN becomes too distracting. Davis opens the shuttered doors.

EXT. CONFEDERATE WHITE HOUSE, BALCONY—DAY

Davis looks down at the street. The Confederate White House is on a hill surrounded by other mansions while at the bottom of the hill are the homes of city poor. The boys of both these groups having each formed a gang—the poor called the BUTCHER CATS, the rich called the HILL CATS—are engaged in a fairly brutal rock fight. About to intervene, Jefferson Davis watches Robert E. Lee ride Traveller through the rock-fighting boys. His presence unites them, at least for now, and they march down the hill behind him.

> STONEWALL JACKSON (V.O.)
Young sir, my religious belief teaches me to feel as safe in battle as in bed.

INT. ASHBY DINING ROOM—NIGHT

Stonewall Jackson is a guest at the table; as Aunt Susan and A SLAVE GIRL serve, he addresses Ben. MRS. ASHBY (50s) smiles proudly as does the ASHBY SISTER (20s), while Tom stares in awe.

> STONEWALL JACKSON
God has fixed the time for my death. I do not concern myself about that, but to be always ready, no matter when it may overtake me.

He pauses, looking Ben full in the face.

> STONEWALL JACKSON
> That is the way all men should live, and then all would be equally brave.

> TOM
> I'm brave.

> MRS. ASHBY
> Thomas, good heavens.

But Jackson smiles. He pulls a printed scrap of paper from his pocket.

> STONEWALL JACKSON
> Do you accept the living Christ as your savior?

> TOM
> I go to Sunday School.

Jackson passes him the paper. It is a Bible tract.

> STONEWALL JACKSON
> Then you will be familiar with what's printed there... Mrs. Ashby, while I prefer to never march or battle on the Sabbath, sometimes such a thing is unavoidable.
> *(re: the bible tract)*
> In those instances I make sure my soldiers receive God's word with their morning rations.

> MRS. ASHBY
> Your devotion is an inspiration to all, General.

> TOM
> You give these to your soldiers?

STONEWALL JACKSON
Yes, making you, by receiving it, a de facto
brother-in-arms.

TOM
What's a de facto?

MRS. ASHBY
It means almost-but-not-old-enough, Tom.

TOM
Oh.

MRS. ASHBY
General Jackson, as honored as we are to have you with
us tonight, aren't you worried to bivouac your men so
close to General Banks's army occupying this country
all the way to Winchester? Why just up the road in Front
Royal the Union 1st Maryland has been encamped for
two weeks.

Stonewall Jackson perks up at the enemy appellation.

STONEWALL JACKSON
My own 1st Maryland believe I march my men too
hard, Madam.
(knowing smile)
I do. But that's what keeps us ahead of our own news.
Far as General Banks is concerned, my ragtag band is
still on the other side of the Massanutton...

Changing the subject—

STONEWALL JACKSON
How old are you, Ben?

BEN
Nineteen years, General, sir.

STONEWALL JACKSON
And yet you do not wear the uniform of your country?

Ben blushes.

MRS. ASHBY
You have guessed my ulterior motive in asking you to
supper this evening, General Jackson.

Intrigued, Jackson gives her a nod to continue.

MRS. ASHBY
Thomas be so good as to get grandfather's sword.

Excited, Tom scampers from the room.

MRS. ASHBY
My grandfather joined the Colonial Army and rode as
cavalry under Light Horse Harry Lee.

STONEWALL JACKSON
Our own Robert Lee's father.

MRS. ASHBY
That is correct, sir.

Tom returns with a cavalry saber. He offers it to his mother, but
she nods him to their guest. Tom gives Jackson the sword. He examines it.

STONEWALL JACKSON
A fine piece of steel.

MRS. ASHBY
I would be proud to see my son wear it in your army,
General.

Jackson looks from the blade to the mother, to son Ben.

STONEWALL JACKSON
Have you ridden as cavalry before?

BEN
I was a lieutenant all last year with the militia.

Stonewall Jackson hands Ben the sword.

STONEWALL JACKSON
At Kernstown I lost some fine officers. The battles
before us will be much larger, much harder fought. Do
you think you could lead men under fire?

BEN
I welcome the opportunity.

STONEWALL JACKSON
Very well, Lieutenant Ashby, as we'll be moving quickly
in the morning and I will not have time to place you
properly, you'll ride for now with my staff...

BEN
(overwhelmed)
Why thank you—thank you very much, General, sir,
I—I...

STONEWALL JACKSON
(smiles)
Would like some dessert? Me as well. What's for it,
Madam?

Mrs. Ashby returns the smile and looks to the kitchen door where, entering from where she's been listening behind it, Aunt Susan beams as she steps behind Ben and—a pie in one hand, her other hand squeezing the young man's shoulder—she pronounces—

AUNT SUSAN

Sweet Lemon Pie, General Jackson.

STONEWALL JACKSON

Why I adore lemons, Auntie.

AUNT SUSAN

I know, General. I know everything goes on in this Valley.

As Jackson cuts into the pie, Aunt Susan removes herself to her mistress' shoulder. Aunt Susan's eyes are filled with emotion. Mrs. Ashby reaches up to hold Aunt Susan's hand and they share a look of true affection and pride.

EXT. CONFEDERATE CAMP—NIGHT

*THE ASHBY FARM,
OUTSIDE FRONT ROYAL—May 22, 1862*

Stonewall Jackson has returned to his army's camp in the fields around the Ashby farm. He sits on a fence rail that sides the Valley Pike. He chews a lemon from a sack given him by the Ashbys as—

CONFEDERATE REINFORCEMENTS

the "LOUISIANA TIGERS" under General Richard Taylor (37), son of President Zachary Taylor, march into camp in perfect order. Taylor dismounts his horse and is directed to Jackson whom he salutes.

TAYLOR
Brigadier General Richard Taylor, reporting, sir.

His voice low and gentle—

STONEWALL JACKSON
By what road and distance have you marched today?

TAYLOR
Keazletown Road, six and twenty miles.

STONEWALL JACKSON
You seem to have no stragglers.

TAYLOR
Never allow straggling.

STONEWALL JACKSON
You must teach my people. They straggle badly.

A bow in reply. Just then the Creoles of Taylor's army start their REGIMENTAL BAND. Surprisingly, these soldiers who wear Zouave uniforms—light, striped baggy pants embroidered jackets and fez head-covering—open their arms to each other and begin to dance a waltz. The reaction from the rest of Jackson's men ranges from LAUGHTER TO DERISION TO CLAPPING IN TIME TO THE BEAT. After a contemplative suck of lemon—

STONEWALL JACKSON
Thoughtless fellows for serious work.

TAYLOR
(bristling)
I hope that the work will not be less well done because of the present gayety.

Jackson gives him a look before returning to his lemon.

STONEWALL JACKSON
We shall see tomorrow.

Finished with Taylor for now, Jackson turns his attention to "Baldy" Johnson.

STONEWALL JACKSON
Baldy! Come over here.

The "arrested" colonel trots up. Jackson looks him over.

STONEWALL JACKSON
No pistol? No sword, Colonel?

"BALDY" JOHNSON
I turned them over to the provost with the rest of the regiment's weapons upon our arrest.

Jackson gives him a raised eyebrow appraisal, then quickly writes an order. Hands it to him.

EXT. ASHBY FARM—DAWN

The far side of the property from where Jackson's army camps. Tom and Georgie move through a field.

TOM
We'll only look like we're swimming, but really we'll be counting the enemy pickets.

GEORGIE
"Pickets?" Like fences?

TOM

No, like the guards posted outside the town. I'll climb
the tree by the creek and call down the number. I'm a
"defacto" in Stonewall Jackson's army. It's my job.

GEORGIE

Can I be a "defacto," too?

A discerning look before...

TOM

You go regular to Sunday school... I reckon you already
are.

Georgie brightens at this. Tom puts his arm around his friend's
shoulder and they continue on.

INT. GENERAL BANKS'S HEADQUARTERS—MORNING

Inside the lobby of the Strasburg Hotel. NATHANIEL BANKS
(41). His is the ultimate rags to riches story; having begun work as a
bobbin boy in a cotton factory he is the former Speaker of the House
of Representatives and three time Governor of Massachusetts. He
wears a bushy mustache above a clean-shaven chin and is trying to
keep the yolk out of it as he dines on soft-boiled eggs with COLO-
NEL G. H. GORDON (36).

NATHANIEL BANKS'S HEADQUARTERS, STRASBURG HOTEL—STRASBURG, VIRGINIA—

9 Miles above Front Royal —May 23, 1862

He is a volunteer general—meaning, of little experience—but eager
to prove himself as he sees military glory as a launch pad to the
White House. An ARMY TELEGRAPH CLERK hands him a telegram. Banks wipes his mustache and reads it.

> BANKS

Hmm. Take down this response, if you please... Inform President Lincoln that: There is nothing to indicate Jackson has been yet reinforced; while Taylor's Louisiana Tiger were sighted, they appear to be passing through. Jackson's force, itself, when last seen, was fleeing Kernstown to hide out on Massanutton Mountain.

He gives Gordon a confident nod that seems to say, "look at how well I've handled this." Gordon butters a piece of toast.

> BANKS
> *(to telegrapher)*

In this, Jackson has been effectively kept on our front. As soon as roads become dry, I will meet and crush him and deliver to you, my dear president, the victory this country is so hopeful for... Here, soldier: let me sign.

The telegrapher hands the pad to Banks who signs with a flourish.

EXT. THE VALLEY PIKE—MORNING

As Stonewall Jackson's augmented army, geared for battle, moves onto the road, they pass with CONTEMPTUOUS COMMENTS—

"BALDY" JOHNSON

standing before the cluster of his arrested 1st Maryland Confederate Regiment beside a covered wagon.

> "BALDY" JOHNSON
> Regiment, 'ten'hut!

The anger and shame evident in his voice and features, compel the men to the command.

"BALDY" JOHNSON

I received an order from General Jackson that very
nearly concerns yourselves, and I will read it to you.

He holds up the order Jackson wrote and reads—

"BALDY" JOHNSON

Colonel Johnson will move the 1st Maryland to the
front with all dispatch, and in conjunction with Taylor's Louisiana Tigers, attack the enemy at Front Royal.
The army will halt as you pass. Signed Jackson.

The unarmed men of the 1st Maryland look ready to mutiny, believing in this that they have been sentenced to slaughter.

"BALDY" JOHNSON

You have heard the order, and I must confess are in a
pretty condition to obey it. I will have to return it with
the endorsement upon the back that the 1st Maryland
refuses to meet the enemy, though ordered by General
Jackson. Before this day I was proud to call myself a
Marylander, but now, God knows I would rather be
known as anything else. When you meet your fathers
and mothers, brothers, sisters, and sweethearts, tell
them it was you who, when brought face to face with
the enemy, proved yourself recreants, and acknowledged yourselves to be cowards. Tell them this, and see
if you are not spurned from their presence like some
loathsome leper and despised. You will wander over
the face of the earth with the brand of coward, traitor
indelibly imprinted upon your foreheads, and in the end
sink into a dishonored grave, unwept, uncared for.

Except for the MARCHING FEET and ROLL OF WAGONS
by the passing army there is utter silence in the ranks and from
the rest of the troops moving nearby as all have heard Johnson's
condemnation.

1ST MARYLANDER CONFEDERATE
We won't disgrace the state!

ANOTHER 1ST MARYLANDER CONFEDERATE
We won't dodge!

THIRD 1ST MARYLANDER CONFEDERATE
Give us back our guns and we'll show you if Maryland's
to be shamed!

The CRY OF "GIVE US BACK OUR GUNS!" is soon taken up by every man of the regiment. Johnson, giving his own dignity time to return, finally gestures to his ORDNANCE OFFICER to uncover—

THE WAGON—THE GUNS OF THE 1ST MARYLAND CONFEDERATE

The men quiet for a moment in anticipation of what comes next. Johnson faces the wagon. He finds his pistol and saber and straps them on. A WILD CHEER goes up from his men. They charge the wagons in a mad rush of patriotism.

EXT. THE VALLEY PIKE—MINUTES LATER

The 1st Maryland Confederate Regiment, moving at double-time, jogs through the ranks of Jackson's Army toward the front, CHEERED on by all whom they pass.

EXT. "HAPPY CREEK"—MORNING

Clothes off, Georgie frolics with some LOCAL BOYS (black and white) in the water of this creek outside the town. For his part, Tom— also buck naked—has climbed partway up a tree to observe—

UNION PICKETS

stationed along the outskirts of the village. They relax and smoke;
some play cards.

TOM
Georgie, c'mon, we need to do this!

GEORGIE
I'm tired a'defacto-ing. I'm catching frogs!

TOM
But we need to tell General Jackson who these Yanks
are!

OLDER BOY
They's the Union 1st Maryland, Tom. Now c'mon
down from there and give us a hand!

The OLDER BOY holds up a bright green frog, its legs squirming.

TOM
That's big enough to eat!

But the frog slips the older boy's grip and splashes into the creek.
Scrambling down—

TOM
Many more that big?

GEORGIE
(giggling; splashing)
They's all over d'place!

EXT. A GRASSY SLOPE / DICKEY RIDGE—MORNING

The 1st Maryland Confederates in the lead, the Louisiana Tigers right behind them, they have left the road and are charging toward a stand of trees atop the ridge. The Tigers SHOUT BATTLE CRIES IN FRENCH—

GENERAL TAYLOR

in the lead, galloping his horse, waves his saber over his head, while—

COLONEL "BALDY" JOHNSON

on foot, jogging backwards before his men, uses his sword like a conductor uses a baton to put them into line-of-battle.

They reach the trees. Johnson turns to Front Royal below—Happy Creek, the Union pickets—and beyond the camps of the Union force, six companies of unwitting Federal soldiers lounging throughout it.

> "BALDY" JOHNSON
> There's the Union 1st Maryland!

A WILD CRY goes up from his men. They charge down the hill toward the town.

EXT. "HAPPY CREEK"—MORNING

Tom is splashing after frogs with the other boys when A CRY OF ALARM goes up from the Union pickets followed by the BANG OF RIFLES. All the boys look to—

FRONT ROYAL

The pickets are clustering together, FIRING over the creek as they back into the town. A CANNON ROARS.

The boys follow the path of its ball over their heads toward Dickey Ridge where they now observe Jackson's army swarming right for them, muskets flashing in the sun. The cannonball passes harmlessly over the treetops.

The boys leap for their clothes as to their immediate left—

THE VALLEY PIKE—STONEWALL JACKSON'S ARMY

charges for the town GUNS BLAZING. Jackson, mounted on Little Sorrel, reins his horse, indicating where he wants—

TWO CANNON

set and aimed.

There is only one escape for Tom, Georgie and the others, and that is into Front Royal. Hopping much like the frogs they've abandoned, they try to pull on trousers as they run.

EXT. FRONT ROYAL—DAY

Tom and Georgie are separated among the retreating pickets fleeing into the town who meet up with the dozen or so UNION PROVOST MARSHALS and UNION OFFICERS who have taken rooms in the one hotel. They turn, prepared to meet the enemy. Jackson's cannon FIRE. The solid rounds BLAST apart a chimney and plunge into the side of a house.

EXT. UNION 1ST MARYLAND ENCAMPMENT—DAY

Beyond the town proper, the lounging men seen early are all on their feet, most moving in frantic confusion as a STUNNED UNION COLONEL gives the DRUMMER the order to beat the LONG ROLL TO ARMS.

EXT. FRONT ROYAL—DAY

Panting, Georgie stops in the middle of the street as behind, Confederates swarm, trading GUNFIRE with the retreating pickets and provosts. BULLETS WHIZZING around his ears, Tom grabs Georgie and pulls him to the safety of a doorway.

CANNON FIRE from both sides begin to EXPLODE in the town. A BULLET THWACKS inches from Tom's head.

TOM
We can't stay here!

Georgie is too scared to speak. Tom notices a cellar across the street. A YOUNG WOMAN with BABE in arms sees them, waves them over. Tom grabs Georgie's hand and pulls him back into the street where they are almost trampled by the hooves of—

BEN ASHBY'S HORSE

BEN
Thomas! Get the hell out of here! Get home now!

He points his sword back the way Tom and Georgie came before riding on. But hordes of Confederates, led by Stonewall Jackson himself, are a tide they can't run against. By the time Tom looks back at the cellar the young woman has closed the door. FUSED CANNONBALLS continue to land and EXPLODE. Terrified, Tom pulls Georgie behind a large tree. They hunker in each other's arms among the thick roots.

INT. TELEGRAPH TENT, UNION 1ST MARYLAND ENCAMPMENT—DAY

The stunned colonel stands over his TELEGRAPHER as he TAPS out a frantic message...waits...TAPS it again...waits.

> STUNNED UNION COLONEL
> Keep at it! We must get word to Banks!

He plunges out of the tent into—

EXT. UNION 1ST MARYLAND ENCAMPMENT—CONTINUOUS

—CHAOS. His men, although outnumbering Jackson's, are panic-stricken and ready to break. TWO JUNIOR OFFICER await him.

> STUNNED UNION COLONEL
> We must hold them until we can get our wagons moving toward Winchester!

INT. GENERAL BANKS'S HEADQUARTERS—DAY

Standing at his telegrapher's shoulder, Banks dictates—

> BANKS
> Dear Mr. President, this attack at Front Royal has been made by a Rebel Force of five thousand which has been gathering in the mountains, it is said, since Wednesday. Reinforcements should be sent us if possible, but I reiterate: I have Jackson where I want him, fixed against my front.

He gives his characteristic curt nod to the telegrapher, then turns to Colonel Gordon as—

> COLONEL G.H. GORDON
> General, before the lines to Front Royal were cut, it was made clear to my command that this force is twice what you've just claimed; it *is* Jackson.

                              BANKS
Bullshit. Jackson is pinned in the mountains against my
front. Front Royal is in my rear.
                         (*then relenting*)
Send a brigade of cavalry to develop the situation, just
in case.

EXT. UNION 1ST MARYLAND ENCAMPMENT—DAY

The Union 1st Maryland has been beaten. Men of "Baldy"
Johnson's 1st Maryland Confederates, GLEEFULLY round up their
late "neighbors" as prisoners and begin collecting spoils of war as at
the far end of the encampment—

EXT. THE SOUTH FORK OF THE SHENANDOAH—DAY

Those Union 1st Marylanders who managed to escape, FIRE with
deadly accuracy upon General Taylor and his men who move forward toward—

THE WAGON BRIDGE

—over the South Fork of the Shenandoah. It suddenly bursts into
flames as Union engineers set off COMBUSTIBLE CHARGES.

Jackson rides alongside General Taylor.

                         STONEWALL JACKSON
We must save that bridge, General, if we're to take
Winchester and force Banks out of Virginia by the
Sabbath.

Taylor gives Stonewall a hard look, then pointing his saber at the
flaming bridge—

                        TAYLOR
                    Tigers: ho!

He spurs his horse toward the burning bridge at the head of his men.

EXT. FRONT ROYAL WAGON BRIDGE—DAY

Fire and smoke abound; timbers CREAK, begin to break off and
fall sizzling to the water. Taylor maintains his saddle in the center
of the span as his Tigers storm the bridge and begin throwing the
burning brands into the river. Meanwhile—

BEN ASHBY

leads a company of cavalry THUNDERING ACROSS to meet the
Union resistance on the far side.

EXT. ACROSS THE BRIDGE—DAY

The sheer dash and daring of it all breaks the opposing Union force.
As the stunned colonel gives the bugler orders to SOUND THE
RETREAT, Ben Ashby's saber takes off the top of his skull. The
colonel dies. His men panic. Those who don't escape and are not
killed or captured, retreat north.

EXT. FRONT ROYAL WAGON BRIDGE—DAY

Much of the fire now extinguished, Taylor smiles as Jackson rides
up beside him.

                        TAYLOR
                Bridge secured as ordered.

                STONEWALL JACKSON
            And a merciful God crowns our victory.

> TAYLOR
>
> Of course to take Winchester within forty-eight hours presupposes our forcing Banks from his headquarters in Strasburg tomorrow—

> STONEWALL JACKSON
>
> Which I have on the Lord's good authority we will.

General Taylor clears his throat and tries again.

> TAYLOR
>
> General Jackson, you realize that for an army who has marched an entire day, fought and won a battle, to march and attack tomorrow at Strasburg, *before* marching and attacking Winchester the next day—the Almighty's authority or not—for what you've proposed: every one of us would have to be cavalry.

Jackson smiles softly.

> STONEWALL JACKSON
>
> But we are, sir. We are—every man of us—cavalry.
> (off Taylor's confusion)
> Foot Cavalry, General. Foot Cavalry!

And Jackson saunters over the bridge amid crowds of his soldiers who now CHEER him his victory.

INT. GENERAL BANKS'S HEADQUARTERS—NIGHT

Banks and Gordon are situated as such that through the parlor windows, by the light of torches, they can see the survivors of Front Royal straggling into town. General Banks is pale, while Colonel Gordon is the exact opposite: red-faced with passion.

COLONEL G.H. GORDON

I was with Jackson at The Point! Saw him fight in Mexico! He means to have your entire army and your supplies—enough to keep the entire Confederate Army armed and clothed for a year, sir!

General Banks flashes Gordon a worried glance, but says nothing, his eyes drawn inexorably back to the beaten soldiers passing before him.

COLONEL G.H. GORDON

Your army can be saved, sir. Listen to me: the proper action now is to fall back—save your men, save your supplies!

BANKS

I would not hear of it.

Beating a hand into his fist like a politician on the stump—

BANKS

I will stand firm! Retreat is a word not found in this army's lexicon!

Moving around behind Banks so that the political general must turn away from the window—

COLONEL G.H. GORDON

Jackson is in our *rear*. It is not a retreat, but a true military movement to escape from being cut off—to prevent stores and sick from falling into the hands of the enemy.

BANKS
(hot)

By God, sir! I will not retreat. We have more to fear from the opinions of our friends than the bayonets of our enemies!

Gordon backs into a chair, sitting as truth dawns upon him.

> COLONEL G.H. GORDON
> I see the trouble here... I see it.... You, sir, are afraid of being accused of being afraid.

Banks considers him with guilty eyes. Gordon rises.

> COLONEL G.H. GORDON
> Which, General, is not a military reason for occupying a false position.

EXT. STRASBURG STREET—NIGHT

Colonel Gordon, on horseback, hurries through the throng of beaten Front Royal soldiers. He passes—

EXT. A COMMISSARY TENT—CONTINUOUS

Where these men are being offered coffee and white army beans. Among the BLACK MEN serving the food can be found—

MARCUS AND ANTHONY

Where Anthony enjoys his work and has a KIND REMARK for each soldier he serves, Marcus looks glum.

> MARCUS
> Stop bein' so friendly.

> ANTHONY
> But I've always been friendly; Mama tells me everyday.

> MARCUS
> I toldja: she ain't yo' mama no more!

CLETUS (45) a grizzled ex-slave, free and employed by the U.S. Army, working now beside the brothers, elbows Marcus.

> CLETUS
>
> You keep chippin' away at that boy's genuine-ness, I'll see he don't have a brother no more neither. Now feel my words or feel worse—your choice, friend.

> MARCUS
>
> Look, we's free and don' even belong here. We got bushwhacked inta this—

> CLETUS
>
> Free men *work* for a living. You's gettin' paid an' kin be proud t'have youse own responsibility.

> MARCUS
>
> This respons'bility is for shit! An' you better butt outta me an' my brother Anth'ny's business!

But before either man can take the argument further, a white Commissary Sergeant, SGT. NEVINS (30), steps behind Marcus whispering in his ear—

> SGT. NEVINS
>
> Word down the line is we'll be pulling out by morning.

Marcus faces him. The two men share a suspicious look.

> SGT. NEVINS
>
> You still up for this?

> MARCUS
>
> I'm up for it.

> SGT. NEVINS
>
> An' the cracked-brain?

> MARCUS
> My brother goes where I—

Cletus grabs Marcus by the back of his neck, hissing—

> CLETUS
> That boy you'll not involve in none o'this sergeant's shenanigans.

Furious, Marcus wrenches out of Cletus's grip, but before Marcus can argue or fight—

> SGT. NEVINS
> Marcus: I don't want the boy. Just the two of us, this job.
> *(to Cletus)*
> And you—I can rely on your confidentiality?

> CLETUS
> Boss, I don' never see nuthin'.

The three of them stare at each other with dislike, while Anthony smiles and dishes out beans to the beaten soldiers.

> SGT. NEVINS
> Well, c'mon then, Marcus.

Marcus, happy to be anywhere else than where he is, pulls off his apron and leaves the chow line.

> ANTHONY
> Marcus! Where you going?!

But Marcus doesn't look back. Anthony makes a move as if to follow, but Cletus puts a gentle hand on his shoulder.

CLETUS
You know me, Anthony?

ANTHONY
Sho, youse Cletus. I need Marcus.

CLETUS
Marcus done take a white man's job. He asked I look
after you whilst he's gone.

His kind eyes bore into Anthony's panicked gaze.

CLETUS
You wanna do right by yo' mama, yous now gonna stay
under my care—till time Marcus is back, cours't.

Anthony bounces on tiptoes trying to espy Marcus in the crowd of
men and tents and wagons beyond, but Marcus is gone. All he is
left with is Cletus's hand on his shoulder, his kind eyes and gentle
words.

RETREATING SOLDIER
Hey, nigger! Beans!

CLETUS
Feed the boys in blue, Anthony: they like your beans.

EXT. G.H. GORDON'S COMMAND TENT—NIGHT

His officers are assembled. He is halfway out of his saddle when he
begins—

COLONEL G.H. GORDON
See to the packing of all stores and baggage. Get the
wagons lined and pointed north.

> UNION CAPTAIN
> Has General Banks ordered the retreat?

Stalking into his tent—

> COLONEL G.H. GORDON
> He will.

EXT. THE VALLEY PIKE—LATER

General Stonewall Jackson sits upon Little Sorrel alongside the road watching his passing army with satisfaction.

> STONEWALL JACKSON (V.O.)
> Men of the Army of the Valley of the Shenandoah: we march today, the sword of Providence, unsheathed to cut from the bosom of the South the ungodly terrorists of Northern aggression—

To a man they are battle-fatigued and hungry, yet they are also keen-eyed and bold: patriots marching toward glory.

> STONEWALL JACKSON (V.O.)
> —that have come to oppress our fair land and fairer women and children.

Stonewall Jackson nods his approval and moves up the line.

INT. ASHBY KITCHEN—NIGHT

On one chair, Mrs. Ashby plies a switch to Tom's bottom. Beside her, Aunt Susan switches Georgie. They stop when both boys are crying—Aunt Susan taking her last swat reaching over for Tom. SMACK!

TOM (V.O.)
No amount of explaining by me or Georgie could save
us from the licking we received upon our return from
battle.

Mrs. Ashby lets Tom off her lap. He wipes his tears and her heart
melts. She is about to embrace her son, but—catching a dour look
from Aunt Susan—pulls back her arms and leaves with—

MRS. ASHBY
Do as your Mammie tells you now, Thomas. Good
night.

She quickly leaves. Aunt Susan lets Georgie from her lap and
addresses both boys.

AUNT SUSAN
The shame you bring this family. The embarrassment
you both cause Benjamin in battle!

TOM
He wasn't embarr—

He chokes off the rest of the sentence as Aunt Susan's switch swishes
for him.

AUNT SUSAN
I know that boy's heart better than any a God's creatures! Don't you be tellin' me nothing about it!

Her words are tough, but Tom notices her eyes are filling with
emotion.

GEORGIE
Mammie why are you cryin'?

> AUNT SUSAN
>
> Was he brave—my boy, Ben? Was he brave and glorious
> in General Jackson's army? I want to hear ev'rythin'.

MOS WITH VOICE-OVER AS THE TWO BOYS RECOUNT
THEIR ADVENTURE

> TOM (V.O.)
>
> She smelled of flour and lemons...like the pie she baked
> Stonewall Jackson. She was the heart of our family, of
> our farm, and of all of us on it.

As the two boys continue talking, Aunt Susan finds taffy for them.

> TOM (V.O.)
>
> She loved my brother Ben most of everyone—our fam-
> ily and her own. She'd nursed him after his troublesome
> delivery that got Mother sick, and as Mother told—
> once if not a thousand times—the bond of those first
> months between Ben and Aunt Susan was special and
> to be respected.

Aunt Susan spreads her arms beckoning the two boys to come into
them. Situated on her lap they enjoy their taffy, all of them thinking
in one way or another about—

CUT TO:

CLOSE ON: BEN ASHBY

Gun smoke swirling around him, he charges his horse at a Union
wagon filled with supplies. The defenders scatter to the Confederate
cavalry and THIS IS—

EXT. THE VALLEY PIKE—DAY—ESTABLISHING

THE UNION RETREAT
FROM STRASBURG—May 24, 1862

THE CAMERA SWEEPS QUICKLY OVER the Union retreat to Winchester: a wagon train of over five hundred Federal vehicles of supplies and material and ordnance—some burning, some crashed, tipped, ransacked (primarily by the oddly uniformed Creoles of the Louisiana Tigers), some being fought for in pockets of battle that have developed at the crossroads from where the Rebels have swept in—all of them strung out from the burning town of Strasburg to as far as the eye can see.

CLOSE ON: BEN ASHBY

He FIRES his pistol into Union TEAMSTERS who scatter for the woods in fear as Ashby and his mounted squad capture a group of wagons.

EXT. A WOODED VALLEY ROAD—EVENING

A supply wagon overpacked with weapons, food, clothing, stolen home furnishings and silver rides alone some distance from the route of retreat. At the reins is Sergeant Nevins. Seated beside him is Marcus. They pass a bottle of whiskey between them, enjoying their "freedom."

SGT. NEVINS
We'll cross the Potomac at Leesburg where I have a "sales agent"... waiting...

His voice trails off as they come around a corner where a Federal roadblock is waiting.

MARCUS
Shit.

INT. WAR DEPARTMENT, TELEGRAPH ROOM—NIGHT

*WAR DEPARTMENT,
WASHINGTON CITY—May 24, 1862*

Lincoln reads a telegram; breathes a sigh of relief and looks to his agitated war secretary, Edwin Stanton.

LINCOLN
Our General Banks is safe.

STANTON
And the wagon train?

LINCOLN
A fifth of it destroyed, lost, abandoned or taken by the enemy...

STANTON
They say Jackson's been reinforced by General Ewell. He must have over 10,000 men by now.

LINCOLN
Bold as he is, Jackson has extended his army marching and fighting for two days and finally is compelled by his only being human like the rest of us to assume his wall-like aspect and, stopping, plant himself firmly outside Winchester.

Lincoln finds a horsehair armchair and, sitting, stretches his legs to their very long length; lacing his fingers behind his head, he smiles, satisfied.

LINCOLN
He's taken the bait. Now we'll spring the trap.

And he's suddenly back on his feet, eager and ushering Stanton to a waiting telegrapher. Lincoln rubs his hands together like an excited schoolboy.

> LINCOLN
> We'll not lose a minute: get orders to General Fremont to move in from the Blue Ridge Mountains; separate orders to General Shields to drop down from the Alleghenies and, sealing Jackson's rear, we'll dismantle that wall stone by rebellious stone.

EXT. AN ORCHARD, JACKSON'S CAMP OUTSIDE WINCHESTER—NIGHT

The night is RAINY making their bonfire steam and fight for every warming flame. The men of Jackson's staff, though triumphant, have endured more than anyone, two days ago, would believe humanly possible. And yet they are weary, haggard and near the breaking point of exhaustion that no amount of martial success can succor.

> STONEWALL JACKSON
> Beyond this fire, beyond this orchard is our prize, gentlemen. Our successes of the past two days are nothing if we do not—not "cannot," I won't use that word—hit the terrorist general, Banks, again at first light.

To a man, Jackson's staff seems to shrink with added fatigue at these words.

> GENERAL LORING
> You ask the impossible, sir!

> STONEWALL JACKSON
> I ask we win this campaign with victory tomorrow. Are you with me, sir?

A long beat. No one really thinks they can do this: Loring knows he cannot.

> GENERAL LORING
> It is folly and madness!

> STONEWALL JACKSON
> After Kernstown, General, you made similar claims against my mentality to our president. Since you did not make them to my face I ignored them.

Paxton, Taylor, Ben Ashby, and others—now including General Richard Ewell (now 45 and affectionately nicknamed "Old Bald Head")—hunker down and avoid eye contact.

> GENERAL LORING
> I said you were mad. You lost that fight, sir, and, though you've won two battle in as many days here, these men you push—and *they are just men*—will be sacrificed to no good end if you force them into battle tomorrow!

Stonewall Jackson smiles, but grimly and without pleasure.

> STONEWALL JACKSON
> There is no forcing the patriot. The patriot volunteer, fighting for country and his rights, makes the most reliable soldier on earth... You, sir, however...

And here he fishes into his coat and withdraws some orders.

> STONEWALL JACKSON
> ...have no more business with this command.

General Loring shoots to his feet.

> GENERAL LORING
> What is that?!

STONEWALL JACKSON
Why, your promotion, sir. General Lee has seen fit to
promote you to Major General.

He hands the orders to Loring.

STONEWALL JACKSON
Your patriots, here, will fall under new command as
you are being sent West. Perhaps against Sam Grant.

A beat as Jackson recalls his West Point and Mexico friend then
mutters.

STONEWALL JACKSON
Bless him, Lord.

"Him" clearly Sam Grant, then Jackson shakes his head at the folly
of it all. Loring looks at his orders. A promotion—usually an event
of distinction—here in the rain and the night and the shared misery
and duty of the others, is received like the curse Jackson intends it.
He points outside the circle of light.

STONEWALL JACKSON
I will not see you in the morning or again. Thank you
for your service.

Loring swallows. Ashamed, he stalks into the darkness of night and
of history.

STONEWALL JACKSON
General Ewell: Winchester is the key to the Shenandoah
Valley. We will envelop it at dawn from two directions.
I can depend on the patriots under my command, and
Taylor—who has fought like St. Michael since you first
sent him—will do God's Will. Will you?

General Ewell rises…a bashful look at his boots, then directly to Jackson.

                    EWELL
          Are you mad, General Jackson?

Jackson gives Ewell an appraising look, before—

               STONEWALL JACKSON
     I am as mad as the Holy Lord against the Golden Calf
     Moses confronted after his descent from Sinai! False
     idols are not just physical; they are infections of men:
     of cowardice, of procrastination, of giving up the fight
     before the fight is fought. Are *you* with me?!

                    EWELL
     By your leave, I will go now and arrange my cannon
     over Winchester. When the battle is commenced my
     shot will more than prove my faith.

He salutes. Jackson returns it and before Ewell has taken two steps the ROAR OF CANNON proves his words as—

                                        CUT TO:

EWELL'S ARTILLERY BELCHING FIRE

and this is a wheat field bathed in fog atop—

EXT. A HILL AT THE TOP OF THE MILLWOOD PIKE—MORNING

Ewell's command tent has been set behind his two batteries. He drinks his morning coffee as he watches the artillery crews do their work.

EXT. UNION ENCAMPMENT BELOW WINCHESTER—MORNING

Men of the 5th Connecticut: camped among wheat-stacks are eating breakfast and boiling coffee as the ARTILLERY SHELLS SCREAM in and begin to EXPLODE among them. To a man, they drop what they are doing and run for their rifle stacks. OFFICERS YELLING at them, these young men form into line of battle as—

COLONEL PAXTON

with his men of Jackson's "Stonewall Brigade," emerge from the fog along a rock wall and begin trading GUNFIRE with the Union soldiers defending their camp. As the configuration of the wall being perpendicular to the Union camp, the Confederates are forced to make their attack in column. This only allows a portion of the men a chance to FIRE. The Union soldiers—lined up as they are—begin to slaughter them.

INT. WINCHESTER HOTEL ROOM—MORNING

General Banks watches the street through the window. Below, Union teamsters, quartermaster and hospital troops are withdrawing in wagons and ambulances. Cletus and Anthony pass by with other civilian—black and white—employees of the Army. To an orderly—

> BANKS
> Have my horse readied. Any supplies and wagons remaining when I ride out are to be burned.

EXT. WINCHESTER STREET—MORNING

Cletus drives a commissary wagon, Anthony beside him. As they pass through a traffic jam at the far end of town Anthony suddenly SCREAMS OUT—

ANTHONY
MARCUS!

Before Cletus can stop him, Anthony has leaped from the wagon
and is pushing his way through horses and wagons. Cletus searches
for the source of Anthony's alarm.

A GALLOWS

hanging from which are the executed bodies of Marcus and Sergeant Nevins.

CLETUS
Oh, dear Jesus. Did he hafta see it Lord?

As Anthony fights his way to Marcus, his voice echoes in a CON-
STANT STREAM OF BABBLE most of it to the effect of "MAR-
CUS! MY BROTHER! I NEED MY BROTHER!" Anthony
scrambles up the gallows and wraps his arms around Marcus's legs,
hugging him and trying to pull him down and CRYING.

A PROVOST MARSHAL moves to apprehend him, but a strong,
dark hand pulls him back. The provost marshal turns to face—

CLETUS
Let him have his peace. He ain't doin' no one no harm,
sir. That boy hangin' there's his only kin.

The provost marshal scowls, but he knows Cletus and...

PROVOST MARSHAL
His kin's a thief. Now get him and your wagon out of
here.

Cletus goes to Anthony. He gently pulls the anguished young man
from his brother's body and takes Anthony into his strong embrace.

CLETUS
He's in a better place, Anthony.

ANTHONY
I want to go home! I need to go home! I want my brother!

Anthony hysterically tries to pull Marcus down, but Cletus pulls Anthony back. As he guides the desolate boy from the gallows, Marcus's body swings back and forth.

EXT. AN ORCHARD, CONFEDERATE LEFT FLANK—MORNING

Less foggy here, the spires and rooftops of Winchester visible in the distant foreground, Jackson rides up to where General Taylor, on horseback, is leading his marching Louisiana Tigers forward on the double-quick. Pointing to a wooded slope to the left of the town known as Bower's Hill—

STONEWALL JACKSON
I expect the enemy to bring artillery to occupy that hill, and they must not do it! Do you understand me, sir? They must not do it! Keep a good look out, and your men well in hand, and if they attempt to come, charge them with the bayonet and seize their guns!

He clenches his fist for emphasis. Taylor salutes and rides forward with his men.

EXT. BOWER'S HILL—MORNING

True to Jackson's prediction, Colonel G.H. Gordon directs the positioning of two battery of artillery supported by four brigades of infantry and one of cavalry. With the SOUND OF BATTLE ECHOING FROM THE OTHER END OF THE BATTLEFIELD, Gordon scans his own front with—

FIELD GLASSES—TAYLOR AND HIS MEN

visible passing the gap in the ridge into which these Union cannon are aimed.

> COLONEL G.H. GORDON
> Hold fire until they enter that ravine and begin to stack up.

EXT. THE RAVINE, CONFEDERATE LEFT FLANK—MORNING

As Taylor's men fill the ravine looking for a path to ascend the hill, Gordon's CANNON OPEN FIRE. Many Rebels fall. The rest duck their heads and seek shelter amidst the WHISTLING SHOT AND SHELL. As Jackson rides up beside Taylor—

> TAYLOR
> *(to his men)*
> What the hell are you dodging for?! If there's any more of it, I'll halt you under this fire for an hour!

His sharp tone has the desired effect, his men going ramrod straight and pressing forward. Taylor notices the look of reproachful surprise his words have put upon Jackson's face. Jackson places a hand on Taylor's shoulder and, gently—

> STONEWALL JACKSON
> I am afraid you are a wicked fellow.

Taylor's hard expression doesn't break. Jackson rides off.

EXT. BOWER'S HILL—MORNING

CANNON CONTINUE FIRING, the Union infantry joining them, as Taylor's men emerge from the ravine. Under withering FIRE, they quickly set their lines and RETURN FIRE.

COLONEL G.H. GORDON
Bugler: sound the charge!

The BUGLER beside Gordon BLOWS HIS HORN.

GORDON'S CAVALRY

charges the Louisianians. With uncommon and unflinching bravery Taylor's Tigers hold their fire until the horsemen are almost upon them, then let go a FUSILLADE that empties half the saddles. The cavalry break. The Confederates charge the guns. As they swarm from the ravine, it is clear they outnumber Gordon's force by two to one. And—

COLONEL G. H. GORDON "BLINKS."

COLONEL G.H. GORDON
Pull back! Save the guns!

As he turns his horse for town leading his infantry in retreat—

THE UNION BATTERIES

are overrun.

EXT. UNION ENCAMPMENT BELOW WINCHESTER—MORNING

Confederate and Union dead and wounded litter the field. Colonel Paxton, bloodied but not beaten, hunkers with his remaining men behind a wall. Peering out, through the fog and gun smoke he can see the 5th Connecticut massing.

PAXTON
Get ready, boys! They're preparing the charge!

As his survivors fit bayonets and load their last rounds, a BUGLE CALL RINGS OUT followed by the REBEL YELL. Paxton and his men peer over the wall. THUNDERING in from the right flank come—

JACKSON'S CAVALRY

PISTOLS BANGING, sabers flashing; Ben Ashby fights hard among them. They overwhelm the Union forces.

PAXTON'S REBELS

climb over the wall and hurl themselves into the fight. Those Union soldiers who do not fall, surrender.

EXT. WINCHESTER STREET—MORNING

Wagon loads of supplies unable to be gotten quickly enough from town are put to the torch. Rebel artillery SHELLS EXPLODE overhead, EXPLODE into buildings, and EXPLODE in the street. Crazed horses BELLOW and gallop, riderless, through town. And the remains of Banks's Union Army falling back from the battlefield retreat through the town, their Confederate pursuers not fifty feet behind them. From—

THE UPSTAIRS WINDOWS OF HOUSES

CONFEDERATE WOMEN throw bottles at the hated boys in blue; they pour pan-fulls of scalding water onto soldiers fleeing through their yards; still others shove forth rifles and pistols and FIRE into them. On a front porch, this happened:

CONFEDERATE WOMAN
That's a lovely pistol, private. May I see it?

In no account does anyone give reason why the UNION PRIVATE carrying the pistol hands it to the woman. It was impossible to ask him after she FIRED it into his head. No one does a thing about that.

As those Union troops who don't surrender make the end of town, Banks becomes visible through the FIRE and smoke, directing a cannon to be aimed up the street.

> BANKS
> Fire!

A round of CANNISTER rips apart Confederates coming in pursuit, causes others to stop and take cover. RIFLE FIRE crackles. To his cannon crew—

> BANKS
> Hold them back for three more rounds, then spike the
> gun and withdraw!

He turns his horse following in the direction of his scattering army a look of ruin on his face. To the fleeing men around him he attempts to rally them with a cry of—

> BANKS
> My God, men, don't you love your country?!

> FLEEING PRIVATE
> Yeah, and I am trying to get to it as fast as I can!

Banks continues on after his broken army. Behind him the CANNON FIRES once more before it is captured.

At the other end of town, CIVILIANS are pouring into the street many carrying Confederate flags they have hidden through the occupation. They swarm around Jackson's triumphant force. Stonewall Jackson rides in on Little Sorrel and is met by RESOUNDING CHEERS... Woman and girls begin offering food to Jackson's worn out and ragged, starving but joyous men. The battle of Winchester is over.

EXT. A TRAIN DEPOT—NIGHT

A train is packed with Union troops—inside and atop it—others walk along the tracks. On the platform, Banks dictates a message to a telegrapher.

> BANKS
> To War Secretary Stanton: the Rebels attacked us this morning at daybreak in great force. Their number, estimated at 15,000, consisted of Jackson and Ewell's divisions...

His shoulders slump, under the weight of his failure. He wipes his brow, takes a steadying breath, and—

INT. WAR DEPARTMENT, TELEGRAPH ROOM—NIGHT

Stanton reads the telegram from Banks aloud to Lincoln...

> STANTON
> "Tonight, we shall all pass the Potomac—"

> BANKS (V.O.)
> Tonight, we shall all pass the Potomac...

> STANTON
> "Safe, I think."

From the president's expression, it is clear he feels the loss just as strongly as Banks. Measuring his words—

LINCOLN

Tell General Banks I am grateful that he has saved so much. Have him remove his army to Harpers Ferry where he must block Jackson and Ewell from any movement on the capital... Tell him to have faith, that I'll send him reinforcements.

Jotting down the message, Stanton nods.

LINCOLN

Then get word to Fremont. He is to chose a field of battle and prepare his attack.

INT. WINCHESTER HOTEL ROOM—NIGHT

The same room Union General Banks occupied the night before, Jackson has fallen across the bed fully clothed—spurs and all—and is sleeping deeply when he is awakened by an urgent KNOCKING. Confused for a moment, Jackson rubs his face and smooths his beard and—

STONEWALL JACKSON
Yes. Come inside.

Entering the room is Jackson's aide, Lieutenant SANDIE PENDLE-TON (22). Son of an Episcopal minister, Sandie is a former student of Jackson's at the Virginia Military Institute. Sandie loves Jackson as a son loves a father and is equal to the general in his religious fervor.

SANDIE PENDLETON
General Jackson, I'm sorry to disturb you. But, here—

He hands a telegraph message to Jackson who sits wearily on the edge of the bed.

> SANDIE PENDLETON

Intercepts from out of Washington. Generals Fremont and Shields are moving on our rear.

Disappointment strikes Jackson hard as he reads the message.

> STONEWALL JACKSON

Just a few more days and the Lord's blessings we'd be _in_ Washington.

> SANDIE PENDLETON

Amen, sir. I am sorry to be the bearer of such bad news.

Gathering his energy to rise—for this interrupted slumber is the first sleep Jackson has had in days—Jackson rises, adjusts his uniform and finds his grubby private's hat.

> STONEWALL JACKSON

Pass the word: we will turn around this army and march before the sun.

A keen look begins to glow in Jackson's eye.

> STONEWALL JACKSON

At four ayem, the troops are to fall in at attention.
> _(with growing passion)_
They are to step off in cadence—holding it for two or three hundred yards...

EXT. WINCHESTER STREET—NIGHT

Candles burn in windows filled with the faces of the women, children and old men of Winchester as they watch Jackson's Army marching forth from Winchester back the way they came. To a man, this army is exhausted, but they are like wolves, lean and tough, mean and indomitable. Their eyes are filled with the same fire that burns in Jackson's.

Eating a lemon astride Little Sorrel, Stonewall Jackson looks upon them with pride and affection.

> STONEWALL JACKSON (V.O.)
> No one is to leave the column for any reason whatsoever without express permission of an officer. Every fifty minutes of each hour they march will be followed by ten minute intervals of rest—preferably each man prone upon the ground as when lying in repose a body gets its fullest rest.

EXT. MASSANUTTON MOUNTAIN—DAY

HAIL pounds Jackson's bedraggled army as they trudge through ice and mud once again over the back of this unforgiving mountain. Jackson rides along the line, encouraging his men here...helping them free stuck artillery there...and all along the line of march he is CHEERED as he urges them—

> STONEWALL JACKSON
> Press on, men! Press on!

EXT. CROSS KEYS BATTLEFIELD—MORNING

CROSS KEYS, VIRGINIA—June 8, 1862

A cluster of tavern buildings—hardly a village—along the Keazletown Road that cuts through low, rolling countryside of ripening fields of grain, bisected by streams and clumps of woods. With the Blue Ridge Mountains as its backdrop, the fields are covered with an even deeper shade of blue: the uniforms of over—

TWENTY UNION BRIGADES (11,500 MEN)

coming into line for battle. It is a frantic scene of much confusion. Across the battlefield, at half the Union number, starved and scrawny with uniforms in tatters, but with lines straight and guns ready is—

STONEWALL JACKSON'S ARMY OF THE VALLEY

FADE OUT.

FADE IN:

EXT. CROSS KEYS TAVERN—MORNING

The dashing, somewhat arrogant, Union General JOHN C. FREMONT (49), surrounded by his STAFF which is made up of both AMERICAN OFFICERS and EUROPEAN MERCENAR-IES (in their flamboyant, Old World uniforms), rides with urgency through a glut of ammunition and hospital wagons toward the battlefield.

> JOHN C. FREMONT
> I have been without reliable maps! Without reliable guides! I have struggled across a mountain range, impassable to anyone else: I have accomplished the impossible and yet Jackson is waiting to meet me?!

Realizing that he is sounding as if he's already lost—which, in fact, he has—Fremont changes his tone.

> JOHN C. FREMONT
> As soon as the lines are set we will coordinate our attack, opening this battle by—

THE SCREAM OF AN ARTILLERY SHELL drowns out anything else Fremont might have said. It EXPLODES directly in front of the Union general and his staff. Fremont struggles to stay in his saddle. Jackson has "opened the battle." From the battlefield comes the sound of MEN and GUNFIRE and POUNDING CANNON.

> JOHN C. FREMONT
> *(suppressed panic)*
> Where is General Shields's Army?!

EXT. A WOODED HILL—DAY

Jackson watches the smoke-clouded battle on the fields below as artillery BOOMS beside him.

JACKSON'S POINT OF VIEW—THROUGH BINOCULARS—THE VANGUARD OF SHIELD'S ARMY

in the far distance, closing rapidly toward a large wagon bridge at Mill Creek which is a river.

> STONEWALL JACKSON
> Mister Pendleton.

> SANDIE PENDLETON
> Yes, General?

> STONEWALL JACKSON
> Send a squad of cavalry and destroy that bridge. General Shields cannot be allowed to join this fight as the Lord has determined that we are to beat *him* tomorrow.

> SANDIE PENDLETON
> Amen, sir. Yes, sir.

EXT. MILL CREEK BRIDGE—DAY

Over a deep, wide, fast flowing river. Ben Ashby and the men of his cavalry unit set explosives on the wide bridge and trade FIRE with skirmishers from Shields's advance. It is hot, dangerous work. Outnumbered, Ashby's men begin to fall one after another. The charges are set. Ashby lights a torch from his cheroot.

> BEN
> Sergeant: withdraw the men!

This as he sets fire to—

FIVE STRANDS OF FUSE

Other troopers throw torches into tar that has been smeared on the supports. As Ben's troopers retreat from one end of the bridge, the first of Shields's skirmishers reach the other. As they attempt to put out the fires and stop the fuses—

ASHBY'S TROOPERS

begin killing them. The bridge burns, but there are too many Union skirmishers and they cut the fuses one after another. On the far side of the creek, Shields's first company of infantry begins to gather; over one hundred men. The GUNFIRE grows furious.

> ASHBY'S SERGEANT
> We did our best, sir. We have to get out of here!

> BEN
> Pull back the men, sergeant.

Yet, Ben spurs his horse *for the bridge*. His men watch—surprised, terrified. They do not retreat until, glancing back—

> BEN
> Sergeant: you have your orders!

But still they do not leave. As Ben Ashby makes the bridge, his men throw out SUPPRESSING FIRE. Ben's horse is shot from under him. Now Union skirmishers are putting out the fire.

Ben Ashby, cheroot clutched in his teeth, draws his pistol and proceeds onto the bridge. Some of the Union soldiers see him and are frozen by his remarkable bravery. These men he SHOOTS. Others SHOOT him. Twice hit he goes down. A beat.

BEN ASHBY'S POINT OF VIEW—HAZY—THE LAST FUSE IS CUT

GROANING IN PAIN, Ben Ashby pulls himself up and lunges forward. He is SHOT again...and again. He falls.

BEN ASHBY'S DYING POINT OF VIEW—HIS SMOULDERING CHEROOT...

on a plank before him and, beyond, an explosive charge five feet farther. A Union soldier moves over him.

BEN ASHBY FIRES HIS LAST ROUND INTO THIS MAN'S FACE. HE GRABS HIS CHEROOT AND CRAWLS THE FINAL FIVE FEET.

> BEN
> ...my valley...stay out.

He touches the cheroot's cherry to—

THE EXPLOSIVES—BOOM!

WITH ASHBY'S MEN

stunned, watching—BOOM! BOOM! BOOM! BOOM! The charges ripple, the bridge EXPLODES. The debris and bodies rain into the water. There is silence. Ashby's troopers face an entire company of Union soldiers across the river. A beat. The Confederate horseman turn their horses back for Cross Keys only to be arrested by an explosion of sound—

THE UNION SOLDIERS

to a man CHEER and take off their hats waving them and their dead leader in salute. Tears tracking his face, Ashby's sergeant waves his own hat in response to them, gives the Rebel Yell, then spurs his horse, leading Ashby's remaining men out of range and away.

EXT. FAMILY GRAVEYARD, ASHBY FARM—MORNING

A beautiful day in the Shenandoah Valley, though tinged with sadness as Tom Ashby, his mother, his sister, an EPISCOPAL PRIEST and the family slaves gather around Ben Ashby's grave.

> TOM (V.O.)
> With his victory against General Fremont at Cross Keys on June 8, followed by another against the general Shields at Port Republic the following day, Stonewall Jackson drove the Yankees from the Valley becoming the greatest hero of the Confederacy.

A coffin is lowered into the ground. Aunt Susan collapses in tears. Uncle Lewis helps her to her feet. Mrs. Ashby takes her in her arms.

> TOM (V.O.)
> He would go on with his Foot Cavalry to join Robert E. Lee and become an even greater hero at the Battle of Chancellorsville... Ben's body was found by Union soldiers two days after he died at Mill Creek. Mother wrote General Shields to ask for him returned. Hesent it by rail to us with a letter saying that while the cause Ben fought for he believed to be wrong, Ben died most heroically and his life and selfless sacrifice were exemp—
> *(the boy has trouble with the word)*
> —exemplary of the greatest and noblest of God's virtues.

The service is read. Dirt is thrown.

> TOM (V.O.)
> My brother Ben was buried in the spot once reserved for mother—between my father and my great grandfather who rode with Washington... Four weeks later, Aunt Susan would join him, having died, as mother said, of a broken heart.

EXT. A UNION RECRUITING STATION, WASHINGTON CITY—MORNING

Cletus and Anthony stand in a huge line of free blacks to sign up for a "Colored Infantry Recruitment! Fight for Father Abraham!"

> ANTHONY
> We *all* gonna be cookin' beans, Cletus?

> CLETUS
> No, Anthony. We'll be soldiers now. Real soldiers gonna win real freedom, everlasting for every man, woman and child a'color in this country. We's gonna fight for every last one of them. Hard.

In the BACKGROUND BEGIN (SOFTLY) THE NEGRO SPIRITUAL: "WE ARE CLIMBING JACOB'S LADDER."

EXT. SLAVES' GRAVEYARD, ASHBY FARM—MORNING

A foggy day in the Valley. All are gathered as before as Aunt Susan is laid to rest under a walnut tree. Here, however, there is music: the Ashby slaves SINGING the CONTINUING SONG. Tom holds Uncle Lewis's hand.

> TOM (V.O.)
>
> There is so much more of the war in the Shenandoah that I could tell—how two years later, Union General Philip Sheridan, arriving under orders of General Grant, boasted he would make so much of destruction to our land that "a crow will have to carry its rations in flying over the Valley." And he did.

INSERT SHOTS:

- *Barns and mills burning.*
- *Farm equipment being destroyed by UNION CAVALRYMEN.*
- *Fruit orchards chopped down*
- *Fields of grain afire.*

> TOM (V.O.)
>
> I could tell how the war would end at Appomattox, our Cause lost but our two countries rejoined in peace; of how that day Mother explained to our servants that their freedom had come and how I couldn't understand how she could cry and smile at the same time...

EXT. ASHBY FARM, THE WALNUT TREE—MORNING—MOS

Mrs. Ashby has the slaves assembled and is speaking to them.

> TOM (V.O.)
>
> How under a large tree in the yard beside Aunt Susan's grave she explained to them that under the order of the President of the United States the Negroes had been liberated and were now free to do as they pleased.

She finishes speaking and Uncle Lewis steps forward to speak for the slaves.

TOM (V.O.)

How Uncle Lewis with his strong sense of honor said
none of them wished to be "free," that all their lives
they had been in my father's family; he had always
been treated with the greatest kindness by my grandfather, and after his death by my father, and after that
by brother Ben; that going into his old age he did not
want to be thrown on the world to make his own living
and be neglected by strangers who had won a war for
a noble cause, but still looked a man by the color of his
skin. And would, he predicted, for a long, long, time.

EXT. SLAVE CABINS, ASHBY FARM—NIGHT—FLASHBACK

TOM (V.O.)

I didn't understand what he meant—that I would make
up for later with mistakes and a fight of my own—just
then, though, I was glad. He had taught me the early
lessons of outdoor life—how to ride, to load and shoot
a gun, to hunt, and do many of the little things about
the farm and home that made up our life... But what I
remember most of the Time Of The Trouble, what I
will carry with me till my time is finished, is my Aunt
Susan. In this I don't think I am alone.

A bonfire burns and the slaves of the Ashby family—including
Marcus and Anthony and Laws—are singing and playing music.
There is food and there is dancing and Tom is in the midst of it, in
Aunt Susan's lap as happy as a boy can be.

TOM (V.O.)

Many a Southern boy and girl of my generation will
recall the old Negro "Mammie"—as she was called—
her gentleness, patience, and faithfulness, her spirit of
unselfishness and kindness, and her interest in the plea-
sures and enjoyments of our young lives.

Aunt Susan notices Ben just outside the circle of light—a young man who understands this world better than his brother and thinks he cannot belong and must be respectful. Aunt Susan laughs at him and, depositing Tom on her cabin stoop, she goes to Ben and takes his hands.

>   TOM (V.O.)
> I remember my old nurse—her songs and stories, her gentle care of my diet and clothes, her mild way of correcting my outbreaks of passion and temper and her ways of training my disposition and character. No mother could have been more considerate of a boy's comfort and happiness.

Aunt Susan pulls Ben into the group and begins to dance with him. Like Tom, Ben loves this woman with all his heart and he is, soon, enthusiastic in his enjoyment of this night. This life. This world lost. As they twirl and laugh—

>   TOM (V.O.)
> I know: the rest of the South was not like our Valley. Slavery was an evil blight on our nation—an American shame forever—which needed to end. But in our Valley, at that time, we did not know better. Life here was different. It was special. We loved and we were loved. We judged with our hearts.

HOLD ON: AUNT SUSAN AND BEN SMILING LIKE MOTHER AND SON

>   TOM (V.O.)
>   *(ashamed)*
> At the time, that seemed worth fighting for.

                                        TO BLACK.

NEGRO SPIRITUAL (V.O.)
We are climbing... Jacob's Ladder... We are climbing Jacob's Ladder / We are climbing Jacob's Ladder... Soldiers of the Cross... Every rung goes higher, higher / Every rung goes higher, higher / Every rung goes higher, higher / Soldiers of the Cross...

FADE OUT.

END OF EPISODE 103

"A NATION DIVIDED"

EPISODE 104

"SHOOTING STAR"

BY

Michael Frost Beckner

FADE IN:

EXT. STRATFORD HALL—DAY

STRATFORD HALL, VIRGINIA—1811

A rented carriage for the FAMILY, a buckboard for their meager possessions—all that is left which could not be sold before the loss of the Lee family home.

> WIDOW LEE
> Robert? Where's Robert? Would someone find him, please?

INT. STRATFORD HALL, GREAT ROOM—DAY

A magnificent home stripped of all comforts; the vacancy of a squandered fortune, silent but for the VOICE WE FOLLOW...

> YOUNG LEE (O.S.)
> Tell father we are traveling to Alexandria.

YOUNG LEE (4) stands at the cold, empty fireplace. Already the aura of responsibility hovers around him. It is a light in his eyes that speaks of a soul destined for greatness.

> YOUNG LEE
> He won't know when he comes back from the jail.

He speaks to CARVED ANGELS holding up the fireplace mantel.

> YOUNG LEE
> Please tell him for me...

LEE SLAVE (O.S.)
Robert..? Robert, where've you got t'now?

YOUNG LEE
I've been good. I care for mother. I mix her medicine
and I do everything I should. I just don't want him to
miss us and feel sad...

The SLAVE enters the room. Sees the child speaking to stone about
a father who abandoned his family.

LEE SLAVE
Robert, your mother and sisters are waiting.

YOUNG
Someone has to look after father and I can't stay here to
tell him where we went.

LEE SLAVE
(re: the angels)
Then this is the right thing. Come along now, your
mother needs you.

You can see in the man's eyes how touched he is by this boy's faith
and nobility.

YOUNG LEE
(to the angels)
Thank you.
(to the slave)
Why can't we stay?

LEE SLAVE
God has other plans for you. For all of his children.

They step away. The last, final, night's log drops. SPARKS jump and die like all shooting stars are destined to death.

FADE OUT.

FADE IN:

EXT. THE CONFEDERATE WHITE HOUSE—DAY

CONFEDERATE WHITE HOUSE, RICHMOND, VIRGINIA—February 19, 1862

Seeping RAIN falls. Framed in an upstairs window General Lee watches GENERAL JOE JOHNSTON (52), a Virginia gentleman once the "first and best" of the U.S. Army and last seen in Mexico, remove his riding gloves and slap mud from his boots and trousers. Reaching the door, Johnston hands gloves, hat, overcoat and saber to an ORDERLY and enters.

INT. CONFEDERATE WHITE HOUSE—DAY

President Jefferson Davis looks up from an ONGOING DISCUSSION with his CABINET as General Johnston enters.

JEFFERSON DAVIS
Have a seat, General. As you see, we've begun without you.

Johnston nods to the various men around the table—a quick handshake exchanged with Lee—before—

JOE JOHNSTON
President Davis, the reenlistment question is obviously of most importance to me. I've looked over the proposed "Furlough and Bounty Act"—

JEFFERSON DAVIS
That bill passed while we waited on you, General.

JOE JOHNSTON
I see.

SECRETARY OF WAR RANDOLPH
Under the act, one-year volunteers who reenlist for three more—or the duration, in case the end comes first—will receive a sixty-day furlough and a fifty-dollar bounty.

JOE JOHNSTON
Yes, and I realize the necessity for some such encouragement. A fifty dollar bounty—extremely generous—and I imagine extremely effective, but this furlough?

He looks to Lee: Lee of all of them must realize his concern.

JOE JOHNSTON
If granted in numbers large enough to be effective it will expose the remainder of my army to slaughter at the hands of the Federals—already three times my strength around Manassas and capable of attacking at any time!

JEFFERSON DAVIS
Capable, General, but…"probable?" McClellan's behavior so far leads me to the inevitable conclusion: George McClellan is afraid to fight.

LAUGHTER from everyone but the two generals.

JOE JOHNSTON
General Lee, it would be imprudent to rely on our assessment of George McClellan's personality flaws to guide our conduct toward this nation's defense.

Lee nods, acceding the point. But the highly disliked and dislikable Secretary of State, JUDAH BENJAMIN (51), pipes in.

> SECRETARY OF STATE BENJAMIN
> Perhaps it's best, General, as we have waited all day for you, you now share with us your assessment of the state of this nation's defense and what you will do...now that you're aware of the passage of my bill.

> JOE JOHNSTON
> From its position along Bull Run and the Potomac—a line I've maintained to this government throughout winter as untenable—my army cannot block the multiple routes by which McClellan could march against this capital. Unequivocally, my army must now fall back to a position farther south before the roads are dry.

> JEFFERSON DAVIS
> Retreat?!

Davis's eyes flash to Lee. Lee's expression, however, does not share the outrage of his president.

> JEFFERSON DAVIS
> To what line would this retreat be conducted, General?

> JOE JOHNSTON
> *(frustrated; snaps)*
> President Davis: being unfamiliar with the country between Richmond and Manassas, I haven't the foggiest idea!

> JEFFERSON DAVIS
> *(jumps to his feet)*
> Sir! That my commanding general should have selected a line which he himself considers untenable, and should
> (MORE)

                    JEFFERSON DAVIS (MORE)
not have ascertained the typography of the country in
his rear is inexplicable on any other theory than that
you have neglected the primary duty of a commander!

A long silence ensues.

                    JOE JOHNSTON
Mr. President, I didn't come here with the belief that as
the Spring Campaign season was opening, my government would unilaterally furlough one third of my army!
That said, this being the position we now *all* are in—
Mr. President—my advice as your commanding general
is retreat.

                    JEFFERSON DAVIS
General Lee, surely you don't advise this?

Lee, having held his counsel, speaks now: softly, directly.

                    LEE
To move from where we are: I would like to see anything else...

Davis's eyes beam, until...

                    LEE
But God has other plans for us. All of us in this coming
fight. And if General Johnston says a withdrawal from
the current line is in order to protect our future, my
advice is to proceed with this withdrawal.

Davis, committed to Lee's opinion, quakes.

                    JEFFERSON DAVIS
I will need assurances, General Johnston, that the army's
                    (MORE)

JEFFERSON DAVIS (CONT'D)
supplies and equipment—particularly the large-caliber
guns along the Potomac and the mountains of subsis-
tence goods now stored in forward depots—won't be
abandoned.

JOE JOHNSTON
Sir, I will do what I can to delay the retreat until the last
possible moment so that the roads will be firm enough
to bear the heavy guns and the high-piled wagons.

With that, he rises. He doesn't like Jefferson Davis; his eyes say he
will make Davis pay, but all he says is—

JOE JOHNSTON
If that will be all, gentlemen, there is much to begin.

INT. LINCOLN'S OFFICE—EVENING

EXECUTIVE MANSION,
WASHINGTON CITY—February 19, 1862

Seated at the cabinet table, President Lincoln takes a report handed
him by Halleck. Stanton stands by.

HALLECK
Officers for promotion to Major General, Mr. President.

LINCOLN
I don't see General Grant's name.

HALLECK
Mr. President, as hard as it is to censure a successful
general, Grant richly deserves it.

Halleck shoots Stanton a glance, hoping to draw him in.

HALLECK

Sadly, a rumor has reached me that, since taking Fort Donelson, Grant has resumed his former habits.

LINCOLN

Ah, the Demon Rum.

HALLECK

Drunk most of the time. I have a letter from General McClellan who, as commander of all our forces, concurs and urges Grant's arrest.

Lincoln considers the letter.

LINCOLN

I'd hoped it wouldn't come to this... Find out what brand of whiskey Grant is drinking.

HALLECK

With speed, sir.

LINCOLN

Then get a barrel to McClellan. Maybe that'll get him to fight.

Halleck scratches his elbows and flashes a look to Stanton.

STANTON

Mr. President, Generals Halleck and McClellan aren't alone in their claims...

LINCOLN

"Unconditional Surrender" Grant will be promoted to Major General... I can't spare this man. He fights.

As Lincoln dips his pen and adds Grant's name to the list, his secretary, JOHN HAY (24), pokes his head into the room.

> JOHN HAY
> Excuse me, Mr. President. Your family needs you...
> Urgently, sir.

INT. EXECUTIVE MANSION, LINCOLN BEDROOM—NIGHT

The "original gorilla" Abraham Lincoln, grips the door frame. Within the darkened room, eleven year-old WILLIE LINCOLN lies in his bed shaking with fever and WHIMPERING in delirium. MARY TODD LINCOLN (44) beats Lincoln family physician DR. ROBERT K. STONE as he attempts to administer her a sedative.

> LINCOLN
> Missus, it's for your own good.

> MARY LINCOLN
> My own good?! What do you know of my good?! What's good for me—you've never cared what's good for me! And now when my son needs me most you're trying to drug me away from him to assuage your own guilt of never paying him the attention any other father would pay his son!

Lincoln's face quivers. Lincoln loves Willie most of all his family.

> DOCTOR STONE
> Mr. President, it would be best were I allowed to treat your son's typhoid without distraction.

> MARY LINCOLN
> Since when is a sick child's mother a "distraction," you quack!

Lincoln is at the breaking point. Voice quavering—

LINCOLN

Mary: come here!

She snaps her gaze at him, but, seeing his real anguish and the power in his exceedingly large clenching fists, she suddenly frightens and rushes to his arms in HOPELESS TEARS.

MARY LINCOLN

I want to be with him; don't take me away. I'll be good, I'll be *myself*; I want to stay—let me stay, father!

Lincoln holds her, very much the father to her.

LINCOLN

Doctor, if she promises to control her emotions?

MARY LINCOLN

I promise. Tell him I promise.

LINCOLN

Allow her to stay with our boy, will you?

DOCTOR STONE

As you wish, Mr. President.

Lincoln holds Mary Todd at arms length.

LINCOLN

There you are, Missus. You stay and do as you're told...

His eyes go to his dying son. His voice cracks.

LINCOLN

I'll be downstairs.

**INT. LINCOLN'S OFFICE/ EXECUTIVE MANSION CORRIDOR /
LINCOLN BEDROOM—NIGHT TO DAY**

- *Lincoln alternately sits behind his desk staring between his
  son's photo and McClellan's plan tacked up on map boards
  and strewn across tables...*
- *He paces the hallway...*
- *He checks in on Mary, Doctor Stone; he strokes his favorite
  son's brow...*
- *Then repeats it all over again until... Sitting in his office,
  having gone through some old papers, he has found—*

A LETTER—"CHICAGO, JUNE 12, 1859"

> WILLIE LINCOLN (V.O.)
> Dear Mother, This town is a very beautiful place. Me
> and father have a nice little room to ourselves. We have
> two little pitchers on a washstand. The smallest one for
> me the largest one for father.

CLOSE ON the boy his breathing slowed with death's approach.

> WILLIE LINCOLN (V.O.)
> We have two little towels on top of both pitchers. The
> smallest one for me, the largest one for father. Me
> and father had gone to the theater the other night. We
> watched Edwin Booth perform "Macbeth."

FLASH CUT:

EXT. CHICAGO THEATER—NIGHT (FLASHBACK)

The marquee: "BOOTH PLAYS MACBETH;" the tall father and
tiny son leaving the theater hand-in-hand.

WILLIE LINCOLN (V.O.)
I liked it, but was sad for the king and all the killing. I
miss you. Love, Willie.

RESUME—MID-AFTERNOON: Lincoln is pacing the hall once
more. A DREADFUL SCREAM emits from Mary Todd Lincoln
upstairs. Lincoln stops. He bows his head. His secretary, John Hay,
sticks his head out his office door.

LINCOLN
My boy is gone. He's actually gone.

Lincoln bursts into tears.

INT. A BALLROOM, WILLARD HOTEL—NIGHT

The military wedding of McClellan's Staff Officer, Captain Wexler.
A 12-piece ORCHESTRA plays an energetic waltz. [**Note: this is
the same waltz with fuller orchestration as was played at Fort Humboldt in Episode One.**]

Among the uniformed men and bejewelled, gowned dancers,
McClellan and Ellen are the spotlight. Their dancing is impeccable.

INT. MCCLELLAN PARLOR—NIGHT

A sad and depressed Lincoln and an impatient Stanton climb from
Lincoln's carriage. They ring the BELL. McClellan's BLACK SER-
VANT answers the door, ushers them inside.

EXT. WILLARD HOTEL—NIGHT

The BRIDAL COUPLE rush under a canopy of crossed sabers to
their waiting carriage. McClellan holds the door for them.

WEXLER
Permission to honeymoon, General?

MCCLELLAN
Permission granted, Captain Wexler. I'll hold this war
until you are out of the saddle and expecting a son!

APPLAUSE and LAUGHTER from the rest of the guests. McClellan shuts the door behind the happy couple, then, twirling his hat,
winks to the guests and they love him for it.

INT. MCCLELLAN PARLOR—NIGHT

Lincoln and Stanton wait in stiff-backed chairs for McClellan's
return. Presently, from within, comes the sound of MCCLELLAN
WHISPERING, ELLEN GIGGLING—Lincoln cranes his neck
around the door frame in time to catch—

MCCLELLAN

carry Ellen upstairs, his hand inside her dress... Stanton looks at—

THE CLOCK 11:25...DISSOLVE TO... THE CLOCK—12:01...
Lincoln broods. Stanton grows more furious by the second. Finally,
he steps into the vestibule and accosts the servant.

STANTON
Will you remind General McClellan that the President of the United States is awaiting his presence in the
parlor?!

MCCLELLAN'S SERVANT
Of course, sir.

The servant climbs the stairs. Stanton glances to his president, but
Lincoln is hunched, elbows on knobby knees, lost under the weight
of too many pressures. Presently...

> MCCLELLAN'S SERVANT

I'm sorry to inform you, but General McClellan went directly to bed, sir.

EXT. MCCLELLAN HOME—MOMENTS LATER

> LINCOLN

If General McClellan isn't going to use his army, do you think he'd let me borrow it for a time?

Stanton snorts, but Lincoln reflects deeper feelings...

> LINCOLN

I would hold McClellan's horse if he will only bring us success.

EXT. MANASSAS JUNCTION—DAY

MANASSAS JUNCTION, VIRGINIA—
February 21, 1862

Longstreet oversees the removal of stores from warehouses. Military wagons overloaded with beef and grain form a column south equal to the column of private citizens' wagons filled to capacity with supplies that for lack of transportation have been given away. Longstreet meets with Joe Johnston.

> LONGSTREET

General Johnston, understand, sir: over one million pounds of meat, all our heavy guns, and seven tons of equipment and stores of weapons and powder are still here.

> JOE JOHNSTON

General Longstreet, President Davis has made very clear his view that we cannot abandon them to enemy hands. We cannot take them. So we will burn them, sir.

LONGSTREET
They're irreplaceable, sir!

JOE JOHNSTON
Burn them, General Longstreet.

Longstreet salutes and moves off. Johnston watches Longstreet give the orders. The warehouse goes up in flames.

INT. EXECUTIVE MANSION, GREEN ROOM—DAY

EXECUTIVE MANSION, WASHINGTON CITY—February 22, 1862

In his coffin, Willie is clothed in evening dress, eyes closed, his hands crossed over his chest and holding a small bouquet of flowers. LINCOLN INTIMATES and WELL-WISHERS pass by the coffin, paying their respects. McClellan, truly touched, stops for a moment, kneels and says a silent prayer. A tear rolls down his cheek. When he looks up he notices Ellen comforting Mary Todd. Counterpoint to the scene—

ELLEN (V.O.)
And I am telling you! The time is now! You must move your armies—

INT. MCCLELLAN PARLOR—DAY

ELLEN
George, they are talking about replacing you!

MCCLELLAN
I told you I should have gone downstairs!

ELLEN
You said, "think of them downstairs while I'm up here in you."

INT. JOINT COMMITTEE ON THE CONDUCT OF THE WAR—DAY

CHAIRMAN WADE
Next order of business..?

SENATOR CHANDLER
We have now documented more than a dozen treason-
ous statements by Mrs. Mary Todd Lincoln. As you
know, she has three brothers serving in the Confederate
Army...

CHAIRMAN WADE
Is she in contact with these enemies?

SENATOR CHANDLER
She writes them...

EXT. U.S. NAVY WHARVES—MORNING

WASHINGTON CITY—March 14, 1862

SINGING, MCCLELLAN'S ARMY moves through vast collections
of supplies, ammunition, wagons, to begin boarding transports—

MCCLELLAN'S ARMY
Brave McClellan is our Leader now,
Brave McClellan is our Leader now,
Brave McClellan is our Leader now,
With him we're marching on!

[Note: They sing these words to the most popular melody of the day
which began as a rather common hymn, "Canaan's Happy Shore."
Throughout this period this melody undergoes—like the nation that
sings it—a remarkable "battle" of lyrics on both sides until a final
transcendent moment that carries through to today as: America's
most recognizable and moving patriotic song "The Battle Hymn of
the Republic."]

As McClellan promised: the finest army the world's ever seen.

INT. THE JOINT COMMITTEE ON THE CONDUCT OF THE WAR—MORNING

Lincoln stands behind the chair where previously George McClellan was called to task. In a sad voice—

> LINCOLN
> I, Abraham Lincoln, President of the United States appear of my own volition before this committee of the Senate to say that I, of my own knowledge, know it is untrue that any of my diminished family hold treasonable communication with the enemy.

The senators can see that Lincoln barely holds his emotions.

EXT. U.S. NAVY WHARVES—MORNING

> MCCLELLAN'S ARMY
> Glory, Glory Hallelujah!

WOMEN and CHILDREN line the sidewalk waving flags.

> MCCLELLAN'S ARMY
> Glory, Glory Hallelujah!

Outside a saloon there is an odd sight: a street peddler of fiddles, music and music lessons, a man we will come to know as the composer of this famous melody, WILLIAM STEFFE (32). His appearance suggests his fortunes have fallen rapidly. He covers his ears and mutters.

> STEFFE
> Jesus wrote that! You've no right, you've no right...

The SALOONKEEPER, embarrassed for Steffe and afraid his words will cause the confused man harm, gently leads Steffe inside.

MCCLELLAN'S ARMY
Glory, Glory Hallelujah! With Mac we're marching on!

INT. JOINT COMMITTEE ON THE CONDUCT OF THE WAR—MORNING

CHAIRMAN WADE
Perhaps, Mr. President, if we let this matter go, you might see your way to doing something for us.

Whatever emotional state Lincoln was headed toward, these words of veiled blackmail stiffen his resolve.

CHAIRMAN WADE
Since the onset of this war, you have failed to acknowledge the fundamental reason and paramount goal for which it is being fought.

LINCOLN
This war is being fought for the restoration of the Union.

CHAIRMAN WADE
No, Mr. President. We fight for the abolition of slavery. This committee charges that you publicly acknowledge this: what all true Americans and Christians desire to hear from your lips.

LINCOLN
(smirks)
You'd enslave me and the reputation of my wife and family to change the aim of this war and tear from the union those slave states that have refused to commit treason and join the Confederacy?

He walks forward into the shadows and, planting his two huge fists on Ben Wade's desk, towers over him.

> LINCOLN
>
> You've no jurisdiction over whether or not I appear before you and tell you anything. I'm here today of my own Executive Privilege—a privilege that while we now speak, my Attorney General is drawing up to include my Mrs. Lincoln and the rest of my family. But, because I'm feeling generous in accord to the hospitality you have shown me, I'll tell you one more thing: If I could save the Union without freeing any slave I would do it. If I could save it by freeing all the slaves I would do it; and if I could save it by freeing some and leaving others alone I would also do that. What I do about slavery and the colored race, I do because I believe it helps to save this Union...

Chairman Wade's face fills with outrage. Chandler and the others are equally shocked as Lincoln concludes.

> LINCOLN
>
> As this "secret" committee has a reputation for leaking its proceedings to the press I've already done you the favor by delivering those words to Horace Greeley, editor of the *New York Times*. Good day, gentlemen.

EXT. U.S. NAVY WHARVES—CONTINUOUS

The loading of troops into transports that cast off onto the Potomac heading south transpires as:

> MCCLELLAN (V.O.)
>
> Soldiers of the Army of the Potomac! For a long time I have kept you inactive, but not without purpose: you
> (MORE)

>   MCCLELLAN (V.O.) (CONT'D)
> were to be disciplined, armed and instructed; the formi-
> dable artillery you now have had to be created. I have
> held you back that you might give the death-blow to the
> rebellion that has distracted our once happy country.

The men his words speak to try hard not to look at the hundreds of
new, empty coffins also being loaded aboard.

EXT. YORKTOWN—MORNING

Visible by its church steeple across three miles of farmland.

>   MCCLELLAN (V.O.)
> The patience you have shown, and your confidence in
> your General, are worth a dozen victories.

**EXT. UNION FIRST LINE OF ENTRENCHMENTS,
YORKTOWN—MORNING**

>   MCCLELLAN
> In whatever direction you may now move, ever bear in
> mind that my fate is linked with yours; I am to watch
> over you as a parent over his children; and you know
> that your "father" loves you from the depths of his
> heart. God smiles upon us, victory attends us, and we
> can ask no higher honor than the proud consciousness
> that we belonged to the Army of the Potomac!

The massive Army of the Potomac is dug-in in strength...but waiting, *defensively*, doing battle with no one.

EXT. CHERRY MANSION—EVENING

Rain. CHARLES DANA (43), a civilian, waits with a STAFF OFFI-CER at the steps to this antebellum plantation house overlooking the Mississippi River where the steamship *Tigress* waits.

CHERRY MANSION, SAVANNAH, TENNESSEE—April 3, 1862

Around a table on the large covered porch Grant prepares to dine with his staff.

> RAWLINS
> He can only be here for mischief.

> GRANT
> He's Assistant Secretary of War.

> RAWLINS
> General, we don't know Dana.

> GRANT
> He treated me fairly when he wrote for the *New York Tribune* about Donelson. Set a place on my right.

> RAWLINS
> My spot, sir?

THE MESS TABLE—LATER

Rain slackened. Beside Grant, Dana is served. All eat steak and potatoes—all but Grant whose plate has only potatoes.

> DANA
> Would you like my steak, General?

GRANT

Thanks, no. I defy any man who grew up a tanner's son
to honestly admit they can stomach the sight, let alone
taste, of bleeding animal flesh... Whiskey, Mr. Dana?
(*Dana hesitates*)
Sherman, pass us that fine bottle.

Sherman passes Grant the whiskey bottle. Grant pours.

GRANT

A Tennessee sour mash liberated from Donelson...

He salutes Dana with his glass: it is filled with water. Sherman and
some of the other officers laugh.

DANA

I see my purpose here is not as clandestine as hoped.

GRANT

I like to drink, Mr. Dana; tell Secretary Stanton I do
not abstain. But tell him this, too: I much prefer making
war on the rebels.

SHERMAN

Here-here!

GRANT

My plan for taking Vicksburg has been held up for
weeks by General Halleck. I'd like you to allow me to
map it out for you.

Dana is stunned, but not half so much as...

RAWLINS

I'm sure, General Grant, in his capacity as a civilian,
Mr. Dana will decline—

GRANT

Rawlins, Mr. Dana's acknowledged he's here among us as a spy for Mr. Stanton. I could be wrong, but I think Mr. Stanton might prefer intelligence on my Vicksburg operation to a story of how I enjoy a weak sour mash...

THE MESS TENT—LATER

Officers mingle. Rawlins takes Dana aside.

RAWLINS

To be frank, Mr. Dana, I'm not enthused to have you among us. It's also apparent the General likes you. Therefore, I see it my duty to take you into confidence.

DANA

If you wish, sir.

RAWLINS

As the son of a drunkard, I know firsthand the destructive power of liquor and I abhor it in all forms more deeply than I hate the enemy.

Dana nods, thoughtfully.

RAWLINS

The General—who *is* an imbiber—knows this. He also knows there are officers he counts as friends who would enjoy nothing better than to drink him into oblivion... My primary duty as Assistant Adjutant-General on his staff is to protect Grant from himself.

The two men regard each other a beat.

RAWLINS

There is no general on either side better suited to winning this war.

DANA

Why do you say that?

RAWLINS

It's not simply that Grant prefers making war to drinking. Grant supplants alcohol with victories.

As their eyes go to Grant smoking and conversing with Sherman beneath a tree—

INT. CONFEDERATE ARMY OF THE MISSISSIPPI— COMMAND TENT—NIGHT

CORINTH, MISSISSIPPI
30 Miles South of Grant

Through the tent flap come CAMP SOUNDS mixed with CRICKETS and FROG-SONG; Confederate General Albert Sidney Johnston (last seen at White Haven discussing Texas, now 59 **and no relation to Joe Johnston**) sits at a camp desk composing a "General Orders." As he writes, HEAR his TEXAS DRAWL...

JOHNSTON (V.O.)

Soldiers of the Army of the Mississippi: I have put you in motion to offer battle to the invaders of your country. With the resolution and disciplined valor becoming men fighting, as you are, for all worth living or dying for, you can but march to a decisive victory over the mercenaries sent to despoil you of your liberties, property, and honor.

EXT. CONFEDERATE ARMY OF THE MISSISSIPPI—CAMP—DAWN

CONFEDERATE SOLDIERS turned out for roll call listen to their OFFICERS read from Johnston's order...

JOHNSTON (V.O.)
Remember the precious stake involved; remember the
dependence of your mothers, your wives, your sisters,
and your children on the result...

**INT. CONFEDERATE ARMY OF THE MISSISSIPPI—
COMMAND TENT—DAWN**

Johnston, dressed for battle, places two letters addressed to his wife
and grown son between their photos inside a folding frame, then
folds closed the frame. He kisses the frame, then leaves frame and
letters on his trunk beside his bible. He attaches his sword to his belt
then steps through the tent flap where a SADDLER waits with his
horse.

JOHNSTON (V.O.)
Remember the fair, broad, abounding land, the happy
homes and the ties that would be desolated by your
defeat.

EXT. A CORINTH MISSISSIPPI STREET—MORNING

CITIZENS read Johnston's order where it is tacked to sidewalk
posts and telegraph poles.

JOHNSTON (V.O.)
The eyes and hopes of eight millions of people rest
upon you.

They CHEER the Confederate Army as it marches from the city.

EXT. A COUNTRY ROAD, MISSISSIPPI—DAY

The Confederate Army of the Mississippi on the march—some in regulation gray, others in yellow-brown butternut, many more in farm clothes with only a Confederate Army cap to show their military affiliation. But all of them are armed and carry regulation packs, ration haversacks, blankets and overcoats. All of them also carry the same weapon: a Pattern 1853 English Enfield Rifle Musket. They march in step and their ranks and files are straight and as true as their hearts. The western sun shines down to warm them.

> JOHNSTON (V.O.)
> With such incentives too brave deeds, and with the trust that God is with us, your generals will lead you confidently to the combat, assured of success... A. S. Johnston, General.

EXT. MISSISSIPPI ROADS TO SHILOH—FROM DAY TO NIGHT TO DAY

—The sun is hot. The men are out of step; wide spaces or cramped bunches of jostling soldiers have replaced the earlier *esprit de'corps* of the march...

—As TIME PASSES, soldiers shuck overcoats in the hot sun; the roadside is littered with the castoff detritus of green, tired soldiers— bedrolls, playing cards, kettles and other personal objects. They continue forward into the NIGHT...

—THUNDER BOOMS as RAIN POURS. The Army of the Mississippi slogs in darkness through calf-high mud. Many now wish they had their coats. Wagons stall. Men CURSE as OFFICERS SHOUT to get some semblance of order to the brigades.

—With DAWN, many soldiers have left the road and their companies and straggle alongside; others wander the fields taking POT SHOTS at squirrels, rabbits and birds...

EXT. A CROSSROADS NEAR SHILOH—MORNING

Johnston, atop his horse at a road junction, meets with two of his subordinates: the swarthy-faced, brooding Creole GENERAL PIERRE GUSTAVE TOUTANT BEAUREGARD (42) and the portly Episcopal Bishop-turned-General, LEONIDAS POLK (55).

> LEONIDAS POLK
>
> This is perfectly puerile! I have stragglers! I have men busting caps on their guns in order to see if their powder's dry! Two of my divisions are just plain missing!

He points to a dense woods less than a mile ahead.

> LEONIDAS POLK
>
> And Grant's Federal Army of the west is beyond that woods! My scouts have heard their drums. If we can hear them, General, don't you think the element of surprise has been lost us?

Johnston's look doesn't deny the "fighting bishop." He turns his attention to Beauregard.

> JOHNSTON
>
> General Beauregard?

> BEAUREGARD
>
> I agree with Bishop Polk. There's no chance for surprise. Now they'll be intrenched to the eyes...but my troops are eager for battle. If they don't find one they'll be as demoralized as if they'd been whipped.

Johnston looks to Polk. Polk's shoulders slump.

> LEONIDAS POLK
>
> My boys would as soon be defeated than retire without a fight.

Some soldiers caught in a traffic jam DISCHARGE their muskets in the air in an attempt to startle a mule sunk to its knees in mud into moving forward.

> JOHNSTON
> Find your lost divisions and get the men quiet and into line of battle... Gentlemen, we'll attack at daylight tomorrow. I mean to hammer 'em!

TO BLACK:

GHOSTLY AND FAR AWAY, SUNG TO THE TUNE MORE COMMONLY KNOWN AS "THE BATTLE HYMN OF THE REPUBLIC"...

> METHODIST CHOIR (V.O.)
> "Say, Brothers will you meet us on Canaan's Happy Shore? Say, Brothers will you meet us on Canaan's Happy Shore?"

INT. MARY LINCOLN'S SITTING ROOM—DAY

Draperies pulled, dark as night. Candles burn. The HAUNTING CHOIR FADES. Mary Lincoln, in black mourning dress, sits across a table from a dark-suited gentleman: a GEORGETOWN SPIRI-TUALIST (30s).

> GEORGETOWN SPIRITUALIST
> (a child's voice)
> Yes, Mama, I see you. I'm here. I miss you, Mama. I love you.

> MARY
> I love you, Willie. I love you and I miss you. Are you happy?

GEORGETOWN SPIRITUALIST
I'm happy, Mama. I'm with Jesus. Everything here is like…music.

MARY
Your Papa misses you, Willie.

GEORGETOWN SPIRITUALIST
I know. I have messages. Messages for everyone about God's promise. About how I'm always with you…

As the Spiritualist continues, BRING UP, ghostly, haunted—

METHODIST CHOIR (V.O.)
"Say, Brothers will you meet us on Canaan's Happy Shore—and wash your sins away!"

INT. LINCOLN'S OFFICE—DAY

Mary, ecstatically happy, rushes in. A careworn Lincoln, going over war plans with Stanton, looks up.

LINCOLN
I am glad to see a bright smile on your face.

MARY
I spoke to him.

Lincoln saddens. He knows who "him" is. So does Stanton. Stanton, embarrassed, quietly leaves.

MARY
He has messages, sir, for us all.

LINCOLN
Willie.

MARY

Most certainly Willie. He's happy. But he misses us
terribly.

Lincoln sighs, it's too much.

MARY

He misses us, do you hear me?!

She clutches at her husband. He puts an arm around her.

LINCOLN

But you said he was happy: that's a good thing, Mary.

MARY

Is it? Is it?!
(breaking down)
I miss him so much. If only I'd been a better mother. If
only *you'd* been there for him! I need to talk more to
him!

Mary attempts to break away, but Lincoln's arm on her back stiffens. He guides her to the window.

LINCOLN

Mother, do you see that large white building on the hill
yonder?

MARY

Don't say it. How dare you?! Listen to me.

LINCOLN

Try and control your grief, or it will drive you mad and
we may have to send you there.

She knows this and, fully succumbing to her grief, she buries her head

in her husband's chest and the SONG THAT HAS BEEN CON-
TINUING SOFTLY IN THE BACKGROUND, RETURNS—

METHODIST CHOIR (V.O.)
Glory, glory Hallelujah! Glory, glory Hallelujah!"

INT. SHILOH CHURCH—NIGHT

An abandoned, one-room log, Methodist meeting house, dim and
empty as the GHOSTLY HYMN once sung there fades to silence.

METHODIST CHOIR (V.O.)
"Glory, glory Hallelujah, For ever, ever more..."

THE CAMERA FLOATS over empty pews and through the
doorway...

EXT. SHILOH CHURCH—CONTINUOUS

WESTERN THEATER—
SHILOH CHURCH, TENNESSEE—April 5, 1862

...where Sherman returns tired from dinner to his tent beside the
empty log structure. He hands his horse to his Orderly, First Sergeant
Bancroft. Bancroft hands Sherman reports Sherman reads with dis-
pleasure before stalking to COLONEL APPLER who salutes.

SHERMAN
All day you've bothered me with these, Colonel. Think
the entire Confederate Army surrounds us?

He leads Colonel Appler to the edge of the hill.

SHERMAN
Show me.

Below are a thousand campfires of the Union forces. Regimental battle flags flutter beautifully in the evening breeze. A Union BAND SOFTLY PLAYS THE WORK CHANTY "SHENANDOAH." A good portion of the men SING. The field is bordered by woods. There isn't a Confederate in sight.

COLONEL APPLER

General: four hours ago I lost seven men to some gray-back cavalry beyond the treeline.

SHERMAN

Enemy scouts do not an army make.

COLONEL APPLER

Sir, I advanced a company into those woods to develop the situation. They ran into scattered firing—from more than scouts.

SHERMAN

From whom, then?

COLONEL APPLER

I earnestly believe a large force of enemy moves on the camp, sir.

SHERMAN

Right there in the woods right now?

EXT. THE FAR SIDE OF THE WOODS—EVENING

CONFEDERATES creep quietly into the forest; so close, their skirmishers hear the UNION MUSIC. Some of the Confederates nervously HUM the song but are HUSHED by their officers.

EXT. THE UNION ENCAMPMENT AT SHILOH—NIGHT

Sherman stands with Colonel Appler at the edge of the woods. They peer into the gloomy shadows. OWLS CALL...but there is no movement and none of the Rebel soldiers can be seen.

> SHERMAN
> You're jumpy is all. Hell, I thought the same as you in Kentucky. After enough of these—
> *(re: Appler's report)*
> They sent me home insane.

EXT. THE WOODS AT SHILOH—CONTINUOUS

A Confederate SHARPSHOOTER raises his rifle. He aims for Sherman's head. An officer crawls up as the Confederate Sharpshooter starts to quietly cock his weapon...

> CONFEDERATE SHARPSHOOTER
> Gonna bag me a Yankee gen'ral, sir.

But the Confederate officer pushes down his barrel.

> CONFEDERATE OFFICER SHILOH
> Not till morning, you ain't.

EXT. THE UNION ENCAMPMENT AT SHILOH—CONTINUOUS

Sherman shoves the negative report into the colonel's coat.

> SHERMAN
> Any more of these, Colonel, you'll be taking your damned regiment back to Ohio.

Leaving Colonel Appler gaping at the woods—was that the glint of a gun barrel?—Sherman stomps through the grass.

EXT. SHERMAN'S TENT—NIGHT

He wakes from a fitful sleep. He throws his uniform jacket over his long underwear and goes out to his campfire.

> SHERMAN
> Sergeant Bancroft?

No one answers. A lantern burns inside the Shiloh Church.

INT. SHILOH CHURCH—NIGHT

Sherman enters to find Bancroft praying inside.

> BANCROFT
> General Sherman, everything okay?

> SHERMAN
> What're you doing, Sergeant?

> BANCROFT
> Couldn't sleep, sir. Figured since we're beside a meetin' house I'd come in and have a talk with God.

Sherman snorts.

> BANCROFT
> You're not religious are you, General?

> SHERMAN
> My wife's got the Catholic Church and enough faith for the entire Sherman family in her littlest finger. I'm sure there's enough in the rest of her hand to include you as well, Sergeant.

BANCROFT
Thank you, General.

SHERMAN
How come you couldn't sleep?

BANCROFT
The quiet.

SHERMAN
Yeah. I think that's what woke me... That colonel
today—

BANCROFT
Colonel Appler, sir.

SHERMAN
I might've been too rough.

Sherman faces out the door. The Union camp can be seen in the
flickering light of its watch fires.

SHERMAN
Have him report to me first thing. Might as well put
him in charge of building some fortifications.

BANCROFT
Yes, sir.

As Sherman watches the night a shower of shooting stars rain for a
brief few seconds across the heavens. He grins.

SHERMAN
Good omen for me, Bancroft... My given name, Tecumseh: means "Shooting Star" in Iroquois.

EXT. THE UNION ENCAMPMENT AT SHILOH—DAWN

SHILOH CHURCH—April 6, 1862

Union troops start morning cook-fires. With delight, some notice rabbits scampering from the woods; some grab rifles in order to bag this fresh meat, but the hare are followed by frightened, plunging deer and the FIRST VOLLEY of Confederate GUNFIRE from the trees cuts the would-be Union hunters down.

BULLETS rip tents killing rising men. The REBEL YELL goes up as the Confederates ATTACK.

[Note: The "Rebel Yell" is a "KI-I!" sound that men who fought this war claim is nothing like a hurrah, but rather a regular wildcat screech with nothing else like it this side of infernal hell. For their part, the Northern armies also charge with a battle cry of "Hurrah!" or in some regiments "Huzzah!" The purpose of battle cries is to affect, when heard by the individual, an awareness of all the men behind and around you, with you, and when you join the yell, your final commitment to close with the enemy or die trying.]

Union regimental battle flags are abandoned, trampled, captured.

Sadly proven right, Colonel Appler, FIRING his pistol, is shot then bayoneted.

Corporal Combs buries his own bayonet into the belly of the rebel soldier he catches tearing the regiment's flag from its stanchion. As the rebel collapses Combs pulls the flag from the man's bloody fingers.

COMBS
Still mine, reb!

He stuffs it into his shirt and flees over ground that now runs red with blood.

EXT. SHILOH CHURCH—CONTINUOUS

Sherman, pulling on his trousers and buttoning his tunic, rushes for the ridge. Union troops in various states of dress flee pell-mell up the hill toward him. MINIE BALLS hit many in the back.

EXT. THE UNION ENCAMPMENT AT SHILOH—MORNING

The only thing that prevents total Union defeat at this point is that half of the Confederates—hungry to a man—stop to steal food and cull through Yankee possessions. General Albert Sidney Johnston rides through the camp scowling.

The Confederate Sharpshooter comes out of a tent carrying stolen boots to almost collide with Johnston's horse.

JOHNSTON
None of that, sir.

Dismayed, the sharpshooter drops the boots by his own bare feet. Johnston, seeing the man has no shoes, reaches down to a table and snatches a tin cup. Shoving the sword that he has been using to direct the attack into its scabbard, he hooks the cup in his finger.

JOHNSTON
Keep the boots, soldier; let this be my share of the spoils today.
(shouts)
We will water our horses in the Tennessee River!

EXT. SHILOH CHURCH—MORNING

SHERMAN
Damn you, boys! Turn and fight!

Fifty yards away, rebels crest the rise.

BANCROFT

General, look to your right!

Sherman turns. Confederates coming from that direction stop to FIRE. Sherman holds up his hand as if to ward off the bullets. His hand is hit as Bancroft is killed.

SHERMAN

Shit.

Sherman wraps his hand with his handkerchief, FIRES his pistol and grabs his horse.

SHERMAN

At 'em, boys! Kill the sonsabitches!

He spurs his horse into the face of the enemy. His men join the fight. Sherman's horse is killed.

A SERIES OF SHOTS—THE FIGHT FOR SHILOH:

- *Sherman, riding a new mount and ignoring the BULLETS flying all around him forms his men into firing lines.*
- *The Confederates, repulsed from the hilltop, form their own line. It is overwhelming in strength and ferocity.*
- *Another horse is SHOT from beneath Sherman. A riderless Confederate horse breaks their lines running straight for the Federal troops. Sherman grabs it. He swings into the saddle as his men continue to FIRE and fall back.*

EXT. PITTSBURG LANDING—MORNING

Smoke rolls from above; BATTLE ECHOES VIOLENTLY. Riding from the steamship *Tigress,* Grant charges his horse into his army. Demoralized TROOPS cower, some tearfully, all useless. Grant grabs a TERRIFIED LIEUTENANT.

> GRANT
> Where's your unit, Lieutenant?

> TERRIFIED LIEUTENANT
> Gone, dead—they've whipped us!

> GRANT
> We aren't whipped.

> TERRIFIED LIEUTENANT
> We're not, General?

Others have heard this. They're stunned.

> GRANT
> We're whipping them. Fill your cartridge boxes and get
> into line! The enemy must not be allowed to escape!

Untrue as Grant's words are, they work like a charm: the soldiers respond with renewed vigor. Passing the trembling members of a regimental band—

> GRANT
> Make yourselves useful: play!

As Grant rides on, the band begins "Hail Columbia." Rawlins and Grant's staff ride hard to keep up with him.

EXT. A SHILOH ROAD—DAY

Confederate General Albert Sidney Johnston sits atop his horse directing Rebel troops to battle with the tin cup. Seeing him, men rushing into line take off hats and CHEER.

Johnston notices movement in the grass beyond the road. He canters over to the spot where he finds a group of WOUNDED FEDERALS. His staff joins him. Johnston dismounts.

> WOUNDED UNION OFFICER
> Brandy, General?

Johnston produces his flask. He fills the tin cup he's been carrying. The wounded Union Officer takes a swig, shares it.

> JOHNSTON
> I want stretchers for these men. Surgeon: you'll stay with them, tend to their wounds.

> JOHNSTON'S SURGEON
> These are enemy, sir. My duty is to tend to you.

> JOHNSTON
> These men were our enemies a moment ago. They were our brothers a year ago and they are our prisoners now. You will take care of them.

> WOUNDED UNION OFFICER
> God bless you, General.

He salutes Johnston who returns the salute before riding after his troops. The surgeon sets to work.

EXT. SHILOH, THE UNION RIGHT FLANK—AFTERNOON

Sherman strides before a fresh line of frightened recruits showing them how to load and fire their weapons. [**Note: the loading of rifle muskets—for both sides—is a nine step process.**]

                    SHERMAN
          Like shooting squirrels, only these squirrels have guns,
          is all.

"Squirrels with guns" and moving forward. Sherman lets his troops FIRE A VOLLEY, then signals them back and grabs his fourth horse of the day. He attempts to mount. The horse shies, the reins tangling round Sherman's neck. BULLETS WHIZZ BY, one plucking his shoulder with a spurt of blood.

                    SHERMAN
          Dammit! Major, God damn help me!

As he leans down to let the major untangle him A CONFEDER-ATE CANNONBALL BLASTS toward him. The cannonball cuts through the reins below the major's hands and blows the crown and back rim off Sherman's hat. Sherman quickly reclaims his saddle, pulling the major up behind him. They retreat.

EXT. THE "HORNET'S NEST"—AFTERNOON

Coming through trees, Confederates roll one Union line and another killing and taking surrenders of dozens of bluecoats.

Now the firing has stopped as they race across a field toward the brush at the edge of a sunken road.

That's where the Union hit them. Union soldiers concealed below the bank of the road wait until the Rebels get within twenty-five yards before they OPEN FIRE; VOLLEYS OF MUSKETRY AND LIGHT CANNON decimate the first Rebel assault.

Another line of Confederates, still tasting the massive victory of the first part of the day, charge, SCREAMING. The CANNISTER and BULLETS, sounding like a million angry hornets, lead them to the same bloody fate as their comrades.

Yet, Confederates keep coming, the next wave getting into the brush above the road and their Yankee enemies. They FIRE down. The Union soldiers FIRE back and the sunken road begins to fill with the dead of both sides.

Johnston rides among his men forming for the next charge.

JOHNSTON

Men of Mississippi, they say you boast of your prowess with the Bowie knife! Today you wield a nobler weapon—

He taps one of the soldier's bayonet's with his tin cup.

JOHNSTON

—the bayonet. Employ it well!

As they CHEER and fix bayonets, Johnston spurs his mount through them to lead the charge. Halfway across the field amid the WHIR AND SCREECH OF SHOT AND SHELL a bullet slaps—

JOHNSTON'S KNEE

At first he pays it little heed as his men surge into the sunken road, bayonets flashing red. Tin cup still hooked on his finger, he's grinning fiercely. A staff officer rides up alongside him. As Confederate cannon are wheeled past—

CONFEDERATE COMMANDER SHILOH
Are you wounded, General?

JOHNSTON
(*to the artillerymen*)
That's it, boys! Give 'em hell!

The cannon—six of them—are positioned. They are loaded with canister shells. Their crews stand back, ears covered, lanyards pulled: BOOM! The bulk of the remaining Union troops surrender while a smaller group flees in panic.

A CHEER goes up from the Confederates as Johnston notices blood running down his leg overflows his boot. He sways; a staff officer catches him as Johnston falls from his saddle.

JOHNSTON'S STAFF OFFICER
General—where are you hurt? Where's your surgeon?!

JOHNSTON
Doing his...duty.

The tin cup drops from Johnston's fingers as he is gently lowered to the grass. It is because there is no pain in bleeding to death that his voice sounds almost disbelieving.

JOHNSTON
I fear it's serious.

EXT. GRANT'S HEADQUARTERS MESS TENT—NIGHT

With darkness, the battle has tapered off. The RAIN, LIGHTNING AND THUNDER, however, are ceaseless. Spirits are low with CRIES FOR RETREAT rippling among Grant's army.

Sherman stands in the rain with Rawlins a short distance from Grant, who stands beneath a tree. Grant puffs a cigar and viciously whittles a stick.

RAWLINS
He's got the look of a man determined to drive his head
through a wall.

SHERMAN
And aims to do it.

RAWLINS
He'll listen to you, General. We must retreat.

Sherman parts from the troubled Rawlins and moves to Grant.

SHERMAN
Well, Grant, we've had the devil's own day, haven't we?

GRANT
Yes.

His cigar glows as he gives a quick hard puff. Grant knows what
Sherman is after. His eyes challenge him to ask for it.

GRANT
Lick 'em tomorrow, though.

With this answer, Sherman knows that his commitment to follow
Sam Grant will lead him to the gates of hell. The long odds don't
bother him anymore. As they stand bonded in the rain—

GRANT (V.O.)
Oh, my Julia... Another terrible battle has occurred in
which our arms have been victorious.

A DISTANT BOOMING OF ARTILLERY precedes...

EXT. THE UNION ENCAMPMENT AT SHILOH—DAWN

Since the previous day, the Confederate encampment, looted and in disarray; SHELLS begin EXPLODING in their midst. Rebel drummers TAP THE ROLL TO ARMS and as wet, groggy Confederates attempt to form for battle—

UNION REINFORCEMENTS LED BY MCPHERSON

perfect formations, weapons bristling, crest the hill from which they were routed the day before. Now it is the Confederates' turn to run. With cries of "RETREAT! RETREAT!" they are killed where they stand or swept from the field.

EXT. THE "HORNET'S NEST"—MORNING

FAST, HARD-HITTING SHOTS—THE CORPSES NORTH AND SOUTH

> GRANT (V.O.)
> For sheer numbers and the tenacity with which both parties held on for two days it has no equal on this continent. The best troops of Lee's rebels were engaged and his ablest generals. But the loss on both sides has been heavy—at least 20,000 killed and wounded altogether... I saw an open field over which the Confederates made repeated charges.

WIDE SHOT: Grant and his officer corps before this field. Among them are Rawlins and Dana. Men openly weep.

> GRANT (V.O.)
> So covered with dead it was, that it would have been possible to walk across that clearing in any direction, stepping on dead bodies, without a foot touching the ground.

EXT. THE ROAD SOUTH—EVENING

The road: filled with battered Rebel columns in retreat. A caisson.
Upon the caisson is a litter. Upon the litter is the dead body of Confederate General Albert Sidney Johnston.

> GRANT (V.O.)
> Among them, I am sad to say, was your father's friend,
> General Johnston... Kiss the children for me. The same
> for yourself. Good night Julia... Ulys.

EXT. PITTSBURG LANDING—DAY

Fresh Union troops come ashore and set camp. Grant meets with
General Halleck outside Halleck's command tent.

> HALLECK
> General Grant, the events of this battle have shown the
> war here must be pressed.

> GRANT
> I'm on record as having said as much for the last year,
> General.

> HALLECK
> You'll be pleased, then, to accept a position as my
> second-in-command.

> GRANT
> Second-in-command, sir?

> HALLECK
> It goes along with your promotion to Major-General.

> GRANT
> I was first in command before.

Halleck crosses his arms and scratches his elbows.

> HALLECK
> I wasn't in the field.

> GRANT
> Have you *ever* commanded in the field, General?

> HALLECK
> My book on tactics is taught at West Point. While superintendant there, Robert E. Lee called it the most important manual ever written.

> GRANT
> Lee reads more than I.

> HALLECK
> Precisely why this Bloody Shiloh of yours has produced more casualties in two days than the total of every American war to date!

> GRANT
> We were attacked, General, because you've had me sitting on my thumbs when I should've been moving toward Vicksburg.

> HALLECK
> Vicksburg is impregnable! The goal of my army now is Corinth.

> GRANT
> Vicksburg makes Corinth irrelevant.

> HALLECK
> Having not read my book, you wouldn't understand Corinth is a strategic target, sir. Wars are won by maneuver and the occupation of cities.

> GRANT

This war, sir, will be won only when their army is destroyed.

> HALLECK

Talk like that only reinforces what the papers are saying—they're calling you a butcher!

> GRANT

General Halleck, a great victory cannot be gained without many casualties. Here the enemy suffered more than we did. I love my men; I grieve at their deaths as well as I grieve the deaths of the men we fight. But we aren't fighting for cities. Our enemies come from the same cities as the rest of us. And until they're beaten man for man back into subjection to our flag, they'll continue to fight and men will continue to die.

Grant steps off.

> HALLECK
> I haven't dismissed you.

> GRANT
> Haven't you?

INT. GRANT'S HEADQUARTERS TENT, PITTSBURG LANDING —DAY

Sherman finds Grant sorting letters for packing as he puffs a fat cigar. He notices a HALF-EMPTY WHISKEY BOTTLE.

> SHERMAN
> What are you doing?

GRANT

Leaving. Sherman, you know. You know that I'm in the way here—in the way of Halleck and his ambition. While he goes digging a trench to belly-crawl to Corinth, the papers claim that as battle raged at Shiloh I was at a dance hall drinking and chasing women.

SHERMAN

I've seen 'em.

GRANT

A dance hall, Sherman! Prostitutes? I don't care whether they lie or disrespect me, but have they no respect for Julia or my children?!

SHERMAN

Where do you plan to go?

GRANT

St. Louis.

SHERMAN

You've some business there?

GRANT

Not a bit.

SHERMAN

And when it's time to face Lee?

GRANT

Let McClellan face Lee.

And, past the point of caring, Grant continues packing.

SHERMAN

Before Donelson I was finished—done in by reports I was crazy. People believed it: Halleck believed. Lincoln believed. I'd have killed myself were it not for the disgrace that would have brought on my children. But you believed in me. You backed me and you sent for me and, like a brother, have become the light I follow... Don't do this.

He makes a sweeping gesture that takes in the booze.

SHERMAN

Hell, Sam—if you go away events will go right along and you'll be left out. Remain, and...well, some happy accident might come along and restore you to favor.

GRANT

We can't win this war on accidents.

SHERMAN

No...we cannot. We need you. I need you. Stay.

Grant considers his friend...then, with a derisive snort, reaches for the bottle.

FADE OUT.

EXT. DARK, ROLLING WATER TATTOOED WITH RAINDROPS—MORNING

The FRAME WIDENS to reveal the Mississippi river under a rainy sky. Somewhere beyond a bend in the river, CANNON FIRE is exchanged. PULLING BACK NOW REVEALS—

EXT. NEW ORLEANS QUAY—CONTINUOUS

NEW ORLEANS, LOUISIANA—April 25, 1862

CROWDS OF ENRAGED CITIZENS—some brandishing weapons, all SHOUTING INVECTIVE or WAILING DISAPPOINT-MENT—watch the river and listen to the DISTANT FIGHTING. Others burn cotton. Others dump rice and molasses into the river. Also, one third of the women are dressed in black mourning clothes and many of the men wear BLACK ARMBANDS or BLACK CREPE ROSETTES on their lapels. **[Note: as the episodes progress, more and more citizens will be seen wearing the vestments of mourning, until, by series' end, two out of every three women in the South and one out of every four women of the North will be clothed entirely in the black symbols of their loss.]**

> NEW ORLEANS VOICES
> Leave nothing for the damn Yankees!

A final SALVO OF CANNON FIRE beyond the river bend is followed by AN EXPLOSION that lights the sky. The crowd falls silent. They watch and wait... Soon—

UNION WARSHIPS

dark against the rainy sky—U.S. SAILORS and MARINES revealed crowding the rails, rigging and yardarms—sail round the bend and slowly head for the New Orleans docks.

EXT. CONGO SQUARE—MORNING

Confederate General JOHN L. LEWIS reads an address.

> GENERAL LEWIS
> Major General Lovell has ordered the evacuation of
> the army, declaring New Orleans an open city in order
> (MORE)

GENERAL LEWIS (CONT'D)
to save it from the destruction wished upon it by the
Yankee vandals. You, volunteer soldiers of our glorious
Native Guard, are disbanded and will return to your
former lives as citizens of New Orleans.

He pauses and looks out at the regiment in the square before him.
BEGIN WITH: THEIR SHOES—their feet spread in "at ease"
position—and PAN UP Confederate uniform pants to their belts
and their tunics and, finally, their faces as—

GENERAL LEWIS
You were free men under us; how free you'll be under
the tyranny of Union occupation... Suffer it nobly.

THE FACES OF THESE CONFEDERATE SOLDIERS: ALL
ARE BLACK

GENERAL LEWIS
Your services to the Confederate States of America are
no longer required.

Andre Cailloux, stoically staring ahead, calls—

CAILLOUX
Company: Attention!

His men snap to the order as one. Without a salute or goodbye, or
even a "dismissed," the general quickly mounts his horse—held by
a SLAVE—and departs.

The free black soldiers of the Native Guard remain at attention until
the HOOFBEATS HAMMER INTO SILENCE. A grin creeps
across Cailloux's face. The soldiers behind him BURST FORTH
WITH CHEERS and throw off their caps of gray.

EXT. COTTON YARD—DAY

—turned boxing ring. BLACK FISTS BOXING A WHITE FACE. Andre Cailloux is the boxer. His opponent, a U.S. NAVY GUN-NER, has a four inch and thirty pound advantage.

The betting is motivated; the crowd an easy mix of local whites and black, Creoles, Union soldiers and sailors.

Despite his opponent's advantage in height and weight, Cailloux whips the fellow mercilessly. The gunner goes down, knocked out in a tumble of his own limbs. The locals CHEER.

The soldiers and seamen give up their money, dumbfounded. Cailloux, goes for water, then lights a cigar. A free black mulatto, PAUL POREE (30s [**last seen opening scene Episode 101**])—a former private in the former Native Guard and full of pride—joins Cailloux. They speak in SUBTITLED FRENCH.

POREE

[Andre! The First Louisiana's been called back into service!]

CAILLOUX

[By whom?]

POREE

[Union General Butler!]

Cailloux, seeing his opponent revived by his Navy friends, walks over, offers his hand. The boxer's friends flash angry looks at Cailloux, but the white gunner shakes his black hand.

NAVY BOXER

Y'taught me something today. I'll think on it...maybe I try again?

> CAILLOUX
> We put on a good match. I'd be happy to oblige.

Andre Cailloux gives the gunner a bundle of cigars.

> NAVY BOXER
> Many thanks.

Pointing to writing on the ribbon that binds them—

> CAILLOUX
> The name of my shop; no finer rolled cigars in the Bayou State.

> NAVY BOXER
> I'll spread the word...

> POREE
> [Listen to me, Andre. The plan is to bring the Big Muddy back into the Union once and for all.]

> CAILLOUX
> [General Grant's going after Vicksburg to do that.]

> POREE
> [Sure enough, but that only gets him into Louisiana; there's still the Reb's up at Port Hudson.]

> CAILLOUX
> [For how long?]

> POREE
> [Depends when you accept our nomination as Captain of Company E.]

INT. WAR DEPARTMENT TELEGRAPH ROOM—NIGHT

Stanton meets with Lincoln in the nerve-center of the war: a room filled with telegraphs and UNION TELEGRAPHERS.

STANTON
McClellan's requested Washington defenses stripped and the men sent to reinforce him.

LINCOLN
What would that leave us for protection here?

STANTON
Ten thousand men at most, Mr. President.

LINCOLN
He can't be serious.

STANTON
I've found General McClellan to be serious. Always.

Lincoln considers the request and, finally, shakes his head.

LINCOLN
He's sat doing nothing for more than a month outside of Yorktown—not Richmond—Yorktown! Tell the general he'll make do with exactly what he now has and no more.

STANTON
McClellan says that without an increase to his army his intelligence reports have him outnumbered two to one by Johnston's massed forces.

LINCOLN
As a matter of fact—

Lincoln grabs a pad and scribbles his own order.

> LINCOLN
> —he will attack the Rebel emplacements at dawn.

EXT. UNION FIRST LINE OF ENTRENCHMENTS, YORKTOWN—AFTERNOON

EASTERN THEATER—
YORKTOWN, VIRGINIA—May 4, 1862

Massive Union siege artillery under General Hooker BOM-BARD the town, their smoke and fire obscuring any tactical view McClellan can have of the situation. Wexler enters.

> WEXLER
> General, the Commander-in-Chief orders you to take Yorktown, now.

> MCCLELLAN
> Does he, Captain?

Wexler doesn't know how to answer.

> MCCLELLAN
> I've already given the order.

True to McClellan's words, CHEERS go up from the mass of Union soldiers who, forming battle lines, march on the town.

EXT. YORKTOWN—VARIOUS SHOTS—AFTERNOON TO EVENING

The scant Confederate defenders holding Yorktown put up little resistance before surrendering to McClellan's arriving army. The town McClellan has sat outside for two months is for all intents and purposes *empty of enemy.*

INT. MCCLELLAN'S YORKTOWN COMMAND POST—EVENING

STAFF OFFICERS bustle with the business of "victory;" McClellan dictates a telegram to his TELEGRAPHER.

MCCLELLAN

To President Lincoln Commander-in-Chief. Victory at Yorktown is mine. Four hundred prisoners and like number of arms taken against heavy odds. Plus seven cannon.

Captain Wexler steps up and salutes.

MCCLELLAN
Captain?

WEXLER

Interrogation of prisoners has turned up some intelligence you should hear, sir.

MCCLELLAN
Go on.

WEXLER

Sir, captured officers and private soldiers have all proposed that, contrary to our own estimates, they were facing us with less than ten thousand men—that Joe Johnston's entire Army of North Virginia is less than fifty thousand. General, press now and you could be in Richmond in three days!

Captain Wexler offers the interrogation reports.

MCCLELLAN
Captain Wexler, I always had high hopes for you.

                              WEXLER
                         Thank you, sir.

                              MCCLELLAN
But you have proven yourself unequal for the hopes I
held. You will transfer immediately to an infantry company where you will learn the truth about this enemy
with whom I'm now engaged.

                              WEXLER
                  General: the war is yours, sir!

                              MCCLELLAN
                     No, Captain: it's yours.

INT. LINCOLN'S OFFICE—DAY

Lincoln faces Stanton, extremely and personally upset.

                              LINCOLN
                  I had high hopes for McClellan.

Stanton says nothing.

                              LINCOLN
While he's delivered me a victory—however small—he
sits in Yorktown three weeks complaining and begging
reinforcements I have repeatedly told him are unavail-
able. Richmond could be his!

                              STANTON
               Shall we remove him, Mr. President?

Lincoln gives Stanton a pained look: has it come to this?

MARY CUSTIS LEE (V.O.)

LINCOLN

I can't. The people...his army... He's so deeply loved; so many look to him, count on him. He's his own worst enemy. Why can't he see? What must I do to help him *see this*?

EXT. MARY CUSTIS LEE'S MANSION—MORNING

McClellan and some staff officers ride up to a large mansion known also as the White House. Alone, McClellan dismounts Dan Webster and walks to—

THE FRONT DOORS—A POSTED MESSAGE

McClellan reads it, the words corresponding with—

MARY CUSTIS LEE (V.O.)

"Northern Soldiers who profess reverence to General George Washington. Forbear to desecrate the home of his first married life, the property of his wife, now owned by her descendants..."

McClellan KNOCKS. While he waits the last words on the message are HEARD—

MARY CUSTIS LEE (V.O.)

"Washington's Granddaughter. Mrs. Robert E. Lee."

The door is opened by a SLAVE. Beside him in her wheelchair is Robert E. Lee's wife, Mary Custis Lee.

MARY CUSTIS LEE

General McClellan?

Doffing his hat, he bows.

> MCCLELLAN
> At your service, ma'am.

They stare at one another a moment.

> MCCLELLAN
> It is my very great honor to meet the granddaughter of the Father of Our Country.

He extends his hand. She takes it as if it were infected.

> MCCLELLAN
> I had the honor of serving alongside your illustrious husband on General Scott's staff in Mexico.

> MARY CUSTIS LEE
> We don't get much Northern news, but I believe you treated the general poorly, George McClellan.

> MCCLELLAN
> Your husband, Mrs. Lee?

> MARY CUSTIS LEE
> You know of whom I'm speaking, sir.

INT. MARY CUSTIS LEE'S MANSION—DAY

The two of them—McClellan and Mary Lee—have been served tea in the solarium. In the shadows of the doorway, Robert E. Lee's THREE DAUGHTERS hover.

> MARY CUSTIS LEE
> I have already lost one home in the path of war.

> MCCLELLAN
> Arlington House. Yes, ma'am, I am aware of that.

MARY CUSTIS LEE

Then please respect my wishes with regard to this one.
Among the ranks of all armies there are the uncouth,
the uncaring, the uncivilized. There are the souvenir
hunters.

MCCLELLAN
Yes, ma'am.

MARY CUSTIS LEE

My request to you is that you personally guarantee the
safety and integrity of this property.

MCCLELLAN

You have my assurance that you will not be molested as
long as I and my army are within the vicinity.

MARY CUSTIS LEE

No, General, you don't understand. I will not be in the
vicinity. Tomorrow morning I will remove myself, my
daughters and my Negro property, to Richmond to
await your defeat. You will be responsible for General
Washington's home. Are you capable?

Ignoring the "defeat" comment, McClellan basks in what he hears
as a comparison of himself to Washington.

MCCLELLAN

I am honored, ma'am. You shall have safe conduct from
my army to your husband at any time you require it in
the morning. While I personally protect this property
by making my headquarters here.

Mary Lee smiles slyly.

MARY CUSTIS LEE
Very good. General, please feel free to camp in my yard.

EXT. MARY CUSTIS LEE'S MANSION—MORNING

McClellan's staff lines the drive at attention in dress uniform as soldiers escort Lee's wife and daughters from the property. For his part, outside his tent, angry and humiliated, McClellan grips a telegram tightly in his fist.

> MCCLELLAN (V.O.)
>
> Darling Ellen, I regret that the rascals are after me again. I had been foolish enough to hope that when I went into the field they would give me some rest, but perhaps I should have expected this. The idea of persecuting a man behind his back. I have been relieved temporarily as General-in-Chief. The great Lincoln baboon—

INT. MCCLELLAN BEDROOM—NIGHT

> MCCLELLAN (V.O.)
>
> —deigns to make re-instatement contingent upon victory. Was not my initial Yorktown victory enough for that incapable?

Ellen McClellan, wearing her dressing gown, puts pen to paper, spelling out her reply in broad and vicious strokes.

> ELLEN (V.O.)
>
> Can you not see what they are doing? Who better than that inept Administration can know how close you are to their crown?! Your victory at Richmond is foregone; your triumph and the assured accolades and gifts of a grateful nation already in your grasp. That most rare bird, Lincoln, pecks at you hoping for your resignation. You *will* attack.

EXT. SEVEN PINES BATTLEFIELD, VIRGINIA—DAWN

SEVEN DAYS BATTLE, VIRGINIA—
June 25 to July 1, 1862

McClellan shows off, riding before his troops arrayed for battle. In their CHEERS and love for him, their uncomplicated faith in his love for them is overwhelming.

> ELLEN (V.O.)
> By victory you will gather your deserved glory around you.

In the distance, Joe Johnston's rebel army prepares to meet them. CANNON BOOM from both sides. As General Meade's Federals charge, Confederate infantry under—

GEORGE PICKETT

counterattack. The battle is engaged: bloody and awful with scores of dying men on both sides, broken bodies and severed limbs flying with each CANNON SHOT and SWARM OF BULLETS. Somehow Pickett makes it through with only a shoulder wound but his men are driven back by Federal troops.

> ELLEN (V.O.)
> And from the ashes of rebellion destroyed, assume your rightful place as *the* leader of this great nation that you—and only you—will have set free!

[Note: as this sequence is the combination of SIX SEPARATE ENGAGEMENTS it should VARY IN TERRAIN, be VISUALIZED SLIGHTLY SURREAL, and the SPIRES OF RICHMOND SHOULD GROW EVER CLOSER.]

GENERAL MEADE

is commanding infantry from atop his horse behind the front ranks. He's waving his sword, PROFANELY URGING HIS MEN FORWARD, when a bullet SLAPS into his right arm. He winces, lifting it to look at the wound.

ANOTHER BULLET buries into his side, half-turning him in his saddle. He goes very erect. Men around him, frightened by the wounding of the general turn and watch—some immediately cut down—but Meade simply clenches his jaw, slowly turns his horse and walks it toward the rear.

WHAM! Another bullet hits him in the back. And yet his disciplined posture and brave gait do not change. He reaches STRETCHER BEARERS and his SURGEON in the rear who help him from his saddle. Meade's troops CHEER. Fight more furiously.

DURING THESE BATTLES one thing is clear: for all his faults, conceits and vanities, McClellan is no coward. Exposing himself continuously to ENEMY FIRE, he leads his troops. And, although he is as he always predicted—and procrastinated until it's become a self-fulfilling prophecy—heavily outnumbered, it is his leadership that pushes his men to grasping reach at victory.

WITH THE 97TH NEW YORK REGIMENT

In total disarray, their formation broken, men falling, others calling—

> 97TH NY SOLDIERS
> Captain!/Where's Captain Wexler?

For everything he was right about and McClellan was wrong, Captain Nathan Wexler has failed his test. He cowers, shaking with fright, eyes squeezed shut, behind a burning caisson, a coward. His infantry company is decimated.

INT. CONFEDERATE WHITE HOUSE, DAVIS'S OFFICE—DAY

Davis looks up from his work at the SOUND OF BATTLE. Lee enters. He's heard it too. Davis opens his balcony doors. The BATTLE SOUNDS INCREASE as the two men step outside. Beyond Richmond, columns of smoke rise into the air.

> LEE
> I've called for my horse.

> JEFFERSON DAVIS
> I'm coming with you.

EXT. SEVEN PINES BATTLEFIELD, VIRGINIA—EVENING

With Longstreet's ARTILLERY. It ROARS as quickly as men can load, pull lanyard, reload and FIRE AGAIN. Riding up—

> JOE JOHNSTON
> How goes it, General Longstreet?

> LONGSTREET
> The enemy fights.

> JOE JOHNSTON
> Send in your reserves.

> LONGSTREET
> Yes, General.

At this, Johnston, gripped by the fever of battle, rides out to be among the last charging mass of his boys.

> LONGSTREET
> General Johnston to the rear!

But Johnston's sword is drawn in one hand, a pistol in the other. He doesn't hear, or doesn't listen. Gripping his reins in his teeth he charges forward. A Federal BULLET SLAMS into his shoulder. As he reels in his seat he loses his sword. He draws his second pistol, then spurs forward, a FRAGMENT from an EXPLODING ARTILLERY SHELL strikes his chest, throwing him violently from his saddle.

The Confederate charge wavers at the fall of their beloved general, but they are committed. They rally, continuing forward to their DESTRUCTION—

LONGSTREET AND JOHNSTON

Johnston lies weakly in grass already bloody from the day's fight. Longstreet holds him.

> LONGSTREET
> Stay with me, sir!

> JOE JOHNSTON
> My sword...I would not lose it for ten thousand dollars... Would not someone please...go back...and get my pistols for me?

Two of Johnston's AIDES linger, frightened and helpless.

> LONGSTREET
> You heard the general: get 'em!

They scurry into the MAELSTROM. ORDERLIES dash up with a stretcher. Longstreet helps lift his general onto it.

> JOE JOHNSTON
> No! Please wait.

And it is at this moment that Jefferson Davis and Lee ride up. Joe Johnston—every breath flecking his beard and cheeks with blood—sees them. Davis takes his hand. The animosity that has lived so long between them: gone.

JEFFERSON DAVIS
My general.

Dodging BULLETS, one of the Aides locates the sword and pistols. He dashes back to the wounded general. The sword is laid across Johnston's breast. Johnston smiles. The pistols are offered. Johnston takes one, but the other—

JOE JOHNSTON
Take it, young man. You've earned it.

The soldier takes the reward and salutes. Longstreet signals the stretcher bearers. They lift Johnston's broken body.

JOE JOHNSTON
I have given my all, Mr. President. But we have been defeated. General Lee: you are the ranking officer on this battlefield. Please call the retreat. Richmond...

He CHOKES up blood.

JOE JOHNSTON
Richmond can still be...defended.

Lee doesn't need to look to Davis to know his duty. He strokes Johnston's forehead and pronounces—

LEE
You will heal and we will continue this fight together.

Johnston can only nod. Then he is carried away.

EXT. SEVEN DAYS BATTLEFIELD, VIRGINIA—UNION LINES—NIGHT

The fighting has diminished to SPORADIC CANNON and PICKET FIRE as McClellan watches his army form and...

IN THE DISTANCE—THE CONFEDERATE ARMY ESCAPES

> BURNSIDE
> General McClellan, my men are willing to press on! Richmond can be ours!

MCCLELLAN'S POV—THROUGH FIELD GLASSES—THE NO-MAN'S LAND

between the two armies. It is filled with the dead and dying of both sides. The SOUND IS AWFUL. But more awful still:

A DRIFT OF PIGS

loose from some pen. They feed on the dead and wounded. It is too horrible to watch; worse still, to HEAR.

McClellan lowers his glasses. From the pain he allows into his face and the way McClellan grips Burnside's shoulder the personal affection between these two men is evident.

> MCCLELLAN
> My brave, brave children...

> BURNSIDE
> Finish this, George. Finish this!

> MCCLELLAN
> This? This..?

BURNSIDE
Yes! *General* you've done it! One more push and...
(knowing McClellan's ego)
everything you've ever wanted is yours.

MCCLELLAN
General Burnside: are you blind? Look at my dead and
broken boys out there! This, sir, is a defeat!

Burnside is stunned. Shaking his head to get the image of the dining
hogs from his mind, McClellan ambles off.

EXT. THE ROAD TO RICHMOND—NIGHT

Jefferson Davis rides beside General Lee. Their conversation is sub-
dued, hardly believing their words.

JEFFERSON DAVIS
Twenty thousand we've lost against McClellan in this
campaign, General.

Lee nods.

JEFFERSON DAVIS
If they press...it's over. I must get back to my offices,
prepare to move the government.

LEE
I'll be forthwith, Mr. President.

JEFFERSON DAVIS
You're staying?

Lee has stopped Traveller, which says as much.

JEFFERSON DAVIS
You've served me well as an advisor. I've guarded you...
jealously.

Lee says nothing.

JEFFERSON DAVIS
I can't hold you in Richmond any longer. Not if we're to
survive. Will you take command of our forces, General
Lee?

LEE
The Army of Northern Virginia?

JEFFERSON DAVIS
All our Armies, General Lee: East, West and South.
Will you?

Lee salutes. But still, he does not move forward.

JEFFERSON DAVIS
Won't you come?

LEE
My youngest son was engaged here, Mr. President.

JEFFERSON DAVIS
As an officer?

LEE
He is too young for that responsibility, sir. An uncom-
mon boy, he fights as a common soldier. By your leave,
I would go find him.

These words bode badly for Lee. Jefferson Davis doesn't know what
to say. He turns his horse. He leaves.

EXT. SEVEN DAYS BATTLEFIELD, VIRGINIA—DAWN

RAIN falls like tears as Lee rides among Confederate and Union troops under flags of truce who mingle without animosity, collecting the dead and dying of their armies.

EXT. A FARM HOUSE/FIELD HOSPITAL—DAWN

SURGEONS appearing like butchers—their smocks covered with gore, blood glistening on their arms up to their elbows, streaking their brows—grimly amputate limbs.

[Note: The preponderance of Civil War amputation was not "butchery" nor lack of surgical knowledge. It was the best and usually only way to save a wounded man's life. And while the mortality rate for amputation was high, more lives were saved by amputation than lost. The injuries these surgeons dealt with were dreadful and the fault of the low velocity, soft lead Minie Ball. This soft lead bullet caused large, gaping holes, splintered bones that could never mend, and destroyed muscles, arteries and tissues beyond any possible repair. Second to the Minie Ball, Germ Theory was unknown; antiseptic surgery would only come into existence in the last months of the war and Blood Types were not discovered until 1901. Surgeons did not know to wash their hands before surgery or between cases, nor did they know to use sterile equipment. When something was dropped, it was simply rinsed in cool, often bloody water. They used sponges that had been used in previous cases and simply dipped in cold water—because cold at that time was "safer" than hot—before using them again on the next person. So, while amputations and operations would be successful on the table, thousands upon thousands of soldiers would die later from infection and blood disease.

Further, at least half of the nurses and cooks in the Confederate Army are slaves or free blacks. They have been impressed into this work against their will. In this episode: most actors are of color. The most caring people on the battlefield.]

A wagon-load of Confederate wounded arrives. Within, among his wounded men is General Ewell. Helped first from the wagon, his staff try to take him into the surgery, but—

> EWELL
> Thank you, gentlemen. I will wait until my boys are seen to.

This, of course, prompts quick action toward the other men in the wagon. To each as they pass him, Ewell has a KIND WORD.

> CONFEDERATE SURGEON
> General Ewell, your leg must come off. The sooner we attend to this, sir, the better your chances.

> EWELL
> Yes, doctor, and I will be ready in a moment... Now, Orderly Sergeant, if you would help me to that gentleman yonder.

> EWELL'S ORDERLY
> Yes, General.

He helps Ewell to the distraught FARMER who owns the house, standing aside as WIFE and DAUGHTERS tend the new arrivals.

> EWELL
> So many years fighting Indians and I lose my leg to an American.

Ewell, known for odd non sequiturs, gets a raised eyebrow.

> EWELL
> This is your farm, sir?

The Farmer nods. Ewell finds his money purse.

EWELL
This is all I have. I wish I had more, but I give it to you
now, sir, for you and your family. See to it all of you and
our boys have everything you need.

As Ewell is carried inside, Lee moves past a wagon filled with severed arms and legs stacked like firewood. He passes Pickett who sits
outside, his shoulder bandaged, arm in a sling. Pickett, his face taut
with pain, his color pale from loss of blood, salutes him. Lee pauses
his horse.

PICKETT
General Lee.

LEE
General Pickett.

PICKETT
If I hadn't been wounded... I would have liked to bring
us victory.

LEE
Mend, sir. You will.

PICKETT
Thank you, General Lee.

Lee hesitates.

LEE
My youngest son Robert... His artillery was attached to
your division...

Pickett's expression becomes hopeless.

PICKETT
My artillery was all destroyed.

> LEE

I understand. If you could direct me, sir, to its last position?

Raising his good arm, Pickett points to a small hill still washed with lingering smoke of stubborn fires and dead.

EXT. SEVEN DAYS BATTLEFIELD—MORNING

Lee stops Traveller. Bodies of Confederate soldiers lie around the smouldering hulks of destroyed Rebel cannon. He recognizes the still body of an eighteen year-old boy lying against a cannon wheel. Choked, to an ORDERLY—

> LEE

The men who carried this position were soldiers indeed... Orderly, would you see to that body—against the wheel...please?

He asks this because he is physically incapable of moving any closer. The orderly walks up the knoll upon which the cannon and boy lie. The orderly takes a sponge staff. Lee grimaces to see him prod the body of his youngest son. Then—

> CONFEDERATE ORDERLY
> You, boy! Wake up, boy!

Robert E. Lee's youngest son, Robert Jr, having collapsed from exhaustion, groggily comes to. General Lee throws himself from his horse. He scrambles up the knoll.

> CONFEDERATE ORDERLY
> Granny Lee wants to talk to you.

Lee's son barely has focused his bleary eyes upon his father when Lee is upon him, embracing him and holding him to his breast and kissing his head repeatedly. OVER THIS—

MCCLELLAN (V.O.)
To War Secretary Stanton: I now know the full history
of the day.

EXT. YORKTOWN—DAY

The soldiers of McClellan's army follow their wagons slowly out of
town in inglorious and unwarranted retreat.

MCCLELLAN (V.O.)
I have lost this campaign because my force was too
small. I again repeat that I am not responsible for this.
And I say it with the earnestness of a general who feels
in his heart the loss of every brave son of mine who has
been needlessly sacrificed today...

INT. MCCLELLAN BEDROOM—DAY

Ellen McClellan, reading this in the newspaper, SHRIEKS and
begins to shred the paper. BUT THE WORDS CONTINUE.

MCCLELLAN (V.O.)
If, at this instant, I could dispose of 10,000 fresh men, I
could gain a victory tomorrow. I know that a few thousand more men today would have changed this battle
from a defeat to a victory.

INT. LINCOLN'S OFFICE—NIGHT

Lincoln doesn't look at the telegram Stanton has laid upon his desk.
A wave of his hand he dismisses his War Secretary.

MCCLELLAN (V.O.)
As it is, the Government must not and cannot hold me
responsible for the result. I feel too earnestly tonight.
(MORE)

> MCCLELLAN (V.O.) (CONT'D)
>
> I have seen too many dead and wounded comrades to feel otherwise than that the Government has not sustained this army.

Lincoln opens the French doors and steps into the RAIN. There is a faraway look in his eyes. PUSH ON LINCOLN'S FACE.

> MCCLELLAN (V.O.)
>
> If you do not do so now the game is lost. If I save this army now, I tell you plainly that I owe no thanks to you or to any other persons in Washington.

FLASH CUT:

INT. CHICAGO THEATER—NIGHT (FLASHBACK)

ABRAHAM LINCOLN AND WILLIE LINCOLN (June 12, 1859) IN A THEATER BOX. On the stage below, EDWIN BOOTH (29) brother of the nation's greatest, most popular star, John Wilkes Booth, prepares to do battle with "MACDUFF."

> EDWIN BOOTH AS "MACBETH"
>
> I will not yield, to kiss the ground before young Malcolm's feet, and to be baited with the rabble's curse. Though Birnam Wood be come to Dunsinane, And thou opposed, being of no woman born, Yet I will try the last. Before my body I throw my warlike shield. Lay on, MacDuff, And damned be him that first cries, "Hold, enough!"

Willie presses his face into his father's chest unwilling to see Macbeth slain. Lincoln smiles at his son's compassion. He strokes Willie's hair, WHISPERING SOOTHING WORDS.

RESUME: INT. LINCOLN'S OFFICE—NIGHT

Lincoln's back is to the open French doors. RAIN falls upon his stooped shoulders, and, SOFTLY—

MCCLELLAN (V.O.)
You have done your best to sacrifice this army.

FADE OUT:

END OF EPISODE 104

BIBLIOGRAPHY

PRIMARY SOURCES

Personal Memoirs of Ulysses S. Grant. New York, 1885.

R. E. Lee (Four Volumes), by Douglas Southall Freeman, New York, 1949.

War of the Rebellion: A Compilation of the Official Records of the Union and Confederate Armies, Prepared under the direction of the Secretary of War, by Bvt. Lieut. Col. Robert N. Scott, Third U. S. Artillery and Published pursuant to Act of Congress approved June 16, 1880.

ADDITIONAL SOURCES

MEMOIRS, REGIMENTAL HISTORIES, PAPERS AND LETTERS:

Abraham Lincoln: Complete Works Comprising his Speeches, Letters, State Papers and Miscellaneous Writings, edited by John G. Nicholay and John Hay. New York, 1907.

An Aide-De-Camp of Lee: Being the Papers of Colonel Charles Marshall, Sometime Aide-De-Camp, Military Secretary and Assistant Adjutant General of the Staff of Robert E. Lee 1862-1865, by Charles Marshall, Frederick Maurice. New York, 1927.

Army Life in a Black Regiment, by Thomas Wentworth Higgenson. Boston, 1870.

Autobiography of Mark Twain, Vol. 1, by Mark Twain, Harriet E. Smith, Berkeley, 2010.

Autobiography of Mark Twain, Vol. 2, by Mark Twain, Harriet E. Smith, Berkeley, 2013.

Autobiography of Mark Twain, Vol. 3, by Mark Twain, Harriet E. Smith, Berkeley, 2015.

A Brief History of the 69th Regiment Pennsylvania Veteran Volunteers From its Formation until Final Mustering Out of the United States Service, by Anthony W. McDermott, *Also an Account of the Reunion of the Survivors of the Philadelphia Brigade and Pickett's Division of Confederate Soldiers, and the Dedication of the Monument of the 69th Regiment Pennsylvania Infantry at Gettysburg July 2nd and 3rd, 1887, and the Rededication, September 10th, 1889*, by Captain John E. Reilly, Philadelphia, 1889.

Campaigning with Grant, by General Horace Porter, LL.D. New York, 1897.

Campaigns of the One Hundred and Forty-Sixth Regiment New York State Volunteers, compiled by Mary Genevie Green Brainyard, New York, 1915.

The Civil War Archive: The History of the Civil War in Documents, edited by Henry Steele Commager, revised and expanded by Erik Bruun, New York, 2000.

The Civil War Papers of George B. McClellan: Selected Correspondence 1860-1865, by George McClellan, Stephan B. Sears. New York, 1992.

"Company Aytch," Maury Grays, First Tennessee Regiment; Or, a Side Show of the Big Show, by Samuel R. Watkins, Tennessee, 1882.

A Confederate Nurse: The Diary of Ada W. Bacot, 1860-1863, by Ada White Bacot and Jean Vince Berlin. Columbia, S.C. 1996.

Down in Dixie: Life in a Cavalry Regiment in the War Days, by Stanton P. Allen. Boston, 1888.

Findings of the Court of Inquiry and Reviews of the Judge-Advocate-General and of the General of the Army, in the case of Major-General G.K. Warren, Washington Government Printing Office, 1883.

Following the Greek Cross or, Memories of the Sixth Army Corps, by Thomas W. Hyde. Boston, 1894.

Forty-six Years in the Army, by Lt.-Gen. John McAllister Schofield, New York, 1897.

Four Years in the Stonewall Brigade, by John O. Casler. 2nd Editon, Girard, Kansas, 1906.

Four Years with General Lee, by Walter H. Taylor, Bloomington, 1962.

From Manassas to Appomattox: Memoirs of the Civil War in American, by James Longstreet. New York, 1895.

General Grant's Letters to a Friend 1861-1880, edited by James Grant Wilson, New York, 1897.

General Sherman as College President: Collected Letters and Documents and Other Material, edited by Walter L Fleming. New York, 1912.

Grant in Peace: A Personal Memoir, Adam Badeau. Hartford, Connecticut, 1881.

Grant in St. Louis, by Walter B. Stevens, St. Louis, 1916.

Hardtack & Coffee: The Unwritten Story of Army Life, by John D. Billings, Boston, 1887.

The Heart Of A Soldier: As Revealed in the Intimate Letters of General George E. Pickett C.S.A., by George Edward Pickett, Sallie Corbell Pickett. New York, 1913.

History of the First Regiment Alabama Volunteer Infantry C.S.A., by Edward Young McMorries, Ph.D. Montgomery, Alabama, 1904.

History of the Fourth Regiment of S. C. Volunteers, From the Commencement of the War Until Lee's Surrender, by J. W. Reid. Greenville, South Carolina, 1892.

A History of the Laurel Brigade, by William N. McDonald, edited by Bushrod C. Washington. Baltimore, 1907.

A History of the Negro Troops in the War of the Rebellion, 1861-1865, by George W. Williams, LL.D. New York, 1888.

History of the 150th Regiment Pennsylvania Volunteers, by Lieutenant Colonel Thomas Chamberlain. Philadelphia, 1905.

History of the Third Regiment of Wisconsin Veteran Volunteer Infantry 1861-1865, by Edwin E. Bryant. Madison, Wisconsin, 1891.

History of the Twenty-fourth Michigan of the Iron Brigade, by O. B. Curtis, A. M., Detroit, 1891.

Home Letters of General Sherman, edited by M. A. DeWolfe Howe. New York, 1909.

Incidents and Anecdotes of the Civil War, by David Dixon Porter, New York, 1885.

Jefferson Davis: Ex-President of the Confederate States of America, A Memoir by His Wife in Two Volumes, by Varina Davis. New York, 1890.

Letters of Mark Twain, by Mark Twain and Albert Bigelow Paine. New York, 1920.

Letters of Sebastian Muller, 1860-1864. Manuscript Collection, Library of Congress, Washington D.C.

Letters of Ulysses S. Grant to his Father and Youngest Sister 1857-78, by Ulysses S. Grant, Jesse Grant Cramer. New York, 1912.

The Life and Letters of Emory Upton, by Peter S. Michie. New York, 1885.

The Life and Letters of George Gordon Meade, by George Meade, Captain and Aide-de-Camp. New York, 1913.

Longstreet's Aide: The Civil War Letters of Major Thomas J. Goree, edited by Thomas W. Cutrer, Richmond, 1995.

McClellan's Own Story, by George B. McClellan. New York, 1887.

Major General Ambrose E. Burnside and the Ninth Army Corps, by Augustus Woodbury. Providence, 1867.

Mark Twain's Autobiography, by Mark Twain and Albert Bigelow Paine. New York, 1912.

Meet General Grant, by William E. Woodword. New York, 1928.

Memoirs, by William Tecumseh Sherman. New York, 1875.

The Memoirs of Colonel John S. Mosby, edited by Charles Wells Russell, Boston, 1917.

Memoirs of Robert E Lee: His Military and Personal History, by A.J. Long. New York, 1886.

Military memoirs of a Confederate, by E. Porter Alexander. New York, 1907.

Our Army Nurses: Interesting Sketches, Addresses and Photographs of Nearly One Hundred Women who Served in Hospitals and on Battlefields during Our Civil War, compiled by, Mary A. Gardner Holland. Boston, 1895.

The Papers of Ulysses S. Grant (1837-1885) Volumes 1-31, edited by John Y. Simon, Carbondale, 1967-2009.

The Passing of the Armies: An Account of the final Campaign of the Army of the Potomac, Based upon Personal reminiscences of the Fifth Army Corps, by Joshua Lawrence Chamberlain, New York, 1915.

The Personal Memoirs of Julia Dent Grant (Mrs.Ulysses S. Grant), by Julia Dent Grant and John Y. Simon. Carbondale, Illinois, 1988.

Personal Memoirs of P. H. Sheridan, General United States Army. New York, 1888.

Personal Reminiscences, Anecdotes and Letters of General Robert E. Lee, by the Reverend J William Jones, DD. New York, 1875.

The Recollections and Letters of Robert E. Lee, by Robert E. Lee. New York, 1905.

Recollections of a Private Soldier in the Army of the Potomac, by Frank Wilkeson. New York, 1887.

Recollections of the Civil War, by Charles A. Dana. New York, 1898.

Reminiscences of an Army Nurse During the Civil War, by Adelaide W. Smith, New York, 1911.

Reminiscences of the Nineteenth Massachusetts Regiment, by Captain John B. Adams. Boston, 1899.

Reminiscences of Winfield Scott Hancock by His Wife, by Almira Russell Hancock, New York, 1887.

The Seventy-seventh Pennsylvania at Shiloh, by Pennsylvania Shiloh Battlefield Commission, edited by John Obreiter. Lancaster, Pennsylvannia, 1908.

The Sherman Letters, edited by Rachel Sherman Thorndike. New York, 1894.

Soldiering with Sherman: Civil War Letters of George F. Cram, edited by Jennifer Cain Bohrnstedt, DeKalb, 2000.

Southern History of the War, The First, Second, Third and Last Year, by Edward A. Pollard. Four volumes. New York, 1865.

Under the Old Flag: Recollections of Military Operations in the War for the Union, the Spanish War, the Boxer Rebellion, etc., (volume one) by James Harrison Wilson. New York, 1902.

The Valley Campaigns: Being the Reminiscences of a Non-Combatant While Between the Lines in the Shenandoah Valley During the War of the States, by Thomas A. Ashby, M.D., LL.D., New York, 1914.

A War Diary of Events in the War of the Great Rebellion, 1863-1865, by George H. Gordon. New York, 1882.

A War of the People: Vermont Civil War Letters, edited by Jeffrey D. Marshall, Hanover, 1999.

The Wartime Papers of R.E. Lee, Clifford Dowdey, Boston, 1961.

What Happened to Me, by La Salle Corbell Pickett (Mrs. Gen. George E. Pickett). New York, 1917.

When Grant Went a-Courtin' by his Wife's Sister: Emma Dent Casey, *The Ulysses S. Grant Association Newsletter,* VI, 1 (Oct., 1968).

When Lincoln Kissed Me, by Henry E. Wing, New York, 1913.

BIOGRAPHIES

American Scoundrel: The Life of the Notorious Civil War General Dan Sickles, by Thomas Keneally, New York, 2002.

American Ulysses: A Life of Ulysses S. Grant, by Ronald C. White, New York, 2016.

A Black Patriot and a White Priest: Andre Cailloux and Claude Paschal Maistre in Civil War New Orleans, by Stephen J. Ochs, Louisiana, 2000.

The Captain Departs: Ulysses S. Grant's Last Campaign, by Thomas M. Pitkin, (foreword by John Y. Simon), Illinois, 1973.

Captain Sam Grant, by Lloyd Lewis, New York, 1950.

Carrying the Flag: The Story of Private Charles Whilden the Confederacy's Most Unlikely Hero, by Gordon C. Rhea, New York, 2004.

Citizen Sherman: A Life of William Tecumseh Sherman, by Michael Fellman, Lawrence, 1995.

Commander of All Lincoln's Armies: A Life of General Henry W. Halleck, by John F. Marszalek, New York, 2004.

Crucible of Command: Ulysses S. Grant and Robert E. Lee-The War They Fought, The Peace They Waged, by William C. Davis, Boston, 2014.

Embattled Rebel: Jefferson Davis as Commander in Chief, by James M. McPherson, New York, 2014.

"First With the Most" *Forrest,* by Rober Selph Henry, New York, 1991.

Fitz Lee: A Military Biography of major General Figzhugh Lee, C.S.A., by Edward G. Longacre, Cambridge, 2005.

General Grant by Matthew Arnold With A Rejoinder by Mark Twain, edited by John Y. Simon, Carbondale, 1966.

General Hancock, by Francis A. Walker. New York, 1894.

General James Longstreet, by Jeffery Wert, New York, 1993.

General Lee's Army: From Victory to Collapse, by Joseph T. Glatthaar, New York, 2008.

General Ulysses S. Grant: The Soldier and the Man, by Edward G. Longacre, Cambridge, Massachusetts, 2006.

General's in Blue: Lives of the Union Commanders, by Ezra J. Warner, Baton Rouge, 1964.

Generals in Gray: Lives of the Confederate Commanders, by Ezra J. Warner, Baton Rouge, 1959.

George Thomas: Virginian for the Union, by Christopher J. Einolf, Norman, 2007.

Grant, by Jean Edward Smith, New York, 2001.

Grant: A Biography, by William S. McFeely, New York, 1982.

Grant and Halleck: Contrast in Command, by John Y. Simon, Milwaukee, 1996.

Grant and Lee: A Dual Biography, by Gene Smith, New York, 1984.

Grant and Sherman: The Friendship That Won The Civil War, by Charles Bracelen Flood, New York, 2004.

Grant and Twain: The Story Of A Friendship That Changed America, by Mark Perry, New York, 2004.

Grant Moves South: 1861-1863, by Bruce Catton, New York, 1960.

Grant's Final Victory: Ulysses S. Grant's Heroic Last Year, by Charles Bracelen Flood, Philadelphia, 2011.

Grant Takes Command: 1863-1865, by Bruce Catton, New York, 1968.

Gray Fox: Robert E. Lee and the Civil War, by Burke Davis, New York, 1956.

"Happiness is Not My Companion:" The Live of General G.K. Warren, by David M. Jordan, Bloomington, 2001.

In the Footsteps of Robert E. Lee, by Clint Johnson, Winston-Salem, 2001.

In the Hands of Providence: Joshua L. Chamberlain & The American Civil War, by Alice Rains Trulock, North Carolina, 1992.

James Longstreet, Part I: Soldier, by Donald Bridgman Sanger / *Part II: Politician, Officeholder, and Writer,* by Thomas Robson Hay, Baton Rouge, 1952.

John Brown Gordon: Soldier, Southerner, American, by Ralp;h Lowell Eckert, Baton Rouge, 1989.

Lee After the War, by Marshall W. Fishwick, New York, 1963.

Lee Considered: General Robert E. Lee and Civil War History, by Alan T. Nolan, Chapel Hill, 1991.

Lee in the shadow of Washington, by Richard B. McCaslin, Baton Rouge, 2001.

Lee the American, by Gamaliel Bradford, New York, 1927.

Lee: The Last Years, by Charle Bracelen Flood, New York, 1981.

The Lees of Virginia: Seven Generations of an American Family, by Paul C. Nagel, New York, 1990.

Lee's Tarnished Lieutenant: James Longstreet and His Place in Southern History, by William Garrett Piston, Athens, 1987.

Let Us Have Peace: Ulysses S. Grant and the Politics of War and Reconstruction, Brooks D. Simpson, Chapel Hill, 1991.

Life and Campaigns of General Robert E. Lee, by James D. McCabe, Jr., Philadelphia, 1870.

The Life and Public Services of Ulysses S. Grant, from his Birth to the Present Time, and a Biographical Sketch of Hon. Henry Wilson, by Charles A. Phelps, Boston, 1872.

The Life of General Ely S. Parker, by Arthur C Parker. New York, 1919.

The Life of Ulysses S. Grant, by Charles A. Dana and Major General James Harrison Wilson. Springfield, Mass., 1868.

The Making of Robert E. Lee, by Michael Fellman, Baltimore, 2000.

The Marble Man, by Thomas L. Connelly, New York, 1977.

Master of War: the Life of General George H. Thomas, by Benson Bobrick, New York, 2009.

Meet General Grant, by W. E. Woodward, New York, 1928.

Men of Fire: Grant, Forrest, and the Campaign That Decided the Civil War, by Jack Hurst, New York, 2007.

The Most Complete and Authentic History of the Life and Public Services of General U.S. Grant, by Herman Dieck, Philadelphia, 1885.

Now the Drum of War: Walt Whitman and His Brothers in the Civil War, by Robert Roper, New York, 2008.

On The Trail With Grant and Lee, by Frederick Trevor Hill, New York, 1911.

A Popular and Authentic Life of Ulysses S. Grant, by Edward Mansfield, Cincinatti, 1868.

A Reporter for Lincoln, by Ida M. Tarbell, New York, 1929.

The Rise of U.S. Grant, by Colonel Arthur L. Conger, New York, 1931.

Robert E. Lee: A Biography, by Emory M. Thomas, New York, 1995.

Sacred Ties: From West Point Brothers to Battlefield Rivals: A True Story of the Civil War, by Tom Carhart, New York, 2010.

Sherman and his Campaigns, by Rev F Senour. New York, 1865.

Sherman: A Soldier's Life, by Lee Kennett, New York, 2001.

Sherman: A Soldier's Passion for Order, by John F. Marszalek, Southern Illinois, 1993.

Sherman: Soldier, Realist, American, by B.H. Liddell, New York, 1929.

Sherman, Fighting Prophet, by Lloyd Lewis, New York, 1932.

Simon Bolivar Buckner: Borderland Knight, by Arndt M. Stickles, Chapel Hill, 1940.

Stephen Dodson Ramseur: Lee's Gallant General, by Gary W. Gallagher, Chapel Hill, 1985.

Stonewall of the West: Patrick Cleburne & the Civil War, by Craig L. Symonds, Lawrence, 1997.

Tried By War: Abraham Lincoln as Commander in Chief, by James M. McPherson, New York, 2008.

Ulysses S. Grant: Soldier and President, by Geoffrey Perret, New York, 1997.

Ulysses S. Grant: Triumph Over Adversary 1822-1865, by Brooks D. Simpson, New York, 2000.

Wade Hampton III, by Robert K. Ackerman, Columbia, 2007.

Wade Hampton: Confederate Warrior to Southern Redeemer, by Rod Andrew Jr., Chapel Hill, 2008.

Warrior in Two Camps: Ely S. Parker Union General and Seneca Chief, by William H. Armstrong, Syracuse, 1978.

The White Tecumseh: A Biography of William T. Serman, by Stanley P. Hirshson, New York, 1997.

Worthy Opponents: William T. Sherman and Joseph E. Johnston: Antagonists in War—Friends in Peace, by Edward G. Longacre, Nashville, 2006.

MILITARY HISTORIES, BATTLE STUDIES, CAMPAIGNS, UNIT STUDIES:

The American Civil War: A Military History, by John Keegan, New York, 2009.

And Keep Moving On: The Virginia Campaign, May-June 1864, by Mark Grimsley, Lincoln, 2002.

And one was a Soldier, by Bishop Robert R. Brown, Pennslyvania, 1998.

An End of Valor, by Philip Van Doren Stern, Boston, 1958.

Army of the Heartland: The Army of Tennessee 1861-1862, by Thomas Lawrence Connelly. Louisiana, 1967.

The Army of the Potomac in Three Volumes: Mr. Lincoln's Army, Glory Road, A Stillness at Appomattox, by Bruce Catton, New York, 1962.

Autumn of Glory: The Army of Tennessee 1862-1865, by Thomas Lawrence Connelly, Louisiana, 1971.

Battle Cry of Freedom: The Civil War Era, by James M. McPherson, New York, 1988.

The Battles for Spotsylvania Courthouse and The Road To Yellow Tavern, May 7-12, 1864, by Gordon C. Rhea, Louisiana, 1997.

The Battles of Appomattox Station and Appomattox Court House, April 8-9, 1865, by Chris Calkins, Lynchburg, 1987.

The Battle of the Wilderness, May 5-6, 1864, by Gordon C. Rhea, Louisiana, 1994.

Beefsteak Raid, by Edward Boykin, New York, 1960.

Bloody Roads South: The Wilderness to Cold Harbor, May-June 1864, by Noah Andre Trudeau, Louisiana, 2000.

The Centennial History of the Civil War in Three Volumes: The Coming Fury, The Terrible Swift Sword and Never Call Retreat, by Bruce Catton, New York, 1965.

Chamberlain at Petersburg: the Charge at Fort Hell-June 18, 1864, by Diane Monroe Smith, 2004.

Chancellorsville, by Stephen W. Sears, New York, 1998.

Chancellorsville 1863: The Souls of the Brave, by Ernest B. Furgurson, New York, 1992.

Chancellorsville and the Germans: Nativism, Ethnicity, and Civil War Memory, by Christian B. Keller, New York, 2007.

The Civil War: A Narrative in Three Volumes: Fredericksburg to Meridian, from Sumter to Perryville, Red River to Appomattox, by Shelby Foote, New York, 1958.

Cold Harbor: Grant and Lee, May 26-June 3, 1864, by Gordon C. Rhea, Louisiana, 2002.

Days of Glory: The Army of the Cumberland 1861-1865, by Larry J. Daniel, Louisiana, 2004.

Embrace an Angry Wind: The Confederacy's Last Hurrah: Spring Hill, Franklin, and Nasville, by Wiley Sword, New York, 1994.

Fields of Honor: Pivotal Battles of the Civil War, by Edwin Bearss, Washington, D.C., 2006

The Final Bivoouac: The Surrender Parade at Appomattox and the Disbanding of the Armies, April 10-May 20, 1865, by Chris Calkins, Lynchburg, 1988.

For Cause & For Country: A Study of the Affair at Spring Hill and the Battle of Franklin,, by Eric A. Jacobson, Richard A. Rupp (co-author), Tennessee, 2008.

Fredericksburg! Fredericksburg! by George C. Rable, North Carolina, 2002.

Gettysburg, by Stephen W. Sears, New York, 2003.

Gettysburg: A Testing of Courage, by Noah Andre Trudeau, New York, 2002.

Gettysburg: The First Day, by Harry W. Pfanz, Chapel Hill, 2001.

Gettysburg: The Last Invasion, by Allen C. Guelzo, New York, 2013.

Gettysburg: The Second Day, by Harry W. Pfanz, Chapel Hill, 1987.

Grant and Lee: A Study In Personality And Generalship, by J. F. C. Fuller, Indiana, 1957.

Grant and Lee: The Virginia Campaigns 1864-1865, by William A. Frassanito, New York, 1983.

Grant Wins the War: Decision at Vicksburg, by James R. Arnold, New York, 1997.

Landscape Turned Red: The Battle Of Antietam, by Stephen W. Sears, New York, 1983.

The Last Cavaliers: Confederate and Union Cavalry in the Civil War, by Samuel Carter III, New York, 1979.

The Last Citadel: Petersburg, Virginia, June 1864-April 1865, by Noah Andre Trudeau, Louisiana, 1991.

The Last Full Measure: the Life and Death of the First Minnesota Volunteers, by Richard Moe, Minnesota, 1993.

Lee's Last Retreat: The Flight to Appomattox, by William Marvel, Chapel Hill, 2002.

Like Men of War: Black Troops in the Civil War 1862-1865, by Noah Andre Trudeau, New York, 2002.

The Long Road to Antietam: How the Civil War Became a Revolution, by Richard Slotkin, New York, 2012.

The March to the Sea and Beyond: Sherman's Troops in the Savannah and Carolins Campaigns, by Joseph T. Glatthaar, New York, 1985.

Mother, May You Never See the Sights I Have Seen: the Fifty-seventh Massachusetts Veteran Volunteers in the Last Year of the Civil War, by Warren Wilkinson, New York, 1990.

No Quarter: The Battle of the Crater, 1864, by Richard Slotkin, New York, 2009.

Nothing But Victory: The Army of the Tennessee 1861-1865, by Steven E. Woodworth, New York, 2005.

One Continuous Fight: The Retreat from Gettysburg and the Pursuit of Lee's Army of Northern Virginia, July 4 - 14, 1863, by Eric Wittenberg, J. David Petruzzi and Michael F. Nugent Michael, New York, 2011.

Out of the Storm: the End of the Civil War, April-June 1865, by Noah Andre Trudeau, New York, 1995.

Pickett's Charge-The Last Attack at Gettysburg, by Earl J. Hess, North Carolina, 2001.

Richmond Redeemed: The Siege of Petersburg, by Richard J. Sommers, New York, 1981.

Sherman and the Burning of Columbia, Marion Brunson Lucas, College Station, 1976.

Sherman's March, by Burke Davis, New York, 1980.

Shiloh 1862, by Winston Groom, Washington, 2012.

Shiloh and the Western Campaign of 1862, by Gary D. Joiner, New York, 2007
Shiloh-In Hell Before Night, by James L. McDonough, Knoxville, 1977.
Shiloh: The Battle that Changed the Civil War, by Larry J. Daniel, New York, 1997.
Shrouds of Glory: From Atlanta to Nashville: The Last Great Campaign of the Civil War, by Winston Groom, New York, 1995.
Southern Storm: Sherman's March to the Sea, by Noah Andre Trudeau, New York, 2009.
Stand Firm Ye Boys From Maine: the 20th Maine and the Gettysburg Campaign, by Thomas A. Desjardin, New York, 1995.
Stonewall Jackson's Valley Campaign: Shenandoah 1862, by Peter Cozzens, North Carolina, 2008.
Struggle for the Heartland: The Campaigns from Fort Henry to Corinth, by Stephen D. Engle, Lincoln, 2001.
The Surrender Proceedings: April 9, 1865, Appomattox Court House, by Frank P. Cauble, Lynchburg, 1987.
The Sword of Lincoln: the Army of the Potomac, by Jeffry d. Wert, New York, 2005.
They Met at Gettysburg: A Step-by-step Retelling of the Battle with Maps, Photos, Firsthand Accounts, by General Edward J. Stackpole, Pennsylvania, 1956.
To Appomattox: Nine April Days, 1865, by Burke Davis, New York, 1959.
To the Gates of Richmond: The Peninsula Campaign, by Stephen W. Sears, New York, 1992.
To The North Anna River: Grant and Lee, May 13-25, 1864, by Gordon C. Rhea, Louisiana, 2000.
Vicksburg 1863, by Winston Groom, New York, 2009.
Vicksburg: The Campaign That Opened the Mississippi, by Michael B. Ballard, Chapel Hill, 2004.
War Like a Thunderbolt: The Battle and Burning of Atlanta, by Russell S. Bonds, Pennsylvania, 2009.
When Sherman Marched North from the Sea: Resistance on the Confederate Home Front, by Jacqueline Glass Campbell, Chapel Hill, 2003.

SOCIAL & PSYCHOLOGICAL STUDIES, CRITICISM &
ESSAY COLLECTIONS, TECHNICAL ANALYSES, ATLASES:

A Victor Not a Butcher: Ulysses S. Grant's Overlooked Military Genius, by Edward H. Bonekemper III, Washington, D.C., 2004.
After the War: The Lives and Images of Major Civil War Figures After the Shooting Stopped, by David Hardin, Chicago, 2010.
Atlas of the Civil War, by Steven E. Woodworth and Kenneth J. Winkle, (foreword and introductions by James M. McPherson), New York, 2004.
Battlefields and Blessings: Stories of Faith and Courage from the Civil War, by Terry R. Tuley, Chattanooga, 2006.
The Bloody Crucible of Courage: Fighting Methods and Combat Experience of the Civil War, by Brent Nosworthy, New York, 2003.
The Civil War Catalog, by Antony Shaw, London, 2003.
The Civil War in Color: A Photographic reenactment of the War Between the States, by John C. Guntzleman, New York, 2012.

The Civil War Years: A Day-by-Day Chronicle, by Robert E. Denney, New York, 1992.

The Complete Gettysburg Guide: Walking and Driving Tours of the Battlefield, Town, Cemeteries, Field Hospital Sites, and other Topics of Historical Interest, J. David Petruzzi, New York, 2009.

Confederate Reckoning: Rower and Politics in the Civil War South, by Stephanie McCurry, Cambridge, 2010.

The Destructive War: William Tecumseh Sherman, Stonewall Jackson, and the Americans, edited by Charles Royster, New York, 1991.

Embattled Courage: The Experience of Combat in the American Civil War, by Gerald F. Linderman, New York, 1987.

Flags of the Civil War (Special Editions [Military]), by Philip Katcher, Richard Scollins, United Kingdom, 2000.

The Flags of the Confederacy: An Illustrated History, by Devereaux Cannon Jr., Tennessee, 1988.

The Flags of the Union: An Illustrated History, by Devereaux Cannon Jr., Louisiana, 1994.

Freedom Rising: Washington in the Civil War, by Ernest B. Furgurson, New York, 2004.

The Generalship of Ulysses S. Grant, by J.F.C. Fuller, London, 1929.

Grant's Lieutenants: From Cairo To Vicksburg, edited by Steven E. Woodworth, Lawrence, 2001.

Grant's Lieutenants: From Chattanooga To Appomattox, edited by Steven E. Woodworth, Lawrence, 2008.

The Imperiled Union, by Kenneth Milton Stampp, Oxford, 1980.

The Land They Fought For: The Story of the South as the Confederacy 1832-1865, by Clifford Dowdey, New York, 1955.

Lee and His Generals, by Captain Wm. P. Snow, New York, 1867.

Lee the Soldier, edited by Gary W. Gallagher, Lincoln, 1996.

Lee's Lieutenants, Volume One, by Douglas Southall Freeman, New York, 1942.

Lee's Lieutenants, Volume Two, by Douglas Southall Freeman, New York, 1943.

Lee's Lieutenants, Volume Three, by Douglas Southall Freeman, New York, 1944.

The Life of Billy Yank: The Common Soldier of the Union , by Bell Irvin Wiley, Louisiana, 1952.

The Life of Johnny Reb: The Common Soldier of the Confederacy, by Bell Irvin Wiley, Louisiana, 1943.

Lincoln's Labels: America's Best-Known Brands and the Civil War, by James M. Schmidt, Roseville, 2009.

This Mighty Scourge: Perspectives on the Civil War, by James M. McPherson, Oxford, 2007.

The New York Times Complete Civil War 1861-1865, edited by Harold Holzer, New York, 2010.

A Place Called Appomattox, by William Marvel, Chapel Hill, 2000.

The Psychohistory of The American Civil War and the Dual Intelligence of Man, by Daniel E. Schneider, M.D., New York, 1981.

Revised United States Army Regulations of 1861: With an Appendix Containing the Changes and Laws Affecting Army Regulations and Articles of War to June 25, 1863, Creator United States War Department, Washington D.C., 2010.

This Republic of Suffering: Death and the American Civil War, by Drew Gilpin Faust, New York, 2008.

Reveille in Washington 1860-1865, by Margaret Leech, New York, 1941.

Richmond Burning: The Last Days of the Confederate Capital, by Nelson D. Lankford, New York, 2002.

Sherman Invades Georgia, by John R. Scales, Annapolis, 2006.

Shiloh: A Battlefield Guide, by Mark Grimsley, Lincoln, 2006.

Uniforms of the Civil War: An Illustrated Guide for Historians, Collectors, Re-en-actors, by Robin Smith, Ron Field, Great Britain, 2001.

The Warrior Generals: Combat Leadership in the Civil War, by Thomas B. Buell, New York, 1997.

Washington in Lincoln's Time, by Noah Brooks, New York, 1958.

The Wilderness Campaign, edited by Gary W. Gallagher, Chapel Hill, 1997.

LINCOLN ASSASSINATION:

American Brutus: John Wilkes Booth and the Lincoln Conspiracies, by Michael W. Kauffman, New York, 2004.

The Assassination of Abraham Lincoln and its Expiation, by David Miller DeWitt. New York, 1909.

The Assassination of Abraham Lincoln: Flight, Pursuit, Capture and Punishment of the Conspiritors, by Osborn Hamiline Oldroyd. Washington, D.C., 1901.

Beware the People Weeping: Public Opinion and the Assassination of Abraham Lincoln, by Thomas Reed Turner, Baton Rouge, 1982.

Come Retribution, by William A. Tidwell, Oxford, 1988.

The Darkest Dawn: Lincoln, Booth, and the great American Tragedy, by Thomas Goodrich, Bloomington, 2005.

The Death of Lincoln: The Story of Booth's Plot, His Deed and the Penalty, by Clara Elizabeth Laughlin, New York, 1909.

Death to Traitors: the Story of General Lafayette C. Baker, Lincoln's Forgotten Secret Service Chief, by Jacob Mogelever, New York, 1960.

His Name is Still Mudd: The Case Against Doctor Samuel Alexander Mudd, by Edward Steers, Jr., Gettysburg, 1997.

History of the United States Secret Service, by General L.C. Baker, Chief National Detective Police, Philadelphia, 1868.

John Wilkes Booth: A Sister's Memoir by Asia Booth Clarke, edited by Terry Alford, Oxford, 1999.

John Wilkes Booth: Fact and Fiction of Lincoln's Assassination, by Francis Wilson, New York, 1929.

The Curse of Cain: The Untold Story of John Wilkes Booth, by Theodore J. Nottingham, Nicholasville, 1997.

Lincoln's Last Day, by John W. Starr, Jr. New York, 1922.

"Right or Wrong, God Judge Me": The Writings of John Wilkes Booth, edited by John Rhodehamel, Chicago, 1997.

Samuel Bland Arnold: Memoirs of a Lincoln Conspirator, edited by Michael W. Kauffman, Berwyn Heights, 2003.

The Web of Conspiracy: the Complete Story of the Men Who Murdered Abraham Lincoln, by Theodore Roscoe, Englewood Cliffs, 1959.

Why Was Lincoln Murdered? By Otto Eisenschiml. New York, 1937.

MAGAZINES AND NEWSPAPERS:

Century Magazine, 1860-1865, 1884-1885.
Harper's Weekly, 1860-1865, 1884-1885.
The New York Herald, 1860-1865, 1884-1885.
The New York Times, 1860-1865, 1884-1885.
The New York Tribune, 1860-1865, 1884-1885.
The Philadelphia Inquirer, 1860-1865.
The Richmond Dispatch, 1860-1865.
Atlanta Daily Intelligencer, 1860-1864.
Memphis Daily Appeal 1862-1863.
Charleston Daily Courier 1861-1865.

SECONDARY SOURCES FOR CHARACTER COMPOSITES:

Various soldiers' letters, diaries, journals-1860-1865. Manuscript Collection, Library of Congress, Washington, D.C.

CIVIL WAR & PERIOD MUSIC:

American War Ballads and Lyrics, v.11 "The Civil War," by George Cary Eggleston, New York, 1889.
History of American Music, by William L. Hubbard (editor), London, 1908.

MEXICAN WAR:

Army of Manifest Destiny: The American Soldier in the Mexican War 1846-1848, by James M. McCaffrey, New York, 1992.
The Mexican War: 1846-1848, by K. Jack Bauer, New York, 1974.
Monterrey Is Ours! The Mexican War Letters of Lieutenant Dana 1845-1847, edited by Robert H. Ferrell, Lexington, 1990.
Mr. Polk's Army, by Richard Bruce Winders, College Station, 1997.
So Far From God: The U.S. War with Mexico 1846-1848, by John S. D. Eisenhower, New York, 1989.

ABOUT THE AUTHOR

After a degree in Novel Writing from the University of Southern California under PEN/Faulkner winner T.C. Boyle, Michael Frost Beckner began in the entertainment industry as the writing assistant to Academy Award winner Barry Levinson on *Good Morning, Vietnam* and *Rain Man*.

In 1989, Michael Frost Beckner's original script for *Sniper* launched a military-thriller franchise now in production on its eighth sequel. Three consecutive record-breaking spec script sales and three films later, Tony Scott directed Beckner's original screenplay *Spy Game*. An international blockbuster that paired Robert Redford and Brad Pitt as CIA partners and rivals, it is now a classic in the espionage genre. Branching into television with his CIA-based drama *The Agency* for CBS, Beckner's pilot predicted Osama bin Laden's terror attack and the War on Terror four months before 9/11. In that series alone, Beckner would go on to predictively dramatize three more international terror events.

Having penned more than twenty-five pilots for network and cable television, miniseries and docudramas, and dozens of original motion picture screenplays, adaptations, and rewrites, he is a Hollywood institution.

In 2001, intrigued by the idea of writing a two-man play focused on the four meetings between Ulysses S. Grant and Robert E. Lee over their lifetimes, Beckner embarked on a twenty-year odyssey which saw his intimate theater piece transform into the most comprehensive Civil War mini-series ever written. Variously known as *To Appomattox* and *Battle Hymn*, and now entitled *A Nation Divided*, for the first time, Beckner's full 12-hour scripts are being released to the public in three book volumes.

He makes his home with his family in the Verdugo Mountain foothills of Los Angeles, California.

9 798985 597493